MARRIED THE MARINA

BEACHFRONT BILLIONAIRES
BOOK 2

ELIZABETH MADDREY

Scripture quoted by permission. Quotations designated (NIV) are from THE HOLY BIBLE: NEW INTERNATIONAL VERSION®. NIV®. Copyright © 1973, 1978, 1984 by Biblica. All rights reserved worldwide.

Cover design by Lynnette Bonner

Published in the United States of America by Elizabeth Maddrey. www.ElizabethMaddrey.com

1

CHRISTIAN

"Who's next?" I scanned the three remaining patients in the waiting room. No one volunteered, though they exchanged looks. I turned and picked up the clipboard from the front desk and found the next un-crossed-off name. "Jeremy?"

A woman stood and tugged the sleeve of the sullen teenager slumped in a seat beside her. "Come on, Jer."

Jeremy's sigh conveyed every ounce of his disgust at being here, but he stood and stomped across the floor toward me.

"Hi, Jeremy. Come on back." I gestured to the hall that led to our two treatment rooms. "Room one."

Mom followed close on Jeremy's heels.

This should be fun.

I closed the door behind me as I entered the small room. I nodded toward the exam bed. "Hop up. How can I help you today?"

"I don't need to be here. It's just a cut."

"A cut from some rusty metal you found on the beach." Mom huffed out. "And I can't remember when you last had a tetanus shot."

I went to the small sink and washed my hands. I dried them, then pulled on a pair of gloves. "Let's see the cut. Rusty metal's never a good thing to get cut with."

Jeremy pulled up the leg of his shorts, exposing a gauze pad taped to his thigh.

"This might hurt." I worked at the tape, trying to avoid ripping the hair off the boy's leg.

"Oh, please." His mom reached over and yanked the tape and gauze away.

"Ow! Mom!" Jeremy shot me a look that clearly implored me to see just how awful his life was.

"Ma'am. I've got this."

"Yes, well, I'm already wasting hours of my weekend away on this. You're understaffed."

Since her words hadn't had a question attached to them, I just nodded. "How old are you, Jeremy?"

"Sixteen." He muttered.

I looked at the cut. It was shallow. "Well, you don't need stitches. I am going to clean it again, just to be safe. Where do you go to school?"

"I hardly see why you need to know that. Can you please just fix this up so we can go back to the beach?" The mom crossed her arms.

I took a moment to unclench my jaw and fight off an audible sigh. "You said you weren't sure when his last tetanus shot was administered. If he's in public school here in North Carolina, his vaccinations should all be up to date. Unless you have an exemption. But if you'd rather I just administer the vaccine, I'll do that."

"Mom." Jeremy swiveled his head and glared at his mother. He looked back at me. "I go to private school. I don't think they require shots."

"Thanks. Then out of an abundance of caution, I'm afraid

you've got a shot coming your way." I collected an antiseptic spray and cotton swab from one of the drawers in the supply cabinet, then a bandage from another. I made quick work of cleaning the cut another time and applying the bandage. "Let me grab the vaccine and then you'll be on your way."

I pulled off my gloves and tossed them in the trash before leaving the room. I pulled the door shut and took a moment to make an annoyed face. Of course I knew there were moms out there in the world who were like this, but it was always startling to encounter one in the real world. I thanked God for my own mother as I went into the locked office-slash-storeroom to get a tetanus shot from the fridge with medications that needed to be kept cool. I put an alcohol swab on a small tray before drawing up the dose into a sterile syringe and replacing the vaccine vial. Then I carried the shot back to the exam room and knocked once on the door before going in.

The mother bit off whatever she'd been saying when I returned. I went through the hand washing and glove routine again. "Go ahead and pull up a sleeve for me?"

Jeremy sighed and yanked up his T-shirt sleeve.

I swabbed the area and quickly administered the shot before covering the injection site with a small, round bandage. "All set."

I used my tablet to check that they'd filled out everything at the kiosk. It looked fine. I just couldn't shake the feeling that the mom was the kind of person who was going to get sent to collections because she didn't believe I'd done the job properly.

I smiled. "Your arm may be sore for a few days. If you do some pushups tonight, it'll help. Any questions?"

The mother stood and sniffed. "No. Come on, Jer."

Rolling his eyes, Jeremy slid off the table and slouched out of the exam room behind his mother. I took a moment to pull the paper covering the exam bed down and tear off the part that Jeremy had used. I cleaned the rest of the room and grabbed the tablet before heading back out to the waiting room.

Only one person remained. I checked the sign in clipboard. "Teresa?"

The woman in the corner was wearing a floppy brimmed sun hat and shades. She stood.

"Room two." I liked to alternate the exam rooms, even though I cleaned them after each use. They didn't look very different, but I convinced myself that it was a little change of scenery.

The woman hunched her shoulders and skittered toward the exam room.

I followed behind, scrolling on my table to find her check-in files. I frowned. She wasn't there. I entered the exam room and pulled the door closed. "Did you check in at the kiosk? I'm not seeing your record."

"No. I'd like to pay cash." Teresa looked up hesitantly. "Can I do that?"

I watched her for a moment. Something about her was tugging at my mind. Wait. "Were you here about a month ago?"

Teresa swallowed, then nodded.

Questions raced through my mind. After I'd treated her on Easter, she'd disappeared. I'd spent entirely too long trying—carefully—to figure out who she was. Where she'd gone. "Have you been on the island the whole time?"

"No." Teresa cleared her throat. "I just—can you please not ask questions?"

"I can try." Even though it was incredibly difficult for me. "Would you take off your hat and sunglasses, please?"

With halting movements that seemed more pain than fear related, Teresa reached up and removed her hat and glasses. Her hair was a different color. On Easter, her hair had reminded me of Rapunzel. Now, it was a glossy deep brown.

I couldn't decide which I liked better.

Not that it mattered what I liked. Obviously.

My gaze went to the place above her eye where there'd been a gash I treated. "Looks like you're healing nicely. No issues with your nose?"

"No. The bruises were bad, but everyone assumed I'd had work done."

My eyebrows lifted. Whether or not she wanted to admit it, that told me a little more about her. But I didn't comment. Instead, I asked, "How can I help you today?"

Teresa took a deep breath and let it out slowly. "I hurt my shoulder."

"Okay." I closed the difference between us and began to gently probe her right shoulder.

She hissed out a breath.

I frowned. "I need to ask you to take off your shirt."

She closed her eyes. After a moment, she pulled off her gauzy shirt. She had a tank top with tiny straps on underneath. "The tank too?"

"No, this is fine." I leaned in to get a closer look at the red, blistered skin. "This is a burn."

"I guess I forgot sunscreen."

I shook my head. "Not a sunburn."

Teresa's pleading gaze met mine. I returned it steadily, working to keep my face impassive.

She bit her lip. "I tripped."

Backward? But sure, I'd play the game. For now. "And fell into...?"

Her voice was barely audible. "The grill."

I winced. I couldn't stop myself. I looked more closely at the burn marks. They could definitely have come from the grate of a grill. I absolutely didn't buy that she tripped, though. I couldn't figure out the logistics that would make that scenario possible. "You're lucky this isn't worse."

"It wasn't on. It had just been sitting in the sun on the deck." She craned her neck to look at the stripes of burned flesh.

"I don't think you need the hospital, but I will want you to come back in a week for a follow-up." I leaned away from her and caught her gaze. "Will you still be on the island?"

She shook her head.

"Then I need you to promise that you'll see your doctor at home."

"Okay." Her eyes slid to the side as she spoke.

"I'm serious. I'm calling these second-degree burns. The blisters are concerning, but I don't see indications that would bump them to third. But I could be wrong. If there's no improvement in a week, you're going to need more intervention."

She blew out a breath. "Fine. I will. Promise."

"In the meantime, you need to keep it covered and dry. If the blisters break, you'll need to apply antibiotic ointment. The over-the-counter stuff at the pharmacy is fine. Also, aloe gel as needed to keep it cool and keep you from scratching if it gets itchy." I went to the cabinet and retrieved a sterile gauze pad and some tape. I made quick work of covering the burns, then pulled off my gloves and walked over to the trash. "Are you safe?"

Teresa had been in the process of pulling her shirt back on, and she froze. After a moment she finished tugging down the garment. "Of course."

"There's no 'of course' here. I've seen you twice in basically two months. And while I'm happy to see you, I'd prefer it wasn't in my clinic." Was it inappropriate to kick myself in front of her? Because that had come out badly.

Her eyebrows lifted. "I have a fiancé."

"Right. I wasn't flirting." I had been, of course. I just hadn't meant to let the words out. "Is he here with you?"

Her eyes blanked. "Of course."

"And at Easter?"

She nodded.

"Anyone else?"

"My parents." She looked away. "We just bought a vacation house."

One corner of my mind started sorting through the real estate turnover. I didn't know every house that sold, but I had a cousin who did. Would it violate his ethics—and mine—if I asked? Was concern for her safety enough to do it anyway? "Welcome to Loring Island."

A ghost of a smile flickered across her lips. "Thanks. Can I go?"

After a moment of typing on the tablet to update the file and switch to self-pay, I offer it to her.

"Oh. Right." She fumbles in her pocket and pulls out a wad of cash. She glances at the total again, then counts out the bills. "I don't have change. So just...consider it a tip?"

"I'll donate it to the women's shelter over in Bennett."

She pales, but doesn't say anything. "Now I can go?"

"Yeah. Enjoy the rest of your weekend. They do fireworks at the lighthouse on Monday night, if you're still around." I shrug. "They're a big draw. Most of the houses nearby can watch from their decks if you're not into the crowds."

"Thanks." She slips off the table and hurries from the room.

I sighed again as I picked up the cash and my tablet. I marked the bill paid and found a biohazard bag to drop the cash into. Who had actual cash these days? I'd assumed she'd tap a card, like people do for their co-pays. But she'd obviously been a lot more serious about not leaving a paper trail than I realized.

Was she hiding it from her fiancé? Or her parents?

Maybe both?

I set the tablet and money aside so I could clean the exam

room, then picked them up to take them back to the front desk with me.

The waiting room was, thankfully, empty.

I took a moment to sit at the front desk. I locked the cash in a drawer and then logged into the main computer to work on the inevitable paperwork. Since I wasn't a medical doctor, all of my cases had to be reviewed by a supervising MD. Thankfully, the hospital on the mainland was happy to keep the "easy" cases over here and cut down on their ER traffic. They had a rotation of doctors who took on the supervision duty.

The rest of the day passed with a handful of scrapes and cuts, but nothing major. It was enough to keep me busy and not bored, but nothing that had me scrambling for an ambulance. Basically, perfect.

I took one final pass through the clinic to check that everything was clean, stocked, and locked. We weren't open on Sundays, but I was on call. More often than not, I had at least one phone consultation. Generally, the locals would either head to the hospital or wait for Monday. But visitors were hit or miss. Either way, I liked knowing that the clinic was ready for me whenever I needed it next.

I collected the trash and carried it with me out to the street, pausing to flip the sign on the front door and lock it behind me as I left. I took the trash around to the dumpster on the side of the building, then started the pleasant walk out of town and out toward my house on the north end of the island.

I was just turning onto the sidewalk of the main road, when a car pulled up beside me and beeped the horn. I looked, grinning at my cousin Travis.

He lowered his window. "Want a ride?"

"You know what? Sure." I checked the traffic, then jogged around to climb in his passenger seat. "Where's Grady?"

"Hanging with Mom and Dad. They wanted to build a sand castle."

"Nice." And it was. Travis's parents had really stepped into the fray when Travis's wife left him in January. We—the whole family—were trying to be there for him. But Aunt Deb was doing the bulk of the heavy lifting. She seemed to enjoy it. "I was actually going to text you."

"Yeah?" Travis pulled out onto the main road leading toward the lighthouse. "You finally going to invest in some rentals?"

"Tempting, but no." I shook my head. Travis would manage everything. I knew that. But the idea of owning a house and not living in it was something I couldn't wrap my head around. "I was wondering if you'd be willing to talk to me about the recent-ish sales to folks who weren't renting, but also weren't living on island full-time."

Travis glanced over at me, eyebrows raised. "Vacation homeowners?"

I nodded.

"Hm." Travis was quiet for a long moment. "The records are public, so it's probably not an issue. But I'd love to know why."

I blew out a breath. "Is it enough if I say it has to do with a patient?"

"You can't tell me. Got it." He shrugged. "There are only two. The Sanderson place finally closed two weeks ago."

I shook my head. "Too recent."

"Okay. Well, that leaves the Hackett place. It sold in late March."

I nodded slowly. The Hackett place had been one of the larger vacation rentals. "Private dock facing the mainland, right? But on the public beach?"

"Mostly right. The beach in front of their place is technically their property. The Hackett's never bothered enforcing it. These new owners have put up signs." Travis shot me a tight smile.

"I've had some complaints from the owners of neighboring property."

I snorted. "Because they have to walk what, fifty extra feet?"

"Maybe a hundred." Travis slowed, then turned onto the road taking us toward the north end of the island where all our family homes were located. "But it's a change. No one likes change."

Wasn't that the truth?

But it gave me a little insight into the kind of family Teresa had. She said she was safe.

I wished I could believe her.

2

TERESA

"Where have you been?"

My guts tightened at the hint of mean lurking in James's voice. "Took a walk down by the marina."

James wore his dark, designer sunglasses, so I couldn't see his eyes, but I imagined that he'd narrowed them as he studied me. "How was it? Still a provincial small town?"

"It's quaint. Yes. But the people are friendly."

James shook his head and brushed at imaginary dirt on his blindingly white shorts. The shorts set off the tan he'd gotten on vacation in the Maldives. The three weeks he'd been gone with his family had been the first break in my stress-level since Mom and Dad decided James was the answer to their prayers when it came to marrying off their spinster daughter.

Oh, they didn't say it all out loud, but the looks told me the story well enough. And since I was back home after failing miserably in my attempt to create any sort of music career in Nashville, I had to go along. At least until December. Then I'd turn thirty and the entirety of my trust would unlock and Mom and Dad couldn't hold it over my head anymore.

I could last six more months.

"Have you changed your mind about golfing with us tomorrow?" James leaned back against the rail of the deck.

Everything he did had an air of calculation that I couldn't understand. There were no photographers lurking here, hoping to get a shot of him. "No. But I hope you and Dad have a great time."

"You really need to learn the game. You know how important golf is in my family."

I smiled slightly, hoping it didn't look as sickly as it felt. "I thought I'd go to church. It looks like the service will be out with plenty of time for me to join you at the golf club restaurant for brunch when you and Dad have finished your game."

James's frown deepened. It was almost a scowl, though he'd never admit it. If he knew, he'd change his expression immediately. Wouldn't want to risk a wrinkle forming. "What is it with you and church? I sort of understand at home—your parents even go there, since there are movers and shakers who need to see and be seen. But what possible reason could you have for church on this ridiculous island?"

"It's important to me." For reasons that had nothing to do with being seen. The biggest benefit from leaving home after college and giving the whole music thing a try—well, aside from getting out from under Mom and Dad's thumb—had been getting introduced to Jesus by people who actually loved Him. "I've told you that."

"Yes, well. I keep hoping you'll outgrow this little phase. Your parents are insisting you will, but maybe they're wrong."

I wanted to confirm that yes, they were wrong. But Dad was working a big deal with James's father, so we needed to keep James happy. At least, that's what Dad said every time I tried to talk to him about not enjoying James's company. Mom was no help, either.

When I didn't answer, James sighed heavily, like a disappointed father. "Anyway. Why don't we go out on the boat for the rest of the afternoon? There's an old off-shore Coast Guard station not too far that I've been reading about. It might be fun to see in person. I'm told there's good fishing out that way as well."

"If that's what you'd like to do." The boat was not my favorite thing. James knew it. That was, most likely, why he suggested it.

He slipped his arm around my shoulders and squeezed. Right on top of the burns. I fought off the urge to twist away from his touch. That's what he wanted. I wasn't going to give him the satisfaction. My lack of response seemed to irritate him, because he took his arm away. "I'll go let your father know our plans. Maybe he and your mother will join us."

"I hope they will." In fact, I was absolutely going to make sure of it. It shouldn't be too hard to convince Dad. He liked to fish. And he was on board the "Keep James Happy" train. Mom might try to get out of it, but...I'd see what I could do.

Her presence seemed to be the only thing that reined James in even a little.

MY STEPS SLOWED as I neared the church. People milled about in front of the steps that led into the building. Kids raced around on the lawn. The parking lot was full enough that I was glad I hadn't begged to use Mom's car. Not that she would have let me. She was irritated that I wasn't joining Dad and James for golf. The fact that I was making good on my comment to attend church just annoyed her further.

A car beeped as it drove past. I frowned. I didn't know anyone here. So, obviously, the beep wasn't for me. Was I becoming just as vain as the rest of my family?

I needed to get away from them.

The problem, of course, was that my music degree was, officially, useless. And I didn't have very many useful backup skills. I could wait tables. But I really didn't want to.

In Nashville, I'd considered seeing if I could get a job at Melody's—a fun diner with singing wait staff—but I never followed through. At the time, I'd had enough money remaining unused in my college fund to hold me over until I landed a record deal. Maybe I should go back and give it a try. Plenty of people in the world waited tables and managed to live. I'd probably need a roommate or two. Or three.

The thought of a small apartment with that many people in it made me shudder.

But what if that's what God wanted me to do?

It wasn't, though.

I knew that, deep down. It was why I'd pulled up my Tennessee stakes and gone home. Of course, I'd thought God was going to make it clear what He *did* want me to do. But so far, that direction hadn't been forthcoming.

I crossed the street and worked my way toward the church steps. I enjoyed the slow, southern drawl of the locals catching up with one another as they walked. Visitors to the island stuck out—like I must—from their choice of clothing. It seemed they were either beach ready in coverups that some website had probably described as "no one will even know you're wearing a swimsuit," or in their "Easter Sunday with Grandma" finest.

I was closer to the latter, though the sundress and tissue-thin sweater to make it Golf Club appropriate for lunch wasn't too far off from what some of the local ladies wore. I blew out a breath. Why was I focused on clothes? It was the kind of observation my mother would fixate on and use to dismiss the whole experience.

Maybe I wasn't as different from her as I wanted to be.

The thought stopped me in my tracks. I closed my eyes and breathed deeply, willing my heart to stop racing. *Jesus...*

"Teresa?"

My eyes sprang open, cutting off my wordless prayer. I glanced around. It had to be another Teresa. Didn't it?

But no.

My gaze landed on the man who ran the island clinic. What was his name? He'd introduced himself. Not as doctor something-or-other. Just a first name. But what was it?

The man jogged over, closing the distance between us. The smile on his face grew. "It is you. You're coming to church?"

"Yeah." I paused and cleared my throat. "That's all right, isn't it? I know I'm not an islander."

He chuckled. "Of course it is. We're always glad to have anyone visit. I'm Christian, by the way."

"Oh. Well. Me, too."

He grinned. "That's good to know. I meant my name. My name is Christian. Christian Thomas."

I took the hand he offered and shook it. My face burned. Of course he hadn't been declaring his love of Jesus. Who did that? Nobody, that's who. "Right. Teresa Duvall. Which you knew. I'm not usually this discombobulated."

"Good word." He didn't immediately release my hand and I had to give a little tug to get it back. His cheeks flushed slightly. "Would you like to sit with us? Or me? I don't have to sit with my family, though I usually do and they'd be happy to have you join us."

I bit my lip. Having someone to sit with would definitely ease the awkwardness of visiting a small church. I'd planned to hide in the back row and scoot out just before everything was over. But...I tipped my head to the side. "Your wife won't mind?"

"No wife. Mom and Dad. Also, an aunt and uncle. And some very annoying cousins and brothers. We're a big crew. Which I realize, as the words leave my mouth, is probably scaring you off. We could just sit together in the back row. It'd be fine. Although I know Gramps would love to meet you."

My head was spinning slightly. "Why?"

"Your family bought the Hackett place, right? Gramps has always loved that place. He'd love meeting the new owner."

"I mean, that's my parents. I'm just kind of hanging out for a bit." I stopped. I didn't want to explain that I was there primarily as eye candy for the son of a business contact to ogle. Not only did I not enjoy playing that role, the fact that I'd agreed to it didn't paint me in the best light either.

Christian shrugged. "Gramps won't care."

Sit alone and get gawked at or sit with the island doctor and...probably still get gawked at. At least sitting with Christian, I'd have a little buffer. "Yeah, all right."

"Nice. Come on." Christian hesitated then jerked his head toward the church.

What had the hesitation been about? Had he been about to offer his arm? Were there guys out there in the world who still did that? Maybe I'd actually ended up in Brigadoon after all.

I fell into step beside him. "Have you always lived on the island?"

"Born and bred." Christian frowned slightly. "Might as well get it out in the open, you'll find out eventually. My family— back some generations, obviously—founded the island."

I stopped. "You what?"

He turned, nodding. "Yeah. Mom was a Loring before she married Dad. Have to say I've always been grateful that Gramps only had daughters so we could escape the family name at least a little. I'm not ashamed of it or anything, but it can be a lot. My older brother got the short straw though, since Mom named him Bennett."

"Bennett. Like the town across the bridge Bennett?"

Christian nodded. "Another Loring family production."

"Poor guy." I muttered. It was bad enough being a Duvall in some circles. I couldn't fathom sharing a name with a town that my family started when I still lived right there.

"Don't feel too bad for him. He's not suffering." Christian started walking again. "But if you've changed your mind about sitting with us, I'll understand. I'll be disappointed, but I'll understand."

I took a couple of fast steps to catch up. "No. It's all good."

He shot me an approving smile.

It shouldn't have warmed me as much as it did. I'd met the man twice—neither time under good circumstances. I cleared my throat. "Do you like being a small-town doctor?"

"It's worse than that, unfortunately." He glanced over at me. "I'm a small-town nurse practitioner."

"Really?" For some reason I couldn't explain, that made me like him more.

"Really." He paused, nodded to a group of older women clustered around the church doors, then put his hand on the small of my back to usher me past them. When we were in the foyer, he removed his hand. "Disappointed?"

About him moving his hand? Yeah. But why would he ask that? Or—oh. "The doctor thing? No. Why would I be?"

He shrugged. "People seem to find it strange."

"I guess nursing isn't a field traditionally associated with men, but that doesn't mean it shouldn't be." It was my turn to shrug. "I'm a big fan of people doing what God calls them to."

He sent me another look that had warmth radiating through my body.

I looked away.

He briefly touched my arm. "Want some coffee before things start? There are lids, so you can take it into the service."

I'd already had the single cup of coffee that I needed to

jumpstart my morning. I wasn't a huge caffeine addict like my parents. On the other hand, a cup of coffee would give me something to do with my hands. "Sure."

Christian led the way through the clumps of people to the corner of the foyer where there was a table set up with urns and cups. And even donuts.

I definitely didn't need a donut.

But I wanted one.

I shoved that thought aside, focusing firmly on the little digs Mom would make about my ability to "catch the right man" if I kept eating like that. Ugh.

I reached for a cup and filled it with steaming black coffee then slid out of the way so Christian could make his own. I grabbed a yellow packet of fake sugar and dumped it in. I'd rather use two or three of the brown raw sugars they offered, but there was the whole swim-suit-man-catching lecture going on in my brain. So yeah. Fake sugar it was. And the nasty powdered non-dairy creamer.

I tapped in the powder and then used a stirrer to try and break up the clumps and mix it into something drinkable.

Christian went for the raw sugar and a generous splash from the pitcher that sat behind a card stating "Heavy Cream."

Lucky.

He stirred briefly, then reached across me for a lid. "Sorry."

"It's fine." I glanced into my cup and frowned. Probably as good as it was going to get. I put the stirring stick into the trash and got a lid myself. This was just for something to do with my hands. I didn't have to drink it. Of course, if I wasn't going to drink it, I could have made it taste better. Doing that, though, would mean I would want to drink it. So yeah. This was the better route.

I looked up to see Christian studying me. "Ready?"

"Yeah."

"You want a donut?"

More than anything. "No. I'm good."

"Hmm." But at least he didn't push. "Do you want to sit with the fam or in the back row?"

I hesitated. Was there a right answer? "I'll leave that up to you."

"Let's go meet Gramps." Christian started back through the crowd.

I followed. Did that mean we were sitting with his family? It didn't have to. Not necessarily. He was good at avoiding answering questions. To be fair, since I'd given him the option, I couldn't really complain about any choice he made.

We went through the double-doors into the sanctuary. I smiled. It was exactly the way I'd pictured it would be. Small-town, long-standing community church. They'd traded out pews for chairs somewhere along the way. And there was a screen on the wall where I imagined they'd project the words for the songs. But it still had that feel of permanence that came from older buildings.

Christian moved down the aisle to a row just in front of the approximate middle of the room. An old man was already perched on the end seat. He had a cane leaning against the seat in front of him.

"Hey, Gramps." Christian touched the man's shoulder, then leaned in for a hug after he looked up.

"Christian, m'boy." Gramps shifted his weight like he was about to stand.

"Don't get up. You're fine." Christian stepped back and gestured for me to come closer. "I'd like you to meet Teresa Duvall. Her family bought the Hackett place."

Gramps grinned broadly. "Oh, now, it's a real pleasure to meet you."

He gripped the seat in front of him and lurched unsteadily to his feet, waving off the hand Christian extended. "I've got it. I'm not doddering yet."

I took his extended hand. "It's lovely to meet you. Christian said you knew the Hacketts?"

"I surely did. It was a sad day when their grandkids decided to turn the place into a rental. Never understood why they grew to hate the island so much that they didn't want to use it themselves." He sighed. "But times change. You live long enough you'll see it all."

Christian laughed. "True. And we'd all just as soon you kept on seeing it change. Sit back down, Gramps."

"Bad as his mother." Gramps shook his head, but he also slowly lowered himself back into his seat. "Have you met my Linda yet?"

I glanced over at Christian, then shook my head. "No, Sir. I haven't been out meeting folks much. My parents brought some business acquaintances along on this trip, so I've been helping out with entertaining them. I hope we'll get a chance to enjoy the island as a family though."

We wouldn't. I knew that. But it didn't make my statement false. I did hope that. I had a lot of hopes where my family was concerned. But it was going to take the miraculous intervention of Jesus to make them reality. I knew that, too.

Gramps turned to look back toward the doors of the sanctuary. "Your family didn't join you this morning?"

"No, Sir. Dad and James are playing golf. Mom's a bit under the weather from our boat excursion yesterday, but she'll probably join us for brunch at the club." Under the weather was code for hungover, but hopefully that wasn't something Christian or his grandfather would pick up on.

"Not everyone's a sailor." Gramps nodded. "Will you join us? We'd love to have you."

"That's the plan, Gramps." Christian chuckled and gestured

for his grandfather to stay seated. "We'll go around and come in from the other side. If you're not going to use the cane, you might as well just sit."

Gramps scowled at Christian, but the twinkle of his eyes gave away his amusement.

I followed Christian as he went to the row in front of Gramps and scooted through to the other aisle, then back down to sit beside his grandfather. I took the seat beside Christian and set my coffee cup on the floor under the seat in front of me, as he had.

Gramps leaned forward to address his next words to me. "What do you do when you're not entertaining people for your parents?"

"I'm kind of at loose ends right now while I figure out what God wants me to do." I hated that it made me sound shiftless, but I honestly had no idea right now. "If I don't have clear direction at the end of the summer, I guess I'll end up taking the receptionist job Dad keeps offering."

"Not what you want to do, though." Gramps's gaze was direct and seemed to understand more than what I'd said.

"No."

"What do you want to do?" Seeing him beside his grandfather, I realized Christian shared the same striking blue eyes.

"I had thought music. But," I spread my hands helplessly. "I don't have what it takes."

Thankfully, the rest of Christian's family chose that moment to filter in from the lobby, so I was saved from elaborating and further questions by a flurry of introductions. No one asked where Christian and I met, which I also appreciated. I'd just as soon not have to lie or dance around explanations for why I'd needed to visit the island clinic. Would he fill them in? Hopefully not. I vaguely recalled signing a HIPAA notice when I'd gone through the required paperwork at intake.

He wouldn't violate that. Right?

The worship band took their places on the platform and I pushed my worries aside. Worship music never failed to soothe the rough edges of my soul. I wasn't going to let today be any different.

3

CHRISTIAN

The quiet babble of after-church conversation started almost as soon as the pastor ended the benediction. I turned to Teresa and lifted my eyebrows. "Well? What did you think?"

"I loved it. You've got a fantastic church here." She had a wistful smile that tugged at something in me. Everything about her tugged at something in me. Since our first meeting when she'd been sporting a black eye and a nasty gash on her forehead, to yesterday with the burns that had—at least in my professional opinion—been deliberately given, she'd pulled at me.

I wanted to help her.

Protect her.

Would she let me?

"Can you join us for lunch?" Mom had scooted down the row and was crowding Teresa between me and Gramps. "We'd love to have you and there's always plenty. We're a big crew, but we don't bite, I promise."

"Mom." I shook my head.

"Even if we did bite, Christian could fix you up." Gramps laughed at his joke, slapping his knee lightly.

I closed my eyes. "Can we not go out of our way to convince her that we're ridiculous. Please?"

Teresa chuckled and briefly touched my arm. "They're fine. I wish I could, Mrs. Thomas, but I'm having lunch at the Golf Club with my parents and their guest."

"Oh. Well, that's disappointing, but the food at the Club is lovely." Mom tapped a finger on her leg. "We'd love to have you —and your family, obviously—another time. Coordinate with Christian."

"I wouldn't want to impose—"

"Nonsense." Mom cut her off. "Loring Island is a friendly place. We'd love to welcome you properly."

Teresa muttered something noncommittal.

Mom eyed me. "Make it happen, Christian."

"I'll see what I can do. Let's not scare them off, though. Okay?" I hadn't missed Mom's calculating look. And while I might not be opposed to seeing what there could be between Teresa and me, we were a long way from the wedding bouquet I could see Mom picturing. I turned my attention to Teresa. "Can I walk you to your car?"

"Car? Oh. I walked." Teresa stuck out a foot. "Comfy sandals."

"You're not walking to the Golf Club." Mom shook her head. "Honey, that's too far. Let Christian drive you."

"Oh, but—"

"I insist." Mom turned to me. "Christian, baby, don't let her walk."

"I'd be happy to drop you off. It's on my way."

Teresa frowned slightly. "Promise?"

"That it's on my way?" I drew an X over my heart. "Absolutely."

Teresa looked between me and Mom. Something in Mom's face must have convinced her not to argue, because she nodded once. "I'd appreciate it."

"Good." Mom patted my arm. "I'll see you at lunch later. And Teresa, if you change your mind, just come along with Christian. There's always plenty. Come on, old man, let's get going."

Gramps scoffed as he lurched to his feet. "You'll be old some-day. See how you like getting bossed around by your children."

Mom laughed and grabbed the cane. She held it out to him with a raised eyebrow. "Forgetting something?"

"Nag, nag, nag." Gramps took the cane and leaned on it as he shifted his weight and started out into the aisle.

"I hope we'll see you around, Teresa." Mom patted her on the shoulder as she scooted past and took up a position beside Gramps.

"I'm so sorry. My Mom is—"

"Lovely." Teresa leaned down and picked up her coffee cup and mine. "She's exactly what a mother should be. Don't apolo-gize for that. I'm just sorry I already have lunch plans."

I couldn't decide if she was serious. I just nodded. "Well, I'm glad you'll let me drop you at the club. It really is quite a walk. Not that there's anything wrong with a good walk—but this weekend especially we have so many visitors in town, the roads aren't always as easy to cross as they usually are."

"I can see that. Everyone loves the beach on Memorial Day weekend." Teresa stepped into the aisle, still holding the coffee cups.

I nodded toward the doors to the foyer. "There's a trash can on our way out. I can take those."

"I've got them. But thanks."

I searched for something to talk about. The easy chatter we'd had before service seemed to have evaporated. Was it Mom? She could certainly come on strong. I was used to it, but it probably wasn't comfortable for someone who'd just been introduced. Especially given whatever was going on in Teresa's life.

Teresa dropped the coffee cups in the trash as we passed them. She paused to shake the pastor's hand and tell him how much she liked the service.

The pastor grinned at me as he shook my hand.

I sighed quietly. I'd be getting questions about Teresa later, I was sure. Now that Bennett was engaged to the town librarian—his high school summer romance gone awry—it seemed like the town was invested in marrying off the rest of the Loring cousins.

Good times.

"I'm over here." I pointed to the left where my car sat alone in the lot.

We crossed the parking lot, and I pulled open the passenger door, cringing as I saw the jumble of papers in the footwell. "Hold on one sec."

I quickly gathered them up and clutched them to my chest. "Sorry about that."

Teresa laughed. "It's fine. It's nice to have a car you don't have to worry about messing up. My parents keep their cars so clean. I'm always worried I'm going to ruin them."

I pondered that as I closed the door and rounded the car. I paused to drop the papers on the back seat before climbing behind the wheel. "Do you not have a car?"

"No. They've offered me one, but right now it's not something I want to afford."

Want to afford? The way she phrased it gave me the impression it had more to do with the money. Maybe I was reading her wrong, but I didn't get the feeling she and her family were the big, close knit, jumble that mine was. "Fair enough. If you're hanging out on the island for long, you should maybe look into a bike. The thrift store often has some good deals. Or, honestly, I could probably scare up something for you to borrow. My family has so many bicycles there has to be one no one is using."

"That's nice of you to offer."

Travis would probably let me loan Teresa Caroline's bike, now that I thought of it. Teresa didn't seem excited about the prospect, but I'd ask. Maybe presenting it to her as a done deal would convince her I was serious.

I started the car. "Have you eaten at the club before?"

"No. Mom and Dad have tried to convince me to come along several times, but I'm not a big fan of dressing for dinner. I gave in today because brunch felt like it might be less," she paused, as if searching for the right word, "ritzy."

I laughed. "It is. Although, to be fair, people tend to dress how they want for the dinners. As long as you don't look like you just walked in off the beach, no one's going to say anything."

"You're a member?"

I wiggled a hand from side to side. "Sort of."

She turned to face me. "How does someone get to be a sort of member at a golf club?"

"It's a family name thing." Would she let it rest at that? I'd mentioned our family relationship to the island. She should be able to connect the dots, right?

"Ah." Teresa nodded. "You're not a fan?"

"Of golf? Or the club?"

"You choose."

I checked the traffic before turning onto the main road. "I guess I don't see the point. Golf's fine. It can be good exercise, if you walk the course. But I don't love how people turn it into a status symbol. Same, really, for the club. Most of the members are just normal people. But there are always a few who want to look down their noses. I'm just not a fan of that. In any setting."

The corners of her lips curved. "Says the scion of the island's founders."

"That's a word." I shook my head.

"An accurate word." She tipped her head to the side. "Don't deny it."

I groaned. "I guess if we're being pedantic."

"Ooh. Now who has a word."

I flashed a grin.

"My parents had several locations they were considering for their beach home. They landed on Loring Island largely because of the ethos of your family founding and remaining here. Plus, piracy adds a certain something. You have to admit that."

"Privateering." I said through gritted teeth. There wasn't a huge difference, historically, between pirates and privateers, but when you were the descendant, the semantics mattered. "Alleged."

"Sore spot, I see."

I glanced over and saw the mirth in her expression.

"Would it help to know my family's company is known as a Beltway Bandit? Bandits aren't any different than pirates, really."

"Maybe." I slowed and turned into the Golf Club parking lot. "Where are they located?"

"DC area. It's a term for the government contractors. Maybe not as much anymore, but when the company was started it was a thing. And for Dad's business, it stuck." Distaste colored her words.

I pulled into the semi-circle in front of the club's main building. "Sorry."

"Don't be. It's my Dad. Not me. And I keep hoping—praying —that he'll find Jesus and tweak some of his practices."

What would it be like to come from a family whose ethics didn't align with yours? "They aren't believers."

Teresa shook her head. "And they're...let's go with displeased, that I am."

I winced. "Sorry. I'll pray for them, if that's all right?"

"Of course." She looked startled. "Thank you."

The valet reached my car and pulled open Teresa's door.

She unbuckled her seatbelt and swiveled, putting her feet on the ground, then she looked back at me. "I appreciate the ride. Would you—would you want to join us for brunch?"

I blinked. Brunch at the club with a family that came across as stuffy and unwelcoming or lunch at Mom and Dad's with our lively, hilarious crew. It was a no-brainer. I opened my mouth to say no. "I'd love that."

Wait. What?

The smile that blossomed on her face made my heart soar. Maybe the disconnect between my mouth and my brain wasn't such a bad thing.

Teresa got out of the car and the valet closed the door before coming around to open my door. I got out and grinned. "Carlton, my man. I didn't realize you were working here this summer."

I bumped Carlton's fist.

"Dad pulled some strings. I wanted to work as a caddy, but those were full. So, I'm parking cars." He shrugged. "It's all for a good cause."

"Still eyeing that Camaro?"

He nodded. "They're going to hold it for me until school starts. Longer, if no one else shows interest."

"Nice." I took the ticket he gave me and slipped it in my pocket. "Come by the clinic sometime when you're off and tell me how it's going, okay?"

"You got it." Carlton slid behind the wheel.

I waited for him to pull away from the curb before joining Teresa.

"Does everyone know everyone on the island?"

I started toward the front doors. "Mostly. The year-rounders, at least. But Carlton's the son of some family friends. I used to babysit him."

"You babysat."

"Sure. It's easy money for a young teen. You didn't?" I pulled open the door and held it for Teresa.

"I did. I hated it though. Stopped as soon as I could find anything else to do."

I chuckled. "It wasn't my favorite. But Carlton was easy."

We crossed the glittering ornate lobby to the restaurant entrance. I stopped at the podium out front.

"Christian." The hostess, Mary Anne, beamed at me. "I didn't see you on our reservation list. I'm not sure we have space for walk-ins, but I'll see what I can do."

"Actually, it's Duvall." Teresa stepped closer. "He'll be joining us if we can have another place added."

Mary Anne's eyebrows shot up. "Of course. The rest of your party is already seated. I'll show you."

Mary Anne signaled to a server and gestured to the podium, then led us through the crowded dining room, past the brunch buffet setup, to a secluded corner. "I'll get another place setting right away."

"Thanks." Teresa sent Mary Anne a bright smile and kept it fixed in place as she neared the table. "Mom, Dad. James. This is Christian Thomas. His mother is a Loring. I invited him to join us."

The stormy glare on Teresa's father's face cleared when she mentioned Loring and was replaced by easy camaraderie. "Mr. Thomas. So wonderful of you to join us."

"Thank you, Mr. Duvall. I apologize for intruding, but I couldn't say no to your lovely daughter." I didn't like playing the snobby rich game, but I knew the rules. I shook his hand, using a firmer grip than I usually bothered with. I mentally rolled my eyes as Teresa's dad worked to out grip me. "It's great to meet you."

Figured.

I turned to Teresa's mother and nodded. "Mrs. Duvall. I see where Teresa gets her beauty."

"Oh, well." Mrs. Duvall waved a hand in front of her face with a sly smile. "Aren't you a charmer."

"Charming or not, it's the truth." I smiled at her, then shifted to face the other man. James. He was older than me. Maybe not by a lot, but probably nearing forty if I was any kind of judge. I extended my hand. "Christian Thomas."

He took my hand, gripping even harder than Mr. Duvall had. "James Willoughby. The fifth."

I smiled politely, as if his name meant nothing to me, which wasn't completely untrue. In the vague recesses of my brain, I had some kind of familiarity with the Willoughby name. From somewhere. Tabloids? Celebrity magazines, maybe? We had subscriptions for most of them at the clinic. I'd been known to page through on slower days. "A pleasure to meet you."

James gestured to the seat beside him. "Teresa, you're here."

I waited a moment, but he didn't stand, so I moved around the table with Teresa and pulled out her chair for her, tucking it in as she sat. Then I took the empty chair beside Mrs. Duvall and across from Teresa.

"Where did you say you met my daughter?" Mr. Duvall eyed me as he spoke.

"At church this morning. I've always enjoyed greeting newcomers."

"And mooching off them for fancy lunches, probably." James's mutter was loud enough for everyone to hear, but quiet enough that I knew I was supposed to ignore it.

"James." Teresa hissed, her mortification obvious.

A server appeared and quickly set the place in front of me. "Will you be having the brunch buffet as well, Mr. Thomas?"

My eyebrows lifted slightly at the formal address. Everyone here knew to call me Christian, but it was obvious that they'd also learned how the Duvalls preferred for things to happen. "If that's what everyone is doing, absolutely."

"Very good. Can I get you a beverage?"

"Orange juice, please."

The server nodded and turned to Teresa. "And you, ma'am?"

"Orange juice is lovely. Thank you."

Mrs. Duvall scoffed. "Why can't you be normal and make it a mimosa?"

"Mother." Teresa's voice was quiet.

The server studiously ignored the interplay. "Please visit the buffet at your leisure. If you need anything, don't hesitate to ask."

Mr. and Mrs. Duvall stood as soon as the server departed.

James paused a moment before joining them. He glanced down at Teresa. "Come along. Just make sure you don't overindulge."

I fought to keep my face expressionless as I stood.

Teresa didn't put the man in his place, which surprised me. Now that I thought about it, her entire demeanor had shifted when we got to the table. Was it because of her parents? James? Some combination of the two?

Was one of them the one who was hurting her?

I bit my lip. Of course, that had to be the case. Didn't it?

Before we got to the buffet line, I peeled off and headed back to the hostess stand.

Mary Anne smiled. "Is everything okay?"

"As always. Could you put the tab for the table on my account?"

Distaste flashed over Mary Anne's face, though she hid it quickly enough. "Are you sure? They've already got a pretty big bar tab running."

Maybe they weren't always this obnoxious then. Alcohol

could change personalities—or at least reveal what people kept as their inside thoughts. "I'm sure."

"All right. I'll make sure the server knows."

"Thanks, Mary Anne." I quickly crossed the main dining room and grabbed a plate from the stack at the end of the buffet.

"I can't believe you still have that ridiculous bandage on your shoulder." Mrs. Duvall didn't appear to be making any attempt to keep her voice down as she chastised Teresa. "You can see it through your wrap and it's ridiculous."

"Mother." Teresa reached for the tongs beside a chafing dish full of crisp bacon. "I'm supposed to keep it covered so it doesn't get infected. I told you that."

Mrs. Duvall sniffed. "It's a simple little burn. They don't get infected."

I studiously focused on the food as I added little bits of this and that to my plate while I inched closer to Teresa and her mother.

"You really are being a baby about the whole thing. I was kidding around." James patted Teresa's shoulder, right over the bandage.

I winced. That had to have hurt.

A lot.

But Teresa didn't react.

James sighed. "Do I have to apologize? Is that what this is? Fine. I'm sorry you can't take a joke. Better?"

"Not really, no." Teresa glared up at James.

Mr. Duvall cleared his throat.

Teresa lowered her head. "Excuse me. I think I'd like an omelet."

I watched Teresa step out of line and make her way to the omelet station, then I glanced down the rest of the buffet. I'd been planning on some roast beef, but maybe eggs would be a better choice.

I made sure Teresa noticed me beside her in the omelet line before I asked in a hushed voice, "Are you all right?"

She shook her head.

"Did he pop the blisters?"

Teresa sighed. "I think one of them, yeah. I'll check it when I get home. The ointment will still be okay to use though, right?"

"It should be. You'll want to be extra careful about keeping it covered. What did he use?" Would she answer me?

"The grate from the grill. It wasn't on, but it sits in the sun all day. He says he didn't think it would be hot." She lifted a shoulder. "Dad really wants this partnership to go through."

"And you're the sacrificial lamb?" I pressed my lips together. "Sorry. That was uncalled for."

"You're not far off. James has...expressed interest. Dad thinks it's just one more way to make sure his company and ours—" She broke off and paled as she took a step back.

My anger must have shown on my face. I took a deep breath and looked away to slowly let it out. "You're okay with this?"

"No! Of course not! But right now, I need my parents' help, so I don't exactly have options." Teresa shook her head, then stepped up to the omelet cook and gave her order.

There was one more empty pan, so I moved closer and gave mine. I touched her arm briefly. "Sorry."

She waved it off.

"Do they know he's hurt you?"

Teresa looked around frantically. If the chef heard anything, he did a good job of hiding it. No one else was close enough to be a worry. "They play it off. Which is what they want me to do. Which is why they can't know that I visited the clinic. They think I looked it up online and am being a hypochondriac."

"But—"

"Christian, please. Let it go." Teresa looked up and met my gaze. "Just let it go. Okay?"

I couldn't do that. I had no idea how to even go about starting to try to let something like that go. I'd feel that way for anyone—it was never okay to hurt another person. But for Teresa? The problem was multiplied. I couldn't get past the idea that she needed my help.

My protection.

And that I needed to do whatever I could to keep her safe. With me.

4

TERESA

I held out my plate for the chef to roll my omelet onto. "Thanks."

Hopefully, Christian would drop it. I shouldn't have gotten into the conversation with him at all. Let alone in public.

And I never should have admitted that James was the one who'd hurt me. Both times. Mom and Dad might make excuses and try to play it off, but I was well aware that James was a ticking timebomb, and I was doing my best to ensure that I kept out of his way whenever possible.

The problem, of course, was that Dad kept making it hard. Much, much harder than it should be. And despite my attempt to get Mom on my side, she just told me not to overreact.

As if a black eye and gash that was going to leave a scar was overreacting. Let alone the burns. It wasn't as if I wanted to go to the police and file a report, either. I just wanted James to leave me alone. And for my family to realize that no matter how much they might want a marriage to solidify the union between our companies, that just wasn't going to happen.

My appetite completely disappeared, but I carried my plate back to our table anyway. I could, hopefully, choke down enough food to keep Mom from commenting. At least I wouldn't be tempted to eat enough that James started making digs about my weight.

He was such a pig.

Christian set his plate on the table and moved around to hold my chair before I realized he was still shadowing my step. I smiled up at him as I sat.

"Thanks."

"You're welcome." He winked before returning to his spot at the table.

I caught the look my mother sent my father as they returned to the table and hurried to look down at my lap, as if placing my napkin was the most important job in the universe right then.

Christian hadn't sat and he moved to hold Mom's chair for her as well.

"Oh, my." Mom laugh was a little too high and much too loud. How many mimosas had she had before we arrived? "What a gentleman."

Dad snorted. "Archaic."

"Not a feminist, huh?" James set his two plates on the table and sat. "Guess there are chicks out there who want someone to do everything for them. Even if they're capable of doing it themselves. I never went for the helpless type, myself. But hey, to each his own, right?"

"I never considered it more than basic manners. But you're right. To each his own." Christian's smile was tight and didn't reach his eyes.

I hid a wince. A statement like that was bound to get James going. And not in a good way.

Dad must have sensed the same thing, because he spoke hurriedly. "What's it like being island royalty, Christian?"

His eyebrows lifted. "I wouldn't know."

"Oh, come on." Dad waved the words away. "Teresa said you

were a Loring. Loring Island. Obviously, you've got some family clout here. Does everyone bend over backwards for you?"

"No. I wouldn't want them to." Christian made a neat slice in his omelet and stabbed the bite with his fork. "My family just loves the island. And we're glad that so many other people do, too. The locals are almost like extended family—so many of them were honorary aunts and uncles when my brothers and I were growing up—and we value the seasonal visitors and are glad to share the beauty of God's creation with them."

I poked at my eggs, then finally cut off a bite. Would I be able to keep them down? That was a question I couldn't answer. But I had to try.

"Not like you're really sharing though. People have to pay to live here or visit. The locals profit off that." James shook his head. "I guess it helps you sleep at night to look at it your way."

"I do sleep well, I won't lie. But I've always attributed that to a solid and satisfying day's work and the sea air through my windows." Christian set his fork down and held James's gaze.

James looked away.

Unfortunately, he looked in my direction.

"You're really plowing through that food. Guess you're not going to want to swim this afternoon." James shook his head. "Maybe I can convince your mother to hop in the pool."

"I can't get my burns wet." I regretted the words instantly.

"Says who? Some website designed to make everyone into sissies who can't handle life? Please. You could swim if you wanted to."

I caught Christian taking a breath, as if he were going to jump into the conversation, and shook my head slightly. *Please take the hint.*

If Christian said something, they'd want to know how he had any knowledge, and then it would come out that he worked at the island clinic...which would definitely mean they'd know I visited there. Even if it didn't? They'd find out Christian was a nurse and that would open a whole new avenue for my parents and James to make this the most uncomfortable lunch in the history of uncomfortable lunches.

Christian's lips flattened, but he stayed silent.

"What do you say, Mrs. Duvall? Are you up for a swim this afternoon?" James glanced down the table at my mom.

Mom drained the last of her mimosa and held up her glass, gesturing with it. "We'll have to see. I'm sure Bernie will join you if nothing else."

Dad frowned at Mom. "Really, Syl."

Mom smiled brightly. "You wouldn't want to let your guest swim alone, right dear?"

"Of course not." Dad's smile was sickly.

He wasn't the biggest fan of swimming. He liked being out on the boat, and he'd wade on the shore up to his ankles, but I could count on one hand the number of times he'd gotten into a swimming pool in my lifetime.

But if it kept James happy and off my case about the burns, I'd deal with whatever little digs Dad was sure to throw my way if he actually ended up in the water.

"Would you care to join us?" Mom sent her words in Christian's general direction.

"Oh, no thank you. I have a family obligation this afternoon. I appreciate the invitation." Christian dabbed his napkin at the corner of his mouth. "In fact, I should probably get going."

"You've hardly touched your food." I blurted out the words before I could stop them. Of course it drew James's attention to my own plate. At least with my appetite gone, he shouldn't feel the need to criticize my own progress.

"I've had enough." Christian scooted his chair back and stood.

The words ping-ponged in my head. Had there been a

double-meaning? Did he mean he'd had enough of me, in addi-tion to the food? My family? All of us?

I started to stand. "I'll walk you out."

Christian hesitated before he smiled. "Thanks." He turned to my parents, "It was nice to meet you, Mr. and Mrs. Duvall. James."

I quickly turned a laugh into a cough. James would not be pleased that Christian had been so informal in comparison to my parents. But what was he going to do about it? He'd intro-duced himself that way, and Christian was only responding in kind.

It shouldn't be a problem.

If it was? Well, I was already doing my darndest not to be alone with James. So far, he hadn't been willing to lash out in front of other people. That was probably why it was so easy for my parents to downplay my injuries.

Neither of us spoke as we crossed the dining room and moved out into the expansive lobby of the golf club. When we were out of view of the restaurant, Christian stopped and turned to me.

"Are you safe?"

I sighed. "I don't know. Probably."

He frowned. "That's a terrible answer."

"It's the only one I have." I shrugged. "I'm getting better at staying out of his way. And as long as I stick near my parents, he won't do anything."

"Are you sure? The fact that they're laughing about your burns suggests otherwise." He scowled toward the restaurant. "Can you make an excuse and come with me?"

I shook my head. "I don't see how. It would just make things worse."

He nodded once as he reached into his pocket and drew out

his phone. "Can I at least give you my number? You can call or text if there's a problem and I'll come."

"Why would you do that?" I took my phone from my pocket, unlocked it, and handed it to him.

He didn't answer while he added his number to my phone. Then his phone chimed. "I sent a text so I have your info on my phone, too. As to why...I don't like seeing people hurt."

Disappointment surged through me. Which was stupid. What had I expected him to say? Of course he was concerned for my well-being, he was a nurse. And a kind man. A believer. All were good reasons for him to care. This wasn't a fairy tale where he'd sweep me off my feet and carry me away from all my problems.

"Promise you'll get in touch. I'm serious. *Before* you get injured again, if possible." Christian shoved his hands into his pockets.

"I'll do what I can. Thanks for coming to brunch with me."

"Thanks for inviting me." His smile flashed—it was gone in an instant—but the image was seared on my brain. He should definitely smile more.

He didn't make a move to leave. I didn't either. I really didn't want to go back in and poke at my plate while my parents and James did their best to consume all the alcohol in the club.

"Teresa!"

I whipped my head around at my name and groaned as I caught sight of James striding across the lobby.

"Did you get lost?" James glanced at me before shooting a glare toward Christian.

"No. Sorry, I was just asking about mid-week services at church. I think I might like to start attending prayer meeting on Wednesdays like I did in Tennessee."

"Starts at seven." Christian tossed the words, like he was repeating them. I hoped he knew I was grateful he went along.

He nodded once. "Hope I'll see you there. Both of you, of course. Everyone's welcome."

James snorted. "Yeah, right. Come on, Teresa. Your food's probably cold."

I hesitated for one moment to watch Christian stride toward the front door, then let James lead me back to the dining room and the awkward afternoon that was waiting for me there.

5

CHRISTIAN

I tossed my exam gloves into the trash and ducked through the curtain surrounding the emergency room cubicle. My days in the Bennett hospital were a nice switch from the slower-paced clinic on the island. Even if they could also be a bit much. Still, that was the deal. For the hospital to oversee the clinic, and for me to be able to run it as a nurse practitioner, I had to agree to some shifts in the ER.

Fair enough, really.

Especially since I had no desire to go to medical school.

I found a vacant seat behind the desk and logged into the computer to finish the paperwork on my last case.

"You free?"

I swiveled to see who'd spoken and fought a wince. She was new. Amy? "I can be in a sec. Just need to finish this paperwork real fast."

"We've got a potential broken arm in seven who asked for you." The nurse—it had to be Amy, didn't it? —raised her eyebrows. "I didn't know we took requests, but Doc Elder said it was fine."

"Huh. Can't say it's ever happened before, but I'll head right over. Did someone already order an x-ray?"

Amy shrugged. "Don't know."

"Great." I muttered and turned back to the computer. I had to log in again. The things logged people out faster than seemed reasonable. Oh sure, privacy, blah blah. It was annoying though. I found my previous patient and double-checked that the antibiotics had been sent to the pharmacy and everything was signed off for discharge, then logged out and pushed back the seat. "You said seven?"

"Yep."

"Thanks." Maybe she'd warm up as she got used to working here. Or maybe it was me. Getting requested at the ER was definitely new, but it wasn't as if I'd been the one to do it. Whatever. I didn't have that many shifts off-island. I could get along with anyone when I needed to.

I strode down the hall, my sneakers squeaking slightly on the floor as I walked, and turned the corner to the line of actual rooms rather than curtained off cubicles that were always the first choice. I knocked on the door of room seven, then pushed it open.

Teresa looked up from her phone.

My heart sank.

"I'm sorry." She set her phone aside. She sat on the bed, cradling her right arm against her body.

"Don't be sorry. Tell me what happened." I swiped my ID through the reader on the room's computer and pulled up her information.

She sighed. "Does it matter?"

"For treatment? No. But to me? Yes." I scanned the information on the machine. "You did the complete intake."

"Yeah." Teresa blinked, but a tear still slipped down her

cheek. "I'm tired of trying to hide it. Dad's going to be so mad. Maybe he won't pay for it. I guess I don't care."

"Good." I got hand sanitizer from the dispenser on the wall, scrubbed my hands together, then pulled a pair of gloves from the box just above it and snapped them on. "Let's take a look. We'll need to get you down to x-ray, obviously, to be sure."

She nodded.

"Can you move it at all?"

Teresa kept her arm cradled against her. "I'd rather not. It hurts. A lot."

"I bet." I could see an obvious deformation three quarters of the way up her forearm. "Let me check on radiology and see how fast we can get you in."

"Okay."

"Be right back." I left the room and went back to the nurse's station. I could put in the order for an x-ray from the room, but instead, I picked up the phone and called over.

"Radiology."

"Curtis? How slammed are you right now?"

"That you, Christian? I didn't realize you were on today. I would've come by during lunch. We're pretty slow. Why?"

"We have a broken arm. Can I bring her down?"

"Yeah, sure, if you have the time. Otherwise, I can send someone over."

I glanced at the case board, then out toward the waiting area. "I'll bring her. We're pretty slow right now, too."

I hung up the phone and adjusted my location indicator to show I'd gone to radiology. That was one of the major benefits of a little local hospital. It could get busy, but it wasn't usually too bad.

On my way back to Teresa's room, I grabbed a wheel chair. I knocked on the door, then maneuvered the chair through. "You're in luck. They can take you right now."

Teresa stood. "I can walk."

"Nope. Hospital policy." I locked the wheels and moved around the front to help her get situated. "Comfy?"

"Not really." She managed a wry smile. "My arm hurts."

"I bet." I unlocked the chair and backed through the doorway, then started down the hall toward radiology. "So, what happened?"

She was quiet for long enough that I began to wonder if she was going to answer. Then she sighed. "James wanted to show my father his new driver. He got his clubs out on the back deck and lined up an imaginary shot. When he swung, he lost his grip and the new club sailed out of his hands and into the ocean."

I snickered.

"Right? Unfortunately, I didn't manage to disguise my own snicker. James wasn't amused. He grabbed another club and before I realized his intention, was swinging it toward my head. I held up my arms to protect my face."

Red hot fury washed through me. I clenched the wheelchair handles and slowed as we approached radiology. "Your father saw this?"

"Yeah."

"And?"

She shook her head.

I clamped my jaw shut on the tirade that wanted to pour out. It wouldn't help Teresa any, and it probably wouldn't even make me feel better. Instead, I pushed her through the door to the x-ray area and nodded to Curtis. "Right arm—you can see where, but maybe go ahead and check the left. Given the nature of the injury, there may be hairline fractures as a result of energy transfer."

Curtis lifted his brows but didn't say anything. "Can do. Want me to bring her back down when we're finished?"

I wanted to wait. But I was still on shift for another hour and there was always something to do in the ER. "Yeah, that'd be great. She's in room seven."

Teresa twisted to look at me. "Thanks, Christian."

"Not a problem. I'll come see you when the x-rays are back." I patted her shoulder, nodded to Curtis, and left the room before I had a chance to convince myself that I could stay.

Things had picked up when I got back to the ER and I dove right in. The anxious mother with her sobbing toddler who wouldn't stop pulling at his ear were a dose of normal that helped calm the simmering rage that Teresa's injury had ignited. I was just finishing their chart, having sent them on their way with a prescription for antibiotics and a recommendation that they follow up with the pediatrician and possibly an ENT. From what the mom said, her child was experiencing nearly back-to-back ear infections. She seemed scared by the possibility of getting tubes. Hopefully, I'd managed to ease her fears there. At least a little.

"Yo." Curtis punched my shoulder lightly. "You hitting on patients now?"

I shook my head. "She's a friend."

"Yeah?" He shot me a skeptical look. "Well, your friend," and I could totally hear his air quotes around the word, "is back in her room. You can read the report, but it's a clean, non-displaced break. Left arm has a hairline fracture, but it doesn't look serious."

I nodded. "Images are in her file?"

"Yeah. I looped in ortho. They said they'd be happy to schedule her when the swelling's down."

"Thanks, man." I tilted my head at him. "You angling for my job?"

He laughed. "No way. I like being in the cool, dark radiology rooms. I don't end up with what looks like either spit up or mashed banana on my scrubs at the end of the day."

I glanced down and chuckled. "I think banana. The toddler I just treated wouldn't relinquish his snack. Scrubs wash."

"Good thing, too. Let me know if your friend needs a date."

"Yeah, I'll get right on that." My voice was dry.

Curtis grinned. "Knew she wasn't a friend."

He pointed at me before he turned and headed back down the hall toward radiology.

I took my time finishing up the toddler, then switched to Teresa's chart. The images were exactly what Curtis had said. I checked the time. It was just about time for me to clock out. I logged out of the computer and pushed back from the desk. I switched my location to gone for the day on the board and headed down to Teresa's room, with a brief detour for a splint and sling.

I knocked and pushed open the door. "Hey."

"Hi." She smiled weakly. "At least I finally got some pain meds."

I chuckled. "That's good. Oral?"

"Yeah. Just ibuprofen. I guess they didn't think I needed anything heavier." She lifted one shoulder. "I don't know if it's helping or I just think it is, but I don't want to crawl in a hole and cry anymore."

"That's good." I held up the splint and sling. "Your right arm is broken. The bones are still aligned though, so that's good. You'll need to wear this splint and keep it still until the swelling is down. Probably two or three days. You should set up an appointment with an orthopedic in three or four days. They've got a great department here at the hospital. Not sure where the closest standalone practice would be, but the internet can tell you."

"Will I need surgery?" Teresa watched as I slid her arm

into the splint and gently tightened the Velcro straps. She frowned as I shook the sling out of its bag. "Do I really need both?"

"You really do." I adjusted the length of the straps and helped her ease her arm into the sling. "Comfortable?"

"I guess."

"As for surgery, that's up to ortho, but when I look at the pictures I don't think so. But don't quote me. It's not my specialty. You didn't drive here, did you?"

"No. Dad dropped me off. At the time, he was angry at James. But he just texted saying I was being dramatic and should figure out my own way home."

I had a lot of not-nice thoughts about her father, but I pushed them away and tried to pray for him. "I can take you. I just got off shift."

"I don't want to be an imposition."

"You're not. Let me just go change. Have they been in with discharge instructions?"

She nodded.

"All right. If you want to wait in the lobby, I'll be out in five."

Teresa stood and awkwardly put her phone in her pocket before grabbing her purse. "Why is being one handed such a pain?"

"You'll get used to it." I gestured for her to go out in front of me, then pointed toward the exit sign. "I'll be right out."

I waited a second to be sure she was on her way, then hurried to the staff locker room to change out of my scrubs and get myself presentable again. In just over the five minutes I'd promised, I strode out into the waiting room.

I scanned the nearly-empty space until I found her. I crossed the room. "Ready?"

"Very." She stood. "I appreciate this. Looks like a ride share would've been a lot."

I nodded. "It's the bridge, I imagine. And the fact that you're technically moving between towns."

"I guess." She shrugged. "I would've paid it. But this is better."

"Can I take you to dinner first?" She probably ought to go home and rest. That was absolutely the instruction I would have given her if someone was picking her up. But I wasn't ready to send her back into that viper's nest just yet. Not if I could get her to agree to something else.

Teresa blinked. "Dinner?"

"Yeah. It's a meal traditionally eaten in the late afternoon or early evening. Maybe you've heard of it."

One corner of her mouth poked up and it looked to me like she was trying not to laugh. "It sounds a little familiar."

"Excellent. So?"

Teresa was silent while we crossed the parking lot to the staff area. I unlocked the car and opened the passenger door.

"Okay."

I grinned. The tension I hadn't noticed disappeared. "Cool."

When I was sure she could manage the seat belt on her own, I closed the door and rounded the car to climb in behind the wheel. "Anything in particular you're in the mood for?"

"Do the locals have a favorite seafood place?"

"Of course we do." I narrowed my eyes in her direction. "I guess you qualify, since your family owns a home on the island. But if we start getting overrun by tourists, I'll know who to blame."

Teresa dragged a finger over her heart in an X. "I won't tell a soul. Promise."

I started the car. "I'm going to hold you to that."

Of course, tourists often found the creatively named Seafood Shack on their own, but it teetered just above the status of dive. Barely. So many of the families on vacation took one look and headed back into town for something a bit more upscale.

Their loss.

Teresa was looking out her window while I drove and I left her to her thoughts. I wanted to talk to her about her family— see why she stuck around—but I couldn't figure out how to bring it up.

I prayed that God would give me the words and open an opportunity for that conversation.

Ten minutes later, I pulled into the gravel parking lot in front of a ramshackle building by the water's edge. There were picnic tables strewn around the grassy area, boats were pulled up along the dock that speared out into the ocean, and a short line was already forming at the ordering window.

"This is...not what I would have imagined." Teresa looked over at me. "You're not trying to give me food poisoning, right?"

I laughed. "Absolutely not."

"Okay." She sounded wary.

"We can go somewhere in town that lets you eat inside if you want. There's a good burger place."

"No." She shook her head to emphasize her words. "No, I asked about seafood. So I'm going to trust you."

"Appreciate it." I grinned and pushed open my door. "Let me come around and help you out, okay?"

She paused in her effort to reach across herself to work the door with her left hand and sighed. "Yeah, all right."

I hurried from the car and around to the passenger door so I could pull it open. Teresa swung her legs around and stood, wobbling once before she found her balance.

"You okay?"

"Yeah." She started across the gravel to the shack. "It smells good."

Chuckling, I closed her door and locked the car before

jogging a few steps to catch up with her. I was about to speak, when a blur of noise and motion rammed into my legs, then arms wrapped around my middle. "Oof."

"Christian!"

"Hey, Grady." I ruffled my nephew's hair and returned his hug, then turned to scan the picnic tables. I found my Aunt Deb and Uncle Rob at the farthest picnic table. Travis, my cousin and Grady's dad, was strolling across the grass toward me.

"Christian. You just get off work?" Travis rubbed Grady's arm. "Let go, buddy."

"Christian!" Grady's arms tightened.

Travis winced and looked up at me. "Sorry."

"Don't be." I swiveled to see if Teresa had gone on without me, but she was a few steps away watching. "Would you mind joining my aunt and uncle while we ate?"

"Of course not."

I studied her face, trying to decide if she was being polite or sincere. I probably didn't know her well enough to say for certain, but there was nothing fake in her slight smile. I gave Grady a tight squeeze then tugged one of his arms loose and bent so I could see his face. "I'm going to get food and then we'll come sit with you, okay?"

Grady nodded slowly.

"Will you go back with your dad while I do that?"

Grady nodded one more time, then turned and took Travis's outstretched hand.

"Thanks." Travis glanced between Teresa and me, then raised his eyebrows.

"We'll go order."

Travis and Grady headed back toward Deb and Rob. I returned my attention to Teresa. "You're sure that this is okay?"

"Absolutely. You ate with my family. This will probably be a lot better." She breathed in deeply. "It smells good."

"That's cause it is." I gestured for her to keep walking toward the order window.

While we waited our turn, Teresa scanned the chalkboard menu, then turned to me. "What do you recommend?"

"Catch of the day."

"That fast?" She looked surprised.

I nodded and pointed to where they'd written "Swordfish" underneath the listing for the daily catch. "Swordfish is a personal favorite. If you're not up for that, you really can't go wrong. The oysters are from local farms. Everything else would be fresh caught today. Maybe yesterday evening at the latest."

"Okay."

When it was finally our turn, I gestured for Teresa to order first.

"Can I get the fish and chips?"

"Course. To drink?"

"Oh. Um." She glanced at me.

"Do you like sweet tea?"

She nodded.

"Do that. Theirs is some of the best."

The teenager behind the register grinned. "For you?"

"I'll do the sweet tea and the swordfish. You doing blackened today?"

The kid nodded.

"Let's do that, then. And can I get a basket of hush puppies with extra tartar?"

"Course." The kid punched numbers on the register, then swiveled it around for me.

I tapped my card to the screen and poked the screen to add a tip. "We're going to sit with Deb and Rob."

"Okay. I'll bring it out. Wait a sec for your drinks."

I watched as the kid filled two enormous cups with ice, then held them under the spigot of an enormous urn of sweet tea. He put them on the small shelf in front of the window.

"Thanks." I took the cups and stepped around the side of the shack where lids and straws and other condiments were kept.

While Teresa put a lid on her cup, I gathered napkins and utensils, then we headed over to sit with my family.

Which hopefully wouldn't end up being an enormous mistake.

6

TERESA

The cup of sweet tea in my hand was larger than any I'd ever considered ordering. How many calories were in there, when everything was considered? Not that I generally cared overmuch about calories, but my parents and James made enough comments about it, that it had started to become second nature.

Christian leaned in to kiss his aunt on her cheek, then shook his uncle's hand. He grinned at the man who'd followed the little boy over. "Aunt Deb, Uncle Rob, Trav, Grady, this is Teresa Duvall. Teresa, this is a part of my family. We're a big crew."

I managed an awkward smile and bobbed my head. "Nice to meet you. Thanks for letting us join your table."

Deb laughed. "I think we're the ones who should be thanking you. Grady didn't give you a whole lot of choice."

"Christian." Grady patted the space on the bench beside him. "You sit here. By me. Austin took us out on his new boat and we got to see dolphins!"

"Nice." Christian sent a confused look at his aunt and uncle. "New boat?"

Deb shook her head. "Apparently. He has a deep-sea fishing operation in mind, in addition to his other boats that he runs."

"Yeah? It'd be nice to have that based on the island. My father has been frustrated that he'd have to come over to the mainland to set something up." I set my tea down on the table and carefully stepped over the bench so I could sit. "I suspect there are more tourists with that same mindset."

"You're likely right." Rob patted his wife's arm. "Deb worries about him overextending."

Christian snorted. "Did you forget whose family he's part of? We like to stay busy. It's almost like it was drummed into us at an early age that just because we were richly blessed didn't mean we could sit on our laurels."

Travis laughed. "He's got you there, Mom."

"Hmpf." Deb's eyes sparkled with laughter, for all she tried to look annoyed. "Next thing you know, you'll be trying to tell me that it's all my fault he's an adrenaline junkie."

"If the shoe fits, hon." Rob ducked out of the way of the playful swat Deb aimed at his arm. He turned and met my gaze. "Deb's a marine biologist. Before she came back to Loring Island to start the science center, she specialized in sharks."

"They're really quite misunderstood." Deb frowned. "I wish more people would take the time to actually learn about them instead of watching *Jaws* and deciding they're just a menace. The odds of being attacked by a shark are something like one in over three million. Compare that to a car accident, which is what, one in a hundred?"

"Nice, Dad. You got her going." Travis shrank away from the glare Deb sent him.

"I'm only saying that I don't think it's right to compare diving with sharks to the things your adrenaline junkie brother does. He didn't get it from me." She crossed her arms.

"Okay. Obviously, you're right. Must be all the stories of near-death house closings I shared with him when he was young. Like the time a client decided to finance a luxury car two days before signing papers for their beachfront house, causing the lender to pull the mortgage." Rob gave an exaggerated shudder. "Nightmares for weeks after that one."

"Oh, hush." Deb muttered. She took a drink from her cup, the spluttering noise letting the whole table know it was empty.

"I'll get you a refill, Mom." Travis popped up and took her cup. He glanced at Grady. "You want more, bud?"

Grady shook his head.

"So is Austin's boat why you're here for supper?" Christian directed his question to Grady, but Rob answered.

"It is. He brought in two swordfish that we caught while we were out."

"Yeah?" Christian straightened and looked at me with a grin. "See?"

"I almost regret getting the fish and chips." That swordfish was practically still swimming if it was caught right before they came to eat.

"Don't." Deb pointed at the empty basket in front of her. "It's fresh this morning, and so good. Tell me how you know Christian."

"Oh." I paused and cleared my throat, then glanced at him. "I met him on the island a couple weeks ago. My family bought a vacation home near the beach."

"The old Hackett place." Rob noted. "Travis did that one. Must have been with your father. Mostly online negotiation."

I nodded. "Dad only came out to see it once. He wasn't overly choosey. He really just wanted someplace that looked impressive."

I winced. "Sorry. That came out wrong. Dad's not—"

"Hey." Christian touched the shoulder of my slinged arm.

"We get family. You can love 'em, and they can still sometimes make you a little nuts."

"A little?" Deb chuckled. "Even so, that's a lovely property. I'm glad someone bought it. Rob and I had been talking about adding it to our vacation rental properties, but it seemed a shame for it not to have a steadier residence."

Rob eyed Christian with a measuring glance. "You met her a couple of weeks ago and still haven't brought her around to meet everyone? Scared she's going to run away when she meets the whole crew?"

Christian chuckled. "It's a valid concern."

Unable to stop myself, I shot him a startled glance. How had he managed to sidestep the question so neatly without actually saying something that wasn't true.

"Well. Now that we've met her, your mother is going to demand her turn. Especially since you haven't even mentioned you were seeing someone." Deb tsked. "Works out for me, though. I love getting one over on my older sister."

Christian looked as though he was about to say something when a bee lazily drifted over the picnic table and Grady began to shriek at a volume and pitch that suggested he was being actively stung, rather than simply in the area of the thing.

"Oh dear." Deb shot to her feet, waving the bee away as she darted to Grady's side. "You're all right. Shh."

I glanced over my shoulder to see Travis coming toward the table at a full-out run, our food tipping precariously in one hand, while iced tea sloshed over the side of his mother's cup. He skidded to a stop, nearly upsetting the cup when he dumped it all unceremoniously on the table and scooped his son into his arms.

"Are you hurt? What happened?" Travis hugged the boy tightly to him, apparently impervious to the ear-piercing noise the boy was making.

"There was a bee." Deb pushed to her feet looking resigned. "It was nowhere near him."

Travis closed his eyes a moment before sinking to the bench into Grady's spot. His son clung to him, shrieks turning into hysterical sobs. "Hey, buddy, hey. I'm not putting you down. It's okay."

Christian bit his lip as he watched the situation unfold. He and Rob exchanged a glance, and Rob stood. "Let's head on home."

Travis sighed as he worked to his feet, Grady still clinging to him. "Yeah, I guess that's the right call. Sorry, Christian. Teresa. It was nice to meet you. I expect we'll see you at lunch on Sunday?"

"Since I'm going to be popping over to Linda's to tease her about the fact that I've already met Teresa and she hasn't, I'm fairly certain that's a given." Deb grinned as she collected their empty baskets, trash, her purse, and the child's backpack that probably belonged to Grady. "I look forward to hearing more about how you met. And how you got Christian to keep you a secret. Although, of the boys in the family, he's definitely the one most likely to be able to keep something quiet."

"Thanks. I think." Christian rubbed Grady's back briefly and waved to the others. "It was good to see you."

Travis let out a mirthless laugh. "Oh yeah."

I watched them cross to the parking lot and all pile into a huge SUV. "Your family is nice."

"They can be. They're also intrusive." Christian slid my fish and chips basket over to me and spent a second dabbing at his swordfish with a napkin. "Guess I'm finding out how sweet tea marinade works with this."

"I can share with you, if you can't eat it. This is a lot of food." I was staring at the three enormous pieces of golden fried fish sitting on top of a huge pile of fries. Three hushpuppies were tucked in one of the curves of the red plastic basket. My mouth watered. It smelled good. And I probably could eat it all, if I let myself. Or at least make a good dent. But it would be better if I didn't.

"Nah." Christian used his plastic fork to pull off a bite of the swordfish and pop it in his mouth. He nodded as he chewed, then took a sip of tea to wash it down. "This tastes just fine. You want a bite?"

"Are you sure?"

"Of course." He slid his basket over a little so it was easier for me to grab some of the grilled fish. Flavor exploded on my tongue when I ate the morsel. Sure, there was a tiny hint of sweet tea, but it didn't matter. "That's amazing."

He grinned and nodded toward my food. "Try yours. I think you'll be saying the same thing. I've never been disappointed here yet."

I picked up one of the fish pieces and bit in. Christian was right. It was delicious.

We ate in companionable silence for several minutes, before Christian cleared his throat.

I looked over at him, eyebrows raised.

"Can you come to Sunday lunch? My aunt's not wrong. My mom is going to expect it now. Honestly, the whole family will. Or, I mean, I could tell them we broke up. Even though we're not dating—I fully understand that. I just..." he trailed off and sighed. "Trying to convince my aunt and uncle of that right then wouldn't have worked."

"Oh. I don't—"

"No. Of course not." Christian held up a hand. "Forget I said anything. I'll figure it out. Who knows, maybe the truth will work, if I stick to it."

I frowned down at my food. How much of the truth would he need to tell? I wasn't proud of being the girl who needed her parents' approval—and support—so badly that she was willing to put up with abuse. If I still had any money from my first trust installment left, I wouldn't. But, if I'd been paying attention to the funds when I was in Nashville, I would have pivoted in my career goals a lot sooner. Then I wouldn't be stuck for the next six months.

Christian gently touched my arm and I ignored the warmth that spread from his fingers. "I won't mention the clinic. That's protected by HIPAA. I take that seriously. Don't worry about that, okay?"

I flashed a smile. "I wasn't."

"Okay. Good." He went back to eating.

I pushed my barely-touched basket away. "What's up with Grady?"

"That's a long story." He glanced at my food, then back at me with questions in his eyes that he didn't ask. He shrugged. "The short version is autism compounded with having his mom walk out on them in January. He gets a new deathly fear every couple of weeks. Usually with time and patience, Travis and his folks can help him over it. I guess bees are new. At least, I hadn't heard about them being a thing yet."

I nodded. "To be fair, bees can be a pain."

"Literally." Christian grinned. "But they generally don't sting unless you're threatening them. I'm glad it wasn't a hornet or wasp though. They'll sting just for the fun of it."

I snickered. I didn't think it was quite that bad, but then, I hadn't ever been stung by something. So maybe I just didn't know.

"Are you finished eating?" Christian scooped the last of his swordfish onto his fork with half of a hushpuppy and popped them both into his mouth.

"Yeah. Think I could get a box?" I wasn't sure how Mom and Dad—let alone James—would react to me coming home with leftovers. Maybe I could spin it as a positive, since I'd eaten so little.

"Sure. I'll go grab one. You need more tea while I'm up?"

I shook my head.

"All right. I'll be right back. Then I'll take you home." He stood and strode unhurriedly back to the shack. He nodded to a few people who hailed him as he passed. Was it nice to live somewhere that people recognized you? It probably depended on whether or not they recognized you because they liked you, or for other reasons.

I blew out a breath. If only things in Nashville had worked out differently. I scoffed at myself. They might have if I'd been smarter with my money. I'd been too sure that I was going to get snapped up with a deal that I hadn't scrimped and saved. I hadn't gotten a day job or found a roommate. So, the money, enough for two years of college, drained away. And since I hadn't gone to college, the tuition for the other two years—or the completion of a degree—got rolled into the full trust.

Six more months.

"What's that you're humming?" Christian set a foam container on the table.

I'd completely zoned out. My cheeks heated. "It's, uh, from *The Music Man*. I like musical theater."

"Who doesn't?"

I frowned at him. "Are you making fun of me?"

"Why would I be?" He looked affronted. "I come from a family with varied and diverse interests. Plus, *The Music Man* is a classic. Who doesn't love trombones?"

"Probably a lot of mothers of young children."

He laughed. "True. But that wasn't the trombone song."

"No." I really didn't want to tell him it was *The Sadder but Wiser Girl*. He'd ask questions that I'd have to dodge. Or make something up. It's not like that was the catchiest tune in the musical. Even worse would be if he *didn't* ask questions. Because that would mean he'd think he already had the answer. And while he might have some hints, he didn't know the full scope of it.

And I'd just as soon he never did.

I'd have to analyze that, later. Because warm and tingly glancing touches were all well and good, but there couldn't be anything between Christian and me. Even if I wanted there to be. Which seemed incredibly unlikely.

I slid my food out of the basket into the to-go container and fastened the lid shut, then stood. "Ready when you are."

"You're not going to tell me the song?" He picked up our trash and stacked it.

I just picked up my cup and started toward his car.

Christian fell into step beside me. "Guess I know what I'll be streaming tonight."

I shook my head. "I don't believe you."

He tossed the trash into a can and stacked the baskets on top of the pile that was on a shelf beside them. Then, as we crossed the rest of the way to his car, he started to hum about the trombones.

Christian Thomas was going to be trouble.

7

CHRISTIAN

"Thanks for the help." Bennett dropped into the deck chair next to me and tapped his soda can to mine.

"Sure thing. You seem pretty settled already though. It's nice to see Gramps's house getting used full again."

"You think it'll be called Gramps's house forever?"

I laughed. "Probably. Sorry."

"Doesn't bother me. Can't imagine it'll bother Jericho, either, for that matter. She loves Gramps."

I nodded. That was clear. "Jericho loves everyone."

"Maybe not you." Bennett grinned over at me.

I rolled my eyes. "She's settling, marrying you. I can't blame her, though. It's expected and if she finally acknowledged her burning passion for me and threw you over, you'd probably shrivel up and die."

Bennett laughed for so long he had to gasp for air.

"It's not *that* funny."

"Sure it is." Bennett chuckled.

I frowned. "I've had girlfriends."

"Key word there is had. When was the last time you went on

a date? An actual date with a woman who knew you were interested in them and who was, in turn, interested in you?"

"That's a lot of conditions." And it ruled out dinner with Teresa on Friday. I'd spent a lot of the weekend trying to think of ways to steer any mention of it into being our first official date. If it had come up. Which it didn't.

Teresa barely acknowledged me at church on Sunday. She'd slipped in the back after we'd already started worship, and had left before the pastor finished the benediction. Not that I'd been obsessively checking. I just happened to notice.

"From your silence, I'm guessing you're all the way back to college trying to figure it out." Bennett shrugged. "Which is fine. Happily single is a thing, you know. Look at Sara."

I must have looked confused, because Bennett tacked on, "Books and Bites?"

"Right." Sara who ran the bookstore. "And you know she's happy about being single how?"

"Because people were always trying to pair us up. Before Jericho came back. You know that. So, she and I talked about it."

"Huh." How had I missed that? Surely it would have come up at one of our family meals? "How'd you keep Mom out of that business?"

Bennett grinned. "Lots of hard work. I think it helped that Mom never thought Sara and I would make a good match. If she'd been in on the matchmaking attempts, it probably would have been a different story."

"That makes sense." I sighed. "Did you and Jericho pick a date yet?"

Bennett lifted his eyebrows at the abrupt change in topic. "No. We're trying to balance what we want—which is honestly to be married already—with Mom's big dream."

"And Jericho's parents?"

He shook his head. "There's still some tension there. She's

working on it. But for now, her mom said she's happy to come but doesn't want to pressure her into anything she doesn't want. Her sisters basically said the same thing."

"And her dad?"

"He hasn't returned any of her calls."

"Ouch."

"Yeah." Bennett blew out a breath. "I'm trying to follow her lead, but part of me wants to reach out and give the man an earful."

"Dude."

He held up his hands. "I know. Bad idea. I won't. But it aggravates me."

"I get that." Better than I was willing to explain at this red-hot second. Of course, Teresa would be better off if her father wasn't in contact with her. He'd been visibly—and audibly—displeased when I dropped her off and he'd seen her sling. She was still wearing the brace and sling on Sunday, at church at least, but was he pressuring her not to at home? She was supposed to go to the orthopedic doctor today. I'd reach out this evening and see how it went. I could claim professional interest, couldn't I?

My phone rang, the tone indicating it was a clinic call. I stood and walked to the far side of Bennett's deck. "This is Christian."

There was a slight pause. "Hi. It's me. Teresa?"

"Hi. Did you mean to call the clinic?" I'd given her my contact info.

She sighed. "Dad accidentally dropped my phone off the side of the boat. So, I have a new one. And there was a glitch in the backup online that somehow only affected your contact."

Her words dripped with air quotes and sarcasm. I winced. "How can I help you? Please let me help you."

"Right now, I just need a ride to the hospital in town for my appointment at the orthopedic. If you can. I don't even know how it works when you're supposed to be at the clinic. Can you... never mind, I'll figure it out."

"Stop. I can absolutely take you. The nice thing about the clinic is that it's not usually busy so I have flexibility. People call when they need me. Like you did. I'll be over to get you in a few minutes. Okay? Sit tight."

"Thanks. I'm sorry about this." Her voice wavered like she was fighting off tears.

"Don't be. I'm happy to help. See you soon." I ended the call and looked over at Bennett. "Gotta run."

"Clinic calls. You're like Batman without the cool symbol in the sky. Or the cape. Or Alfred."

"So, basically, nothing like him." I tucked my phone in my pocket. "Especially given my huge, still alive, family. And the fact that I don't like caves."

Bennett chuckled and stood. He beat me to the door into the house and held it open for me. "A few discrepancies."

My lips twitched up. I held my thumb and forefinger a tiny space apart. "Just a few. See you later. July fourth would be a good wedding date. Think of the fireworks."

Bennett snickered, like I'd hoped he would.

I jogged down the steps to my car and climbed in. Nothing on the island was far from anything else, but the distances were enough that if you didn't want some exercise, or to spend a while walking, a car was useful. Sometimes, vacationers near the beach complained that the town wasn't really walkable from their rentals. I wasn't sure what they expected us to do about that, but it was a recurring theme.

I entertained myself with various ways to relocate our main street to the beach, and the ensuing complaints about houses being too far away from the surf, while I drove toward Teresa's place. As I slowed prior to turning off the main road, I spotted her waving from the corner. Frowning slightly, I turned and pulled over to the curb.

She opened the door and climbed in. "Thank you. Really."

"Like I said, I'm happy to do it. But I would have come to your house." I glanced in the mirrors to be sure we were clear before making a tight U-turn, then getting back on the main road that would take us to the bridge to the mainland.

"I know. I just...Dad's, well, and James too, honestly. It's complicated." Teresa bit her lip and stared out her window.

"And your mother?"

Teresa sighed. "Drunker than usual."

No help from that quarter, then. Not that I'd been under the impression that Mrs. Duvall was going to be help on the best of days. "You need to leave. You know that, right?"

She nodded. "That's complicated, too."

I hesitated. What was the line? Was there one? With something like this, where it was a real possibility that she was in increasing danger, was there a point where I needed to be quiet? I prayed for discernment and guidance and chose my words carefully. "Do you want to tell me why? Or how, I guess?"

"Not really."

I didn't respond. Something about the way she sat—motionless, refusing to look at me—gave me the impression that she wasn't finished. We reached the bridge and I joined the light traffic heading over to the mainland.

"I don't know what you know about my family. Mom and Dad both come from money. Big money, not just doing okay. But trust fund money." She glanced over at me.

I nodded.

"Dad does pretty well in the business world, too. The money just keeps expanding. Which I guess is the point. Regardless, it's all he cares about. Dad checked out of the family—beyond the need to keep up appearances—when it became clear that his only offspring was going to be a girl. Mom did, too, once she realized that I wasn't going to be a perfect little debutante daughter." Teresa shrugged. "I'm not looking for a poor little rich girl situation here. I've always been taken care of. But we're not a tight family unit."

I couldn't quite stop the snort. "I picked up on that much."

She offered a weak smile. "Yeah. Anyway, my grandparents —or maybe their grandparents—set up the money for future generations to sort of trickle down. I got access to enough of my trust to pay for college. But I never wanted college. There were allowances for that, sort of, and I took advantage of them to try and make it in Nashville."

"That can be hard, I imagine."

"You have a way with understatement. But basically, yes. I ran out of money and, with nowhere else to go until I hit thirty and can access all of my money, I ended up back home. I'm grateful my parents gave me a place to land. I owe them for that."

I disagreed with that. A lot. But my family was different, so maybe I simply didn't understand how one like hers worked. "You could get a job, though. Move out and support yourself until you get the trust?"

"Oh, sure. All those jobs I'm super qualified for. Can people live on burger flipping pay? It doesn't seem like it. And to be honest, I'm not even sure I could manage flipping burgers. I tried waiting tables in Nashville when the money ran out, and that was a disaster." She turned slightly. "And the reality is, I don't know how to live like someone who has no money. That's part of how I got myself into this situation in the first place. If I'd been smarter in Tennessee, I probably could have afforded to go to school and figure out some kind of backup plan."

I nodded. "Is school your plan? When you get your money?"

"I guess. I need to do something that'll make it possible for me to support myself. I could live on the trust, but that's...I don't want to do that."

I smiled, both proud and relieved that she felt that way. "Any thoughts on what that would be?"

"Not really. Music has always been what I love most, and I've already proven that I don't have what it takes to make that my career." She let out a heavy sigh. "I'll have to figure out what I can do that I won't absolutely despise. Given my performance in school, that's a very small pool to choose from."

"I doubt that." I glanced over at her, trying to read her expression. "You graduated, right? You have to be good at something."

"Sure, I graduated. But I was a solid C student. Some Bs, when the teacher was kind or there was teamwork so classmates helped me out. The only thing I ever did well in was music. Oh, and theater. That's even less probable as a career than music. Maybe flipping burgers isn't such a bad idea after all. I can probably learn how to do that. Then all I'd need was a cheap place to stay. Most likely someone renting a room in their house." She wrinkled her nose.

Sharing a living space could be tricky. I'd had roommates in college and grad school. Definitely not my favorite, but we'd made it work. I frowned slightly. "Lots of the shops in town hire seasonal workers. You could start there."

"Aren't those jobs all full by now? It'll be June tomorrow."

"Not sure. I haven't paid a lot of attention, honestly. But it'd take what, half an hour, to walk through town and look for help wanted signs? I'll go with you, if you want." Where had that come from? Not that I'd mind walking around town with her. I wouldn't mind that at all. But would she want me to?

"You would?"

"Yeah. Of course." I flashed a smile in her direction.

We finally reached the end of the bridge and bumped softly

onto the main road. It didn't take long to get to the hospital after that. I drove around to the patient parking and found a spot near the main, non-emergency entrance.

Teresa cleared her throat. "Do you want to come with me?"

"I can. Or I can hang around town and you can text me when you're done. Tell me what you prefer."

She hesitated. "I guess it makes more sense to text you. You can run errands or something."

"All right." I could use a quick trip for some groceries, since I was over here. "When you're done, maybe we can swing by MacLachlan's and get some ice cream before we head back."

"That sounds really good. I appreciate this." She pushed open her door and got out. "Probably won't be too long."

I chuckled. I wasn't going to bet on that, either way. Sometimes the doctors in the building ran on time. Sometimes they ran late. It all depended on how their day had been going to date. "See you soon."

I watched her walk into the building, then reached for my phone. I hesitated a moment as I looked between my mom and Aunt Deb's contacts. I finally tapped Aunt Deb.

"Hi, Christian." Aunt Deb sounded a little out of breath and I heard screeching in the background.

I winced. "If you're busy, I can call back."

"No. It's just a rough day for Grady." The screeching faded and was replaced by the quiet sound of the surf. "There. I walked outside on the deck. He has to get it out of his system. To what do I owe the pleasure of your call?"

I laughed. "Do I need to call more often?"

"Probably not. But you have to admit it's unusual."

"It is." I made a mental note to do better. Although, our family was big and intertwined, so it wasn't as if we ever went long without seeing and talking to one another. I cleared my throat. "I wondered if you might be open to having a guest for a while."

"A guest?" Aunt Deb paused. When she spoke again, her voice had a teasing lilt. "Would this be a female guest?"

"It would. But it's not like that."

"Of course not."

"I'm serious. Teresa and I are just friends." Were we even that? I'd certainly like us to be. So yeah, I'd stick with that. "Her home situation is complicated. It would be good if she could have a safer place to stay. Get on her feet."

"Of course."

"Just like that?" I smiled slightly. I hadn't necessarily expected something different, but it was still a big ask.

"Just like that. Although, I would like to know why you asked me and not your mom."

I bit my lip. "I thought, with Gramps living there now, it might be a bit much. But I hadn't factored in Grady."

"Ah. But Grady doesn't live here. And you're right. Dad's still settling in with Linda. I'm probably the better choice. You know she's going to ask, though. It's good you have a reason."

Should I have asked Mom? Gramps settling in wasn't the whole reason behind my choice. Asking Mom would open up so many questions about Teresa. Our relationship. Our plans. When she could expect a grandchild.

"I also thought she might be more comfortable with the idea since she's met you before."

Aunt Deb snickered. "That one would not fly with your mother."

I was leaving that alone. One way or another, Teresa would end up meeting Mom—Sunday after church if nothing else— but if I could put it off, I was going to. "She's also looking for a job. Any ideas of who might be hiring?"

"Hm. I haven't seen any signs in the windows lately. But actually, you should ask Bennett. Travis was saying something about him complaining that his receptionist was flaky. Not sure if that translates to wanting to replace her, but it's worth asking."

"Yeah?" Why hadn't Bennett mentioned anything about that when I was helping him at the house. Then again, we didn't really talk about work. Bennett and I both had jobs with confidentiality requirements, too. Neither of us were big on work talk. "I'll shoot him a text."

"When will she want to move in?"

"Not sure. Would today be too soon?"

"No." Aunt Deb's voice held questions.

At least she didn't ask them outright. "I'll let you know as soon as I know. Does that work?"

"Of course." She paused. "Why don't you bring her for dinner? Either way."

Was that a good idea? On the one hand, my aunt was an amazing cook, and I'd be dumb to turn down a meal she wanted to prepare for me. On the other? I didn't need her getting ideas about the relationship between Teresa and me. Was I attracted to her? Yeah. But attraction wasn't the end all, be all. I'd learned that in college. We had some things in common—our faith being one of them. That was key.

But also? She was in a situation with her family and life right now that potentially made her susceptible to making less than well-thought-out decisions. I didn't want any romantic relationship we might or might not have to be influenced by that.

"Christian?"

I cleared my throat. "Sorry. Look, I'll see what she has to say. She hasn't asked me to solve her problems."

Aunt Deb laughed. "You're a Thomas through-and-through, aren't you?"

"And a Loring. Both sides of the family are big on helping when we can."

"True enough. Though your dad is more about saving than just helping."

I frowned.

"That's not a bad thing. It's a big part of why you're an amazing nurse. And probably why you never wanted to be a doctor. You like being more hands-on and less specialized." She sighed. "I'm still going to make a nice supper. Why don't you come, either way? There'll be plenty if Teresa decides to join."

"That I can do. What time?"

"Let's say six thirty. Does that work?"

"Absolutely. Thanks, Aunt Deb. Love you."

"Love you back. You're one of my three favorite nephews."

I laughed. She only had three nephews, but it had taken my brothers and me into our teens to really piece together that she wasn't calling any of us her absolute favorite. "And you're my favorite aunt. I'll see you later."

She chuckled and ended the call.

I took a second to text Bennett and ask about the potential of a receptionist-slash-assistant position opening at the law firm, then started the car and headed toward the market. If I was grabbing dinner at Aunt Deb's, I could at least bring something nice for dessert.

8

TERESA

I gave Christian a weak smile as he pulled up to the curb
outside the hospital entrance. I reached for the car door
and pulled it open, then got in.

"Thanks."

"I see you went for purple." He nodded toward the cast on
my arm. "Good choice. Though I'm partial to the lime green,
myself."

I wrinkled my nose. "Really? It looks a lot like puke."

"That's the fun."

"Boys never stop being teenagers, do they?"

He laughed. "Probably not. So. Ice cream?"

"Definitely. Bonus if there's some kind of hot fudge
involved."

"That can definitely be arranged." He waited until I'd gotten
my seatbelt fastened before starting to drive. "Everything go all
right at ortho?"

"That's what the doctor said. I don't have any reason not to
believe her. The bones were all still in alignment, the swelling
was down, I'd been doing a good job keeping it immobile, blah
blah blah."

"Blah blah blah? I'm not sure that's part of the standard medical dictionary."

I shrugged. "That's what it sounded like to me. At least with this cast, I can take showers. Somewhere in the dim recesses of my memory, I thought I knew that casts had to stay dry."

"Sure. In the bad old days of plaster. Not that they don't still use that sometimes, but mostly it's fiberglass these days with a waterproof liner when there's no swelling. Or surgery. I don't think they can do that if an operation was necessary." He frowned. "It's been a minute since I did anything with casts. At the clinic and in the ER, we just stabilize and refer."

Something in his voice made me look over at him and really *look*. "You love what you do, don't you?"

"Yeah."

I waited a moment to see if he'd go on. He didn't. What must that be like? Well, I knew, actually. It's how I felt about music. No explanation necessary, because when I was doing it, my whole being was at peace.

How was I going to manage a life without music in it?

Ugh. Dramatic much? I didn't have to remove music from my life. I got that. At the same time, it wouldn't be the same. I'd have some random job filling my days for eight hours. Or more. Look at Dad—an eight-hour day was short. Gosh, I didn't want that.

I groaned.

He looked over. "Are you all right? Need pain killers?"

"No. Sorry. I was just thinking."

He slowed, then turned into the parking lot of a retro-styled drive-in. The rotating sign above the ordering window proclaimed it "MacLachlan's" and the line of teens declared that this was a hot spot for kicking off Friday festivities.

"Wonder what flavors he's got for the weekend." Christian pulled into a spot toward the back of the lot and parked.

"They're not always the same?" I undid my seatbelt and

pushed the door open. "How do you know if they'll have something you want?"

Christian got out of the car and grinned at me across the roof. "It's ice cream. Plus, he always has at least one of the standards."

The standards? Hopefully, that meant chocolate. Or strawberry. I could deal with vanilla in a pinch, but why would anyone want to? I was used to choosing from among thirty-one delectable flavors when I went out for ice cream. Even better, though, was standing in the freezer aisle in the grocery store surrounded by possibilities.

I shut my car door and fell into step beside Christian. "I guess he doesn't encourage forming an attachment to a particular favorite."

He wiggled a hand from side-to-side. "There's a rotation. Things come and go. And Jon's good about taking requests. I've let him know a time or two that I missed his peanut butter and strawberry jelly flavor and he's brought it back for me."

Peanut butter and jelly? *Strawberry* jelly? I wrinkled my nose. "Not grape jelly?"

"Grape's okay." He stopped behind the last person in line. "Strawberry's better."

"Not possible."

He looked at me, eyebrows lifted. "You've tried it?"

"Well, no. Because pb&j means grape jelly. Period."

He chuckled. "What about peanut butter and banana? Or marshmallow fluff?"

I gagged. "Why? Why would anyone do that?"

"Because Elvis?" The "duh" was clearly implied in the way he said it.

I shook my head. "There is nothing about Elvis that makes him an authority on...anything."

Christian gasped and clutched a hand over his heart. "I thought you were a musician."

"I wanted to be."

He narrowed his eyes at me and we inched forward in line. "There's a difference between doing something as a career and having something be part of what makes you you."

Was there? What was the point of "being a musician" if I couldn't make music? Not that there was any law saying I couldn't still make music, but if it didn't make a living, what was the point? "I'm just someone who enjoys singing."

"Isn't that one definition of a musician?"

"I guess it depends on who you ask." Why wouldn't he drop it? Asking him to let it go felt like making it an even bigger deal though, so I kept quiet.

He seemed to pick up on my desire to change the topic, because he pointed at the board listing the flavors. "What do you think you'll have? He can make a sundae out of any of them— hot fudge and strawberry options. Sometimes pineapple, although I question people who think a pineapple sundae is a delicious choice."

"There we're in agreement." I grinned and scanned the options. "Pineapple is fine in some circumstances, but not in a syrup for ice cream and not with ham. Ever. In any combination."

Christian gave an exaggerated sigh and swiped a hand over his forehead. "I will forgive your lack of pb&j sophistication since you do not, at least, approve of pine and swine. My brother Evan insists that it's an underrated choice for pizza. Bennett and I are reasonably sure that is proof that he was adopted. No matter what Mom and Dad say."

I laughed. What would it be like to have siblings? Especially ones who clearly enjoyed being around one another?

We moved forward again. There were only two people in

front of us now. I considered the flavor options again. "What do you recommend?"

"Of those?" He tipped his head to the side as he looked at the choices. "I'm going with beach tracks, myself. It's kind of a tropical twist on moose tracks—coconut base. If you like coconut, then I'd recommend it. And it would go well with hot fudge."

Coconut was fine. I didn't love it. But I didn't hate it, either. "All right. I'm sold."

Within a few minutes, we were at the window. The man inside grinned out at us.

"Christian! Haven't seen you here for a while. Been keeping you busy?"

"Always. But Teresa and her family just bought a house on the island and she hadn't been here before, so I had to introduce her. Teresa, Jon. Jon, Teresa."

I lifted my good hand. "Hi. Nice to meet you."

"Welcome to our little corner of paradise. Although, I'm a mainlander. I couldn't do the bridge as much as I'd need to if I lived over there." Jon chuckled. "What can I get you?"

Christian gestured for me to order.

"Can I get the beach tracks as a hot fudge sundae?"

"Of course. You want to add a banana and make it a split?"

I heard Christian's intake of breath but spoke before he could. "No thank you."

"All right. Christian?"

"Just a small beach tracks."

"Coming right up." Jon pressed buttons on the old-timey register and told us the total.

Christian had his wallet out before I could offer to get it. He handed Jon a twenty and dropped a lot of the change into the tip jar before we scooted over to join the folks waiting at the next window to grab our orders.

"You were going to make a comment about bananas, weren't you?" I glared at him.

"Maybe. Maybe not. You'll never know."

"Oh, I know." I shook my head. "Just because I don't think bananas belong on a sandwich with peanut butter doesn't mean I don't like them at all."

"Noted. So, you do like bananas?"

"Not really."

Christian laughed.

He kept laughing long enough that I crossed my arms. "It's not that funny."

"It kind of is." He took a deep breath and blew it out with a few final chuckles. "But I'm sorry."

I waved off his apology. "It's fine."

"Would you like to have dinner at my aunt's house tonight?"

My eyebrows lifted. "That came out of nowhere."

"I guess it did. I was chatting with her when you were in the ortho office." He hesitated. "She has a room you can stay in, if you want."

I froze. "She what?"

The teen in the second window called out Christian's name and he turned, with visible relief for the brief reprieve, to grab them. With a bowl of ice cream in each hand, he nodded toward an empty round table on the far side of the parking lot. "Want to sit over there?"

"Sure." My voice was clipped and I stalked in that direction without making eye contact. He'd talked to his aunt about my predicament? Found me a place to stay? The nerve!

A tiny voice in my mind whispered that it was a nice thing he'd done.

Maybe.

But it was also presumptuous.

I slid onto one of the four curved benches that were attached to the table. Christian set my sundae down in front of me and slid onto the seat opposite.

I poked my spoon into the ice cream with enough force that a little splash of fudge flicked onto my hand. I looked up and glared at him. "Did you find me a job, too?"

A flush crept up his neck and onto his face. "I have a couple leads."

"Because I'm such a failure at life, I can't figure this out on my own?"

Wisely, he didn't reply. Instead, he spooned up a bite of ice cream.

I followed suit. The juxtaposition of cold ice cream and hot fudge soothed. As did the explosion of tropical flavor. I took another bite.

He was trying to help.

I'd known from the first time we met—back at Easter—that Christian was a fixer. It had been responsible for a small part of my hesitance to give him all the details of my situation. I'd wanted to avoid this exact scenario.

I made the mess.

I had to fix it.

"Look, I'm sorry. The dinner offer is open regardless. But you don't have to take me up on any of it." He sighed quietly. "I thought I was helping."

I nodded. "I imagine you did."

Christian stuck his spoon into his ice cream and stood. "I'm going to wait at the car. When you're finished, I can take you home."

He picked up his cup and walked toward his car, pausing only to toss the barely-touched treat into a trash can as he passed it.

I sighed and looked down at my sundae.

That could have gone better.

Not that he had any right to jump in and try to rescue me, like I was an incompetent little girl. And sure, looking at my life so far objectively, that was probably a reasonable conclusion to reach. But it didn't mean I had to like it. I was going to change things. Myself.

I just needed six more months.

Once I had access to my trust—and my parents no longer had any say in how I used it—I would get on with fixing my life.

I didn't need some white knight charging in to save the day.

I was going to save the day.

All on my own.

I took my time finishing the sundae. It was delicious. And Christian could wait. If he hadn't wanted to meddle so badly in my life, he could have been here eating his own treat.

I ignored the part of me that realized how unfair I was being. He hadn't committed me to anything. He'd simply found options. Options that were available now, not in six months. I should be grateful.

But what did he expect in return?

I tossed my trash as I passed the can and joined Christian at his car.

"I'm sorry I overstepped." His voice was stiff.

I nodded once, pulled open the passenger door, and got in.

I should say something. Let him know it was okay. But it wasn't okay. I could handle my own life. He might have had good intentions, but good intentions were nothing but pavement on the road to bad destinations.

Without another word, Christian started the car. He reached over and turned on the radio, then tapped his phone. After a few seconds, Elvis started singing loudly through the car speakers.

I glared at him.

He didn't even look my way, just kept his gaze locked straight ahead as he navigated through town to the bridge.

I crossed my arms.

Fine.

9

CHRISTIAN

"You can just drop me off here."

They were the first words she'd said to me since we left MacLachlan's. Maybe streaming the Elvis station had been a bit much, but I'd hoped it might at least get her to smile. Also? I liked his music. I liked all the oldies. Of course, today that spread to include just about anything in the 20th century, so I had a lot to choose from. Elvis had just seemed like the right choice at the time.

I turned onto the neighborhood streets.

She sighed.

"I'm not dropping you on a street corner."

"You don't think I'm capable of making it home?"

"That's not what I said. Nor is it what I meant." I frowned over at her. "And that's not why I talked to my aunt, either."

"Okay."

She didn't sound like she believed me. I couldn't do anything about that.

I slowed, then pulled to the side of the road in front of her family's home. "I really am sorry for butting in. The dinner invitation stands. As does the rest of it."

"Okay."

Awesome. One-word answers. I didn't bother to sigh. "It's a small island, so I'll probably see you around. Or you can call me. Whenever. For whatever reason."

She looked at me. At least she wasn't scowling anymore. Then she gave a slight shake of her head and got out of the car. "I appreciate the ride."

"No problem."

I don't know if she heard me, because she slammed the car door as I was speaking and started toward the house. I waited until she'd gone inside before pulling away. Even then, I was reluctant to leave. What would her parents' response be to her cast? Was James still there with them, even after he'd broken their daughter's arm?

None of those were questions I could answer. Nor were the answers my business.

But I wanted them to be.

Because I was stupid, apparently.

Back at the main road, I turned left and headed into town. I'd go sit in the clinic for a few hours, in case there were walk-ins, then I'd head over to Deb's for dinner. At least I'd get a meal I didn't have to cook. Hopefully, when Teresa didn't show up, they'd leave it alone.

Who was I kidding? There would be questions. So many questions.

Too bad I didn't have the answers.

I parked in my spot by the clinic and got out of the car. I went to the trunk and got the two grocery bags out of the cooler. The ice was still doing all right, but there was no reason not to put them in the fridge in the clinic and ensure that the chocolate cream pie I'd picked up was still a decent dessert offering when I got to my aunt and uncle's.

When I'd unlocked the door and stowed the groceries, I

checked the voicemail. Any calls should have rolled over to my cell, but sometimes there were glitches. Not today, though. Was that a good thing? Probably. But I still would have loved to have something to do to take my mind off Teresa.

I dug out my phone and opened my texts with Bennett.

DON'T THINK SHE'S GOING TO BE GETTING IN TOUCH ABOUT THE JOB.

His response was fast. OH? WHY NOT?

NEVER GOT A CHANCE TO TELL HER ABOUT IT.

SOUNDS LIKE A STORY.

I gave a short laugh. NOT A GOOD ONE.

SORRY. WANT TO HANG TONIGHT? JERICHO AND I ARE GRILLING.

THANKS, BUT I'M OKAY. HEADING TO AUNT DEB'S.

WAIT. HOW'D YOU SWING THAT INVITE?

I'M HER FAVORITE NEPHEW.

Three laugh-crying emojis rolled side to side on Bennett's side of my screen. SURE YOU ARE. MORE LIKELY? YOU'RE THE MOST PATHETIC, SO SHE FEELS SORRY FOR YOU.

I grinned. WHATEVER WORKS. I STILL GET A HOMECOOKED MEAL OUT OF IT.

SUCK UP.

YOU KNOW IT. I'M BRINGING A CHOCOLATE CREAM PIE.

THAT'S LOW. MAYBE WE'LL CRASH THE PARTY.

I'LL REMIND HER TO LOCK THE DOOR WHEN I GET THERE.

Three dots appeared, then disappeared. I waited a moment, then set my phone aside. He probably got busy. That was fine, texting with him had at least shifted my mood some. And if he did crash dinner tonight, I was going to bring up a wedding date again. That should get the heat off me and Teresa and on to Bennett. Which was right where it belonged.

I had a couple of walk-ins that were easy to handle and kept my mind off Teresa. For the most part. After prescribing aloe gel and vitamin e for the bad sunburn and wrapping up a sprained ankle and suggesting that beach volleyball was probably off the menu for the next week or so, I cleaned everything up, grabbed my groceries, locked the doors, and headed back to my car.

I didn't bother putting the groceries in the cooler this time. It wasn't a long drive to my house and I had time to stop to put everything away before walking over to Aunt Deb's. We all had houses on the north end of the island, away from town and the main tourist locations. There were some other year-round residents out our way, but generally the lots were bigger and the homes farther apart. It was much nicer, in my opinion, than being down by the public beach.

When I got home, I pulled into the garage that made up the ground level of my house. Most of the houses on the island were built that way—it made sense, given the possibility of flooding with hurricanes that sometimes made their way far enough up the east coast of the US to hit us. Not everyone closed it in with a garage door, opting instead for more of a car port situation. But I liked the privacy. No one automatically knew if I was home. It generally kept folks from stopping by with medical questions outside of clinic hours.

At least if they called, I could answer the question—and decide to go in if necessary—rather than having the decision forced on me.

I climbed up the stairs from the garage and unlocked the door that led into the kitchen. I set the groceries on the counter and unloaded them into their proper locations. I left the pie out, so I wouldn't forget to take it with me.

The house was quiet.

Normally, I liked that. On days when the clinic was busy—or when I spent time on the mainland in the ER—this was a refuge. Today? It just felt empty.

I crossed to the wall of windows that made up the rear of the house and looked out over my slice of beach to the ocean. I stood there for several minutes, just watching the waves. I wasn't responsible for how Teresa responded to my attempt to help.

Had I been wrong to do it?

I frowned.

How was I supposed to answer that? Jesus said we should help people. Do what we could for them. But maybe we were supposed to wait until we were asked? No. If there was a need I could meet, wasn't I supposed to do just that?

I scrubbed my hands over my face.

I wasn't going to come up with a decisive answer. That much was clear. The reality was, I'd done what I thought made sense and she'd been irritated by it. So. Lesson learned. I wasn't going to cut her off or freeze her out though. If Teresa needed my help, I'd still willingly give it.

But only if she reached out.

With that settled in my mind—for now, at least—I checked the time. I'd be early if I left now, but I couldn't handle the quiet. I'd just end up getting in my head about everything. I grabbed the pie off the kitchen counter and went out through the kitchen door onto the deck, then down the stairs to the beach so I could walk over to my aunt and uncle's.

Maybe I should get a pet.

Dogs were out. I wasn't home enough for a dog. But a cat would probably be okay. Dad had always angled for us to have a cat when we were little, but Mom wasn't a fan. It wasn't an allergy thing. At least not to my knowledge. I should probably check. I didn't want to make it so my family couldn't come over.

But I needed to do something to break up the solitude in my house.

"There he is." Uncle Rob's voice carried down to me from their back deck.

I lifted a hand and started up their beach. "I'm early."

"You wouldn't be you if you weren't." Rob chuckled. "It's something I've always admired about you."

I climbed the stairs and joined him over by the grill. "Aunt Deb said she was cooking."

"She is. I'm just grilling the corn." Rob clicked his tongs together. "It's a beautiful summer night. I have to use the grill for something. Feels like it'd be wrong, otherwise."

"Probably." I glanced toward the kitchen door. "I should go put this pie in the fridge."

Rob glanced down, then grinned. "Chocolate cream pie. You really are my favorite nephew, you know that?"

"At least for tonight?"

He nodded and pointed the tongs at me. "At least for tonight. Keep on bringing over pie though, and we'll see about a permanent crown."

"Maybe I'll do that." I could handle being someone's favorite. I crossed the deck and went into the kitchen. The scent of sauteed garlic filled the air. My mouth watered. "Heya."

Aunt Deb poked her head out of her walk-in pantry. "There you are."

I laughed. "Uncle Rob greeted me the same way."

"It's what we do. What do you have there?"

I closed the difference between us and held out the pie.

She shook her head. "Your uncle's going to be in heaven. Stick that in the fridge then go keep him company. Is your girl coming?"

"She's not my girl. And probably not, no. She's...irritated with me."

Aunt Deb came out of the pantry, her arms full. "Why?"

I took the large flour container from her and carried it over to the counter. "Because I talked to you about her staying here. And to Bennett about a job."

"Hmm." She brought the rest of her load over and set it

down. "She thinks you don't believe she's capable of handling it herself."

"How do you know that?" I frowned. "You know I'm not like that."

She patted my cheek. "Sweet boy. I do know that. Deep down, she probably knows that. But women don't like men handling things for them. Unless we do."

"Oh, well. That clears it right up. Thanks." I rolled my eyes. "Was I really not supposed to have tried to help?"

"I can't tell you that, hon. Did you apologize?"

"I did."

"And she's still angry?"

I thought about our silent ride back to the island. "At least."

"Well. Give her some time. The door's always open, if she decides she wants to take you up on it. And I don't think Bennett's going to fill that position any time soon. He's not looking super hard."

"Speaking of Bennett," I moved around the counter to the other side so I wasn't in her way, "He said he and Jericho might crash dinner."

"Won't that be fun?" She grinned at me.

"I told him I'd get you to lock the door."

Aunt Deb laughed, long and low. "You'll do no such thing. Evan texted earlier saying he might swing by, too. It's nearly time to start the turtle walks, so I'm guessing he wants to talk about that."

I blinked. Was it really almost time for the sea turtles to come ashore to nest? I guess it was. Evan and Aunt Deb would know. Plus, it was basically June, and that was the start of the season. "He's been running things single-handedly for a few years now, why would he need to talk about it?"

Deb leveled the scoop of flour with the back of a knife. "He always has ideas. Sometimes they're things I tried. Sometimes they aren't. He just likes to kick them around. And since he's the only one of the six of you who followed in my footsteps, I love it."

I nodded. "Does it bother you that none of your kids wanted marine biology?"

"Nope." She dumped the flour into a bowl and dipped into the flour container again. "Everyone has their own calling that they need to find. I'm glad Evan wanted it, though. I'd hate for our family's influence on the science center to end. And, really, Austin loves the ocean as much as I do. He was just never one for school. The idea of grad school? He couldn't deal with that."

"He's figured out how to make his life on the ocean." Both my brothers and all three of my cousins had found their way. As had I. And we were all different. But my parents and Deb and Rob had always encouraged us to chase our interests and pray about how God wanted us to use them. Grami and Gramps, too. It was wonderful, really, to have a supportive family.

I wished Teresa had the same.

"I love to see it." She dumped another scoop of flour into the bowl. "Now, you get another three place settings and take them on out with your uncle while I finish up in here. It's a nice evening, so we'll eat out there. The table's mostly set."

I did as I was told, collecting plates, cutlery, and glasses from the cabinets that were as familiar to me as those in my parents' house. Or my own.

Uncle Rob looked up from where he sat, legs stretched out in front of him. "More people coming?"

I shrugged and set the additional places at the table. "They're maybes. Bennett got jealous that I was coming over, so he and Jericho may come. Aunt Deb said Evan would probably show up."

Uncle Rob snickered. "So, I get all my nephews and not any of my own sons? I'll take it."

I laughed and plopped down in the seat next to my uncle. "Travis isn't coming?"

"Nope. He came and picked up Grady—much to Grady's dismay—and said they were going to head into town for burgers. That perked Grady right back up."

"Yeah? I heard there's a new burger place where the Thai restaurant used to be."

"I happen to know that's the case, since I handled the sale." He grinned at me. "But knowing Grady? They'll be eating at the golden arches. That's all he wants when you say burgers."

"Nothing wrong with McDs. Best fries in town, anyway."

"Ha. You're not wrong, unfortunately. You'd think being on the beach there would be someone who could manage to make decent peanut oil fries." He shook his head. "As it is, I have to find somewhere with an actual boardwalk to get my fix. Or sweet talk your aunt into making them. But she hates frying."

"You could always do the frying." I gave him a look. "It's just as manly as grilling. Get one of those big outdoor fryers like they use for turkeys?"

"Hm." Uncle Rob drummed his fingers on the arm of his chair. "I just might at that. If I do, you'll come over and help me perfect the recipe, right?"

"Hundred percent." I wasn't going to turn down French fries. Ever. I focused my attention on the ocean, watching the gentle waves lap at the shore. "Is there anything resembling a cheap rental around here?"

"Thinking about your girl?"

I glanced over at Uncle Rob.

He shrugged. "Your aunt and I talk. And don't bother with the 'she's not my girl' bit. She might not be, but you want her to be."

"I—"

Uncle Rob rolled over whatever I would have said to object.

"As to a cheap rental? Not really. Certainly not in the summer. Even if there was something affordable, it's unlikely that there'd be something vacant. No. Her best bet is going to be taking us up on the room until she gets on her feet."

"Or waiting it out until they go back to wherever home is." Because she certainly didn't need to stay here. I knew that. Maybe it would even be better if she didn't. She probably had some kind of support system—friends, a church, something— back home.

"Depending on where that is, yeah. Seem to recall Travis saying they were from up near DC. Not sure affordable is some- thing that happens there, either."

"Probably true enough." I sighed. Why was I back to looking for solutions for her? This was her problem to solve. She'd made that very clear.

"Hey, y'all." Aunt Deb pushed open the kitchen door, then shooed Bennett and Jericho out onto the deck. "Look who I found."

"Party crashers." Uncle Rob sent me a wink, then stood to offer a hand to Bennett and hug Jericho. "More the merrier. I feel like we need to call up your parents though and let them know that we scooped you all up for a Friday night."

"Please don't." Bennett groaned. He pulled a chair away from the table and flopped down. "Mom said the next time we saw her, we had to give her a wedding date or she'd choose one and we could deal with it."

"You should just get Austin to marry you. He got ordained online, remember, so he could do weddings on his boats? Go get your license, get hitched, then let Mom plan whatever party she desperately wants to hold." I brushed my hands together. "Done and dusted."

Jericho pointed at Bennett. "See? I told you I didn't think eloping was a bad idea. Now your own brother is suggesting it.

Although, I figured we could just have them do it at the court-house while we were there."

Bennett frowned. "Don't you want the whole floofy dress and all of that? Like we planned when we were kids?"

"Not really. We're not kids anymore. I'm ready to get on with our life together." Jericho sat in the chair next to Bennett and took his hand. "Maybe we get Austin to do it on the beach and your family can be there so they don't miss out. And then if your mom wants to plan a party, she can have full rein there."

Bennett glanced at me, then over at our aunt and uncle. "How horrible of an idea is this, really?"

"I think it sounds like a lovely compromise, if the two of you really don't care about the big wedding." Aunt Deb looked at Jericho. "Your parents won't mind?"

"No." Jericho's smile faded. "Things are strained with my mom. And my sisters are busy with their own lives. I was pleased Maddie and her boyfriend came out at Easter. Becca says she's going to come visit sometime. Maybe a big party will be incentive for her. She and Mom get along the best of any of us."

"Then I think you should talk to Austin and see what he thinks." Uncle Rob knocked on the table and glanced over at Aunt Deb. "Food about ready?"

"Just about. Why don't you come in and help me bring everything out?"

Uncle Rob stood. "On my way."

I watched him head into the kitchen before looking at Bennett. "You know Aunt Deb made more than enough food. Why don't you text Austin and see if he wants to come eat? Then you can run it by him."

Bennett looked at Jericho. "You're sure?"

She nodded. "Text your cousin."

Bennett leaned over and kissed Jericho.

I looked away. Maybe I could pretend to be mature enough

not to make gagging noises, but that didn't mean I wanted to watch the lovebirds being sickening. Especially since my current love life was whatever level went below non-existent.

I pulled out my phone and navigated to the courthouse website. "Huh."

Jericho cleared her throat. "What's up?"

"Apparently, the marriage license office is open until noon tomorrow. You could be there at eight when they open and Austin could marry you on Sunday at lunch when we're all at Mom and Dad's."

A slow grin spread over Bennett's face. "Wouldn't it be hilarious to act like nothing was going on, and then when Mom demands a date, we just say today?"

Jericho started to chuckle.

I grinned. Mom had a good sense of humor. I could see her being temporarily taken aback, but she'd get in the spirit of things quickly enough. "Evan has that really nice camera at the science center that he uses for his research. I bet you could talk him into taking some pictures."

"I guess I should text him, too?" Bennett reached for his phone.

"He's supposed to be stopping by. It's almost turtle walk time." I stood as the kitchen door opened and hurried over to take a big bowl from my aunt. "This smells amazing."

"Chicken with fifty cloves of garlic. Because I know you love it. And I made biscuits, even though they don't necessarily go with the fancy, because I know you love them, too."

"Absolutely still my favorite aunt." I kissed her cheek.

Uncle Rob came out with two more bowls and sent a mock scowl at me. "Get your own girl, that one's mine."

Aunt Deb giggled and set her dishes on the table.

Uncle Rob went to the grill and loaded the grilled corn onto a platter, then carried it over to the table and set it beside the rest of the food. He took his seat at the head of the table. Deb sat beside him. Bennett and Jericho were on the other side of Rob, so I moved around to sit beside Deb.

We all joined hands. My phone buzzed in my pocket as Rob began to pray. I squinted an eye open and slid it out enough to check the readout. It was the clinic. As quietly as I could, I stood and moved to the far side of the deck.

"This is Christian."

"Christian? It's me. I'm sorry. I...can you come get me? Please?"

10

TERESA

"Of course. It'll take a minute to get home to my car, but I'll hurry." Christian sounded so calm on the other end of the phone.

I clung to that calm with every ounce of my being as I threw my clothes into my suitcase. Dad was downstairs screaming and James was screaming back. I couldn't make out their words, but I didn't need to. My face throbbed. I turned to look around the room for anything else I didn't want to leave behind. I wasn't coming back.

"Okay. Please hurry."

"I'm on my way."

The call ended. I swallowed and stuffed my phone into my pocket, then grabbed a few books and a picture frame off the shelves and tossed them on top of my clothes. I flipped the suitcase shut and zipped it. At least I'd packed light for the trip to the beach. Knowing we'd have a house, with a laundry room, had meant I didn't need to pack the way Mom had.

Was I forgetting anything?

The screaming downstairs got louder. I grabbed the handle of the suitcase and set it on the floor. I turned to collect my guitar, grateful that I'd upgraded the case to a backpack style in Tennessee, and the journal I used for songwriting from the corner by the desk. I shrugged the straps on—more of a challenge with my dumb cast than without, but I finally got it—and stuffed the journal into the front pocket of the suitcase. With one final glance around the room, I wheeled the suitcase behind me through the door. I snuck down the stairs, trying to avoid drawing attention to myself as I made my way past the study, where Dad and James were having their disagreement.

That's what Dad would call it tomorrow. A disagreement.

"Teresa?" Mom's slurred voice came from the darkened lounge.

I paused and looked over.

"Men can't help it, honey. You just have to learn to deal with it." Mom offered a weak smile.

"No, Mom. I don't." I probably shouldn't have said anything. Mom wouldn't remember. She probably wouldn't remember that she saw me leaving. That part, at least, was good. But nothing I could say or do would convince Mom that this was abnormal.

With a furtive glance toward the room where Dad and James were yelling, I darted to the front door and out, dragging my suitcase behind me.

Christian would want me to stay here, but I needed to keep moving. Dad could decide at any point that he was going to haul me downstairs into the argument. What he would want me to do, I couldn't say. All of this had started because I came home with my arm in a cast and James had been confronted with the reality of his actions. For one brief moment, I'd believed Dad might just put an end to James's stay at our house and defend me. Then he'd hit me. Because I went to my follow up appointment. Now James and Dad were arguing about the best way to get me to fall in line with whatever story they cooked up.

I hurried down the sidewalk and turned toward the main road. I didn't know exactly where Christian lived, but it wasn't in town. He'd been coming from the other direction when he picked me up earlier this afternoon. Thinking of that, when I reached the main road, I turned toward the lighthouse and kept walking.

I'd made it a little over a block when I spotted Christian's car heading the other direction. He slowed and after a moment, made a U-turn, then pulled up beside me with his flashers on.

I grabbed the door handle and wrenched it open. "Thank you."

"Of course. You sit. I'll get your bag." He pushed open his door and got out of the car, hurrying around to grab my bag. He gestured to the guitar and waited while I wriggled out of the straps, then he carried both to his trunk and put them in. He was back in the driver's seat before I was completely settled.

Traffic was light. That was, at least, a bonus. Only a few cars had zipped past, and no one had really even looked twice.

I waited for him to start in with questions, but he didn't. Which was just fine. Of course it was. It wasn't as though I needed to pour my heart out to him and have him smirk and say "I told you so."

Except...I sincerely doubted he'd say that. Because he just wasn't that kind of guy.

I sighed.

"How bad does it hurt?"

I looked over at him. "What?"

He sent a quick glance my way before returning his attention the road ahead. "Your face. Do you think anything's broken?"

"Oh." I gently laid one of my hands on my cheek. I'd broken my nose, so I knew how that felt. And my arm. This didn't hurt like that. "I don't think so, no."

"Okay. When we get to my aunt's, we'll get some ice on it and see how that helps." His knuckles were white on the wheel.

Was that why he wasn't speaking? Anger? At me? Or the situation?

Probably both.

I should have taken him up on the dinner offer, and the place to stay, right away. Why had I thought I could make it work until we left for home?

"I'm sorry." I couldn't have said exactly what I was sorry for. Except maybe everything.

"None of this is your fault." We reached the lighthouse and he turned onto the road that would take us to the northern end of the island.

"I know that. I meant..." My shoulders slumped. "From before. You did a nice thing, and I threw it in your face. And now, I'm asking you to bail me out anyway."

"I told you the offer was always good. I meant it." His voice was still clipped, but he did send a slight smile my way. That was enough to get me to relax. Maybe he wasn't as angry as I'd thought.

Or, at least, not as angry at me.

"I'm still sorry. And grateful." I looked out the window as the houses got larger and farther apart. This was the end of the island where the residents who didn't live in town—or near town—had their homes. Most of the houses near the public beach were rentals. With a few exceptions, like my family's, that were family-owned vacation homes. These houses seemed more settled, friendlier. Which made no sense. A house was a house. It didn't have a personality.

Before too much longer, we slowed, and Christian turned into the driveway in front of an enormous shingled house. Lights glittered in the windows and the landscaping burst with color. And regardless of what I'd tried to tell myself about houses not having personality, there was no question that this one was a welcoming home. It gave off the air of a comfy sweater and chocolate chip cookies.

Christian parked behind another car, and cut the engine. "I imagine there's still plenty of food. Aunt Deb goes all out when she's having people over. Come on in. My brother Bennett and his fiancée are here, too. And another cousin."

I hesitated. "That's a lot of people. I'm interrupting a family dinner."

"No, you're not. C'mon. Deb was upset when she heard you weren't coming. She'll be glad you changed your mind." He got out of the car and went to the trunk to get my things.

It wasn't like I had options. Not good ones. I could go back and hope no one had noticed my absence yet, but that would only delay the inevitable. If Dad wasn't going to stand up for me now, and Mom had proven her only answer was to drink more, then I was on my own.

I pushed open the door and climbed out of the car.

Christian waved me ahead of him and followed with my suitcase and guitar.

I went up the stairs to the front door and stopped on the porch, turning to wait for Christian to catch up. He was already there.

He reached around me to push open the door. "Go on in."

I stepped into the foyer, moving only as far into the house as necessary for Christian to come in behind me and close the door.

He set my cases to the side and put his hand on the small of my back. "They're out on the deck. It's straight through."

Ignoring whatever it was that his touch was doing to my insides, I started walking. His hand dropped away, though he stayed by my side. When we reached a door that clearly led to the deck, he opened it and followed me through.

The group at the table was laughing. For a moment, no one noticed us, then his aunt sprang to her feet and rushed over to grab my good hand.

"You came after all! I'm so glad. Come and sit, there's still so much food."

It was a little like being sucked into a tornado and I let her drag me along.

"You sit here." Deb pulled out a seat and patted the top of it. "Christian was already here, so you'll be next to someone you know better."

"Thanks." My words weren't quite a mutter, but it was close.

"What can I get you to drink?"

I looked at Christian, pleading for his help.

"I'll get it. Sit down, Aunt Deb." He moved closer to his aunt and leaned in, though his voice still carried to everyone at the table. "You're scaring her."

Deb laughed and swatted at Christian. But she resumed the seat she'd popped out of, which I appreciated. Hovering made me feel like a burden.

Christian disappeared back into the house.

Rob gestured across the table. "Have you met Bennett and Jericho? And Austin and Evan? Austin's ours. Bennett and Evan are our nephews, and Jericho's marrying Bennett."

"It's nice to meet you." I lifted my good hand in an awkward wave. "I'm Teresa."

"You're in the Hackett place, right?" Bennett lifted a bowl off the table and moved it closer. "Dig in. Unless you've already eaten."

"I'm good. But thanks." I cleared my throat. "Everyone says it's the Hackett place, so I guess so."

Rob laughed. "It'll be the Hackett place until your family has owned it for a few years. Maybe longer. There are a few houses in town that everyone still refers to by the owners from, gosh, the eighties?"

"At least." Deb nodded. "Of course, some of those have at least been in the same family that long, so it's not unreasonable, even if the last name changed with marriages over time."

Christian came back out and set a can of sparkling water in front of me before taking the seat between me and Deb. He popped the top of his own can and looked over. "Did you get introduced?"

"I did. Thanks."

He reached for the bowl that Bennett had moved and scooped fragrant chicken and sauce from it. My mouth watered. Maybe I was a little hungry after all. He looked at me, the spoon in his hand. "Can I serve you some?"

"Sure. Yes. Please."

He chuckled and dipped back into the bowl. "This is one of my favorites that Aunt Deb makes. You should try her biscuits, too."

"Hey. My grilled corn is also renowned." Rob nudged the platter of corn our way.

"Dad." Austin shook his head. "Anyone can grill corn."

"I grill other things, too." Rob crossed his arms. "Watch it, kid. I seem to recall you losing to all comers last summer when we had a grilling competition."

"It was rigged. Mom and Aunt Linda are never going to vote against their husbands." Austin blew out a breath. "Maybe we should include catching fish in our next little foray. You cook what you catch."

Rob's eyes lit with anticipation. "You are on."

"Don't say it hon. These kids don't even know who Donkey Kong is." Deb shook her head and looked my way. "I'm sorry. My men never seemed to leave their teenage years behind."

"That's because you keep me young." Rob took Deb's hand and brought it to his lips.

"Flatterer." But Deb sounded more amused and pleased than anything else.

The men were all grumbling about how they absolutely did know who Donkey Kong was, but no one appeared to be listening. I smiled slightly. Who didn't know who Donkey Kong was? He was an integral part of American culture at this point, wasn't he?

Regardless, I took an ear of corn off the platter and added it to my plate.

"That's a girl." Rob nodded approvingly at me. "Since you came for dinner, does that mean you've changed your mind about moving in, too?"

My eyebrows lifted. Had Christian not given his aunt and uncle details about my situation? Rob seemed so matter of fact about the whole thing. Of course, no one had commented on my face, either, and I surely had to be working on another black eye. So maybe he was just polite. "Yeah. Um. If that's still okay?"

"Absolutely." Rob glanced at Deb. "Right, hon?"

"Definitely. And since Bennett's here, you could chat with him about the job opening he has after dinner." I must have flinched or something, because Deb hurriedly tacked on, "If you want."

"No pressure. I promise." Bennett held up a hand, smiling. "And you'll have to excuse our family. We're ridiculous busy bodies sometimes."

"Sometimes?" Jericho scoffed. "Would that be just times that can be represented on a clock?"

"Something like that, yeah." Christian chuckled and looked my way. "I come by it honestly, at least. Sorry."

"He really does." Jericho flashed a grin. "They all do. You

haven't even met Linda yet. She couples her generic feeling that she knows what's best for everyone with older child syndrome."

"Which means she also thinks she's always right." Deb's eyes sparkled with laughter. "Then again, she'd say I have younger child syndrome and think I deserve to have everything I want when I want it. And you don't say anything, buster."

Rob held up both hands. "I wasn't planning on it. I like being married to you. You're pretty."

Everyone around the table laughed.

"Can I help you with the dishes, Aunt Deb?" The quieter man at the end of the table—was it Evan? —stood and picked up his plate. "Then we can talk turtles and not deal with the peanut gallery."

"That sounds great. Does everyone have all the food they want?" Deb stood and started to stack the plates at her end of the table.

"I'm good. Thanks." Christian glanced at me. "You?"

I nodded. "It's very good. Thank you."

"You're welcome. I'm glad you came." Deb picked up the big pile and started for the door into the house. Evan trailed after her, his own arms loaded down with dishes.

"If you don't need me anymore, I'm going to bail, too." Austin stood and grabbed a few of the dishes left on the table. "Any particular dress code on Sunday?"

"Wear a suit." Rob pointed at him. "At one point, you had a nice charcoal one. What did you get that for?"

Austin groaned. "Bennett's law school graduation. I'll see if it still fits. Is someone going to tell everyone else to dress up? I don't want to be the only guy in a suit."

"Oh. We should, shouldn't we?" Jericho bit her lip. "Your mom is going to be annoyed if she's under dressed."

Bennett wrinkled his nose. "You're right. But if we don't do this as a surprise, she's going to put her foot down about it. Uncle Rob?"

I let the conversation swirl around me. I had no idea what they were talking about, but I appreciated how well they all got along. The teasing was never mean-spirited. And Christian kept brushing my arm. It was reassuring.

Was he doing it on purpose?

"Deb'll figure something out. Since Evan's taking pictures, maybe she'll just say she got a hankering to have photos done." Rob shrugged. "Leave it to Deb. But suits all around, guys. Just because you're eloping doesn't mean it needs to be casual."

Jericho frowned. "I guess that means I need to find a dress of some sort. I don't think any of my library outfits will work."

"I like your library outfits." Bennett leaned over and gave Jericho a not-so-perfunctory kiss.

"Get a room." Austin muttered as he walked behind them. "See y'all later. It was nice to meet you, Teresa. Even if I do feel sorry for you getting sucked into a relationship with that one."

"Hey!" Christian glared as Bennett and Rob laughed. "Last time I talk up your fishing skills."

"They don't need talking up. They speak for themselves." Austin grinned and pointed at me. "If you decide you're ready for the real catch in the family, hit one of these guys up for my number."

He turned and was through the door into the kitchen before I could come up with any sort of response. It was only as I tried to think just what sort of response would have been appropriate that I realized just how relaxed I was feeling. Maybe they hadn't been teasing one another to put me at ease, but it had worked anyway.

I sighed.

Christian rubbed my arm. "I never got you that ice pack. Why don't I do that now? Then, when you're done eating, Deb can get you settled in your room. You don't have to talk about the job tonight if you don't want to."

"I'm okay." I reached over to rest my hand on his for the briefest moment. "I guess I'd like to talk to Bennett now—if that's okay with him?"

I looked at Bennett, eyebrows lifted.

"Of course." He leaned back slightly in his chair. "It's basic front desk stuff. Answer the phone. Greet clients. Make appointments."

I considered a moment. I could probably do all of that. I was decent on a computer. I wasn't going to make it a career or anything, but email and social media and that kind of thing. Making appointments couldn't be that much harder. "I can probably handle all of that."

Christian scooted his chair back and stood. "I'll be right back."

Bennett grinned. "I'm sure you can. There might be some scanning and copying, too. I can show you how the machine works. It's reasonably straightforward. That's really about it. You might be the only one in the office at times, but we aren't exactly a hotbed of walk-in traffic. If you want to keep the front door locked when you're in there alone, I'm fine with that. We have one of those smart doorbell camera things. If anyone comes by, you can talk to them without opening the door."

The muscles that had clenched when he'd mentioned being alone in the office loosened again. I'd been trying to figure out how I was going to keep Dad and James from being a nuisance. Not that they couldn't just wait until the door was unlocked. But at least then, I'd have Bennett there as backup.

Christian returned and handed me what looked like a bean bag. It was cold, but soft, and the little gnomes doing gnomey things all over the fabric made me smile. I held it to my face.

"Thanks." I smiled slightly at Christian, then turned to

Bennett. "I guess I should tell you there's a possibility that my dad and his business partner might make trouble. They aren't going to be happy I left."

Bennett just shrugged. "We can deal with that if we need to. The nice thing about working in a lawyer's office is that you've got immediate access to someone who's great at writing up official sounding requests to leave someone alone."

Rob chuckled. "And if that doesn't work, I'm friends with the Sheriff. And the chief of police over on the mainland. But if your family's smart, they'll understand that messing around with someone the Loring family adopted is a bad plan."

"You make us sound like we're some kind of mafia, Uncle Rob." Christian shook his head.

"Are you talking to me?" Rob's voice took on a thick, New York accent as he spoke.

Everyone at the table laughed.

"But seriously." Rob leaned forward. "Let us help you. However we can. Okay?"

I nodded and looked down. My eyes were burning with hot tears that I had no intention of letting fall if I was able to stop them.

Bennett cleared his throat. "When can you start? Our current employee is pretty motivated to move on. Her boyfriend got a job in Charlotte. She wants to follow."

"Monday?" I didn't imagine they were open on the weekend, and I was ready to start earning my keep.

"Sounds good. Give me your email address, and I'll send you the details and some forms that we need filled out. If you bring them with you Monday morning—I like us to be open at nine—we'll be good to go."

"Thank you." I looked up and held Bennett's gaze. "I really appreciate this."

"You're helping me out, too, so it's an easy win for everyone. Christian has good ideas sometimes."

"Only sometimes?" Christian shook his head. "I believe I also pushed you to get over yourself when it came to things between you and Jericho."

"Like I said, you sometimes have good ideas." Bennett shifted away from Jericho's playful swat, then he pushed back his chair and stood. "We'll head out and let you get settled. Get my number from Christian and text me your email address. You'll come to lunch on Sunday, right?"

I blinked. I hadn't been planning on it, once I figured out that it was turning into a surprise wedding. "Oh. Um. I thought it was a family—"

"She'll be there." Rob cut me off.

I frowned at him.

He shrugged. "There's no way Deb will let you out of it. Linda either. And since Linda doesn't know about the wedding, if you don't show up, she's going to be both annoyed and suspicious."

"You don't want Mom to be either of those things." Christian covered my hand with his. "Trust me."

I sighed. "If you change your mind, let me know. I won't be upset."

Jericho stood and took Bennett's hand. "We're happy to have you there. Maybe...would you want to go into Bennett tomorrow and look for dresses?"

Honestly, that sounded like the worst time imaginable. But I could recognize an offer of friendship when it happened, and with my life the way it was right now? I could use all the friends I could find.

"Yeah. I'd like that."

Jericho beamed. "Cool. I have to work until two. Can you swing by the library around then, and we can go from there?"

"I'll get her there." Christian spoke before I could.

"Perfect. Night, y'all." Jericho tugged Bennett's hand slightly and the two of them headed into the kitchen.

"Why don't we get you settled?" Christian stood.

I stood as well and reached for my plate.

"I've got that. You go on in. Deb will set you up." Christian picked up the last dishes on the table.

I started toward the kitchen door, then paused and looked over my shoulder. Christian and Rob were laughing—I'd missed whatever was said—but something squeezed in my heart. Christian was a good man.

If only I could deserve someone like him.

11

CHRISTIAN

"**A**re you riding to lunch with Aunt Deb, or can I give you a ride?" I stuffed my hands in my pockets as I turned to Teresa.

Church had just ended, and everyone was busy gathering their things and heading out. They'd switched on recorded music at a volume so low it was easily lost in the hum of voices.

"Oh. I hadn't thought about it." Teresa bit her lip. "Would they mind if I went with you since they brought me?"

"I can't imagine they would." I glanced around and finally spotted my aunt and uncle chatting with one of the elderly couples who were long-time island residents. I was debating going over to ask versus texting, when Aunt Deb looked up. I caught her eye and gestured to Teresa, then myself, and mimed driving.

Aunt Deb grinned and nodded.

I looked back at Teresa. "I think we're good to go. Ready?"

"Yeah." She pressed a hand to her stomach. "Unless there's a way for me to get out of it. I really don't think—"

I chuckled, cutting her off. "Mom will have my head if you don't show up. Please don't do that to me."

One corner of her mouth poked up. "All right."

"I promise it'll be okay." I put my hand on her back as we stepped into the flow of people heading out of the worship center.

"I'll hold you to that."

It took a little longer to get to my car than I anticipated, since we had to stop to chat with various people as we passed them. Everyone wanted to meet Teresa. That was one of the joys of small town living I was used to, but didn't love. There were no secrets on Loring Island. Not for long, at least. Not that Teresa living with Deb and Rob needed to be a secret, but the speculative glances when people saw us together were frustrating.

Not that I'd mind if Teresa and I ended up a couple, but I wasn't honestly sure where she stood on the idea. Her life was in a weird place, and it would make sense if she just wanted to focus on that and not add in the complication of a relationship.

When we finally reached the car, I opened the door for her, shutting it when she was situated, then went around to the driver's side and got in. "Have you heard from your family?"

She froze in the process of fastening her seatbelt. "A couple times, yeah."

I started the car and backed out of my parking space, taking the time to analyze her tone. "They're upset."

"That's one way to put it." She sighed and her fingers tightened around the small purse she held in her lap. "I haven't actually answered any of their calls. Doesn't seem to bother them, they just leave horrible voicemails. And texts."

"I'm sorry."

"Me, too. I'll talk to them tomorrow, after I start the job with Bennett. I want to be able to tell them that I'm employed and have a place to stay. That I'm making it on my own."

I could understand that. "Will it make a difference to them?"

"Not sure. I hope so, but it may depend on how things are going with finalizing things between Dad and James."

"Can I ask you something?" I wasn't sure if I wanted to know the answer, but I'd been wondering since she brought up James —and then meeting him—so maybe it was better to find out than not.

"Go ahead." She sounded wary.

"I guess I'm just wondering why the whole James situation had anything to do with you in the first place."

"Ah." She paused. "I think, at first, Mom and Dad were hoping I'd be interested in James. One of those things where a business connection was even more solid because it was also a family connection. But I got that out of their minds quickly."

Had she? I wasn't so sure about that. From the interactions I'd seen—which were admittedly few—James felt like he had some kind of possessive hold on her.

"What?"

I glanced over at her and shook my head. "Nothing. Sorry. Just thinking."

"You don't think they told him I was interested, do you?" She frowned, then made an exasperated noise. "Of course they did. Because why would they take anything I say at face value? Well, I'll be setting them straight on that tomorrow, too."

"Sorry."

"No. You don't need to be sorry. I should have realized it. I've been so caught up wondering why they didn't seem to care about my injuries. But I thought it was just the deal. I mean, it's a lot of money and some great opportunities for Dad's business, so maybe that really is it." She sighed and shook her head. "But if Dad got it in his head that he could make a relationship happen? Mom would go along with it. That's what she does."

I reached over and squeezed her hand briefly. "If there's anything I can do to help, please let me know."

"You've already done too much." She shifted and slipped her hand out from under mine. "Your whole family has, now."

"I can promise you, we're all happy to do it."

She nodded, but it was obvious to me that she didn't like having to rely on anyone.

The last little bit of the drive was spent in silence, and I was almost relieved when I pulled into Mom and Dad's driveway. At least with the big family gathering, I wouldn't be the only one responsible for conversation.

"This is lovely. I guess I didn't realize your mom was basically next door to Deb." Teresa unbuckled and pushed open her door. "I can see why your family doesn't leave the island."

I considered the sprawling beach house a moment, then nodded. Sometimes I took it for granted, but she was right. "We're definitely blessed. I think we'd leave if there was a reason. So far, though, God's kept us here. I'm glad of it."

I started up the steps ahead of her. Mom would be annoyed if she saw me, but it felt like Teresa might appreciate not being the first in the house. I could do that for her. I knocked twice on the door, then pushed it open. "It's me!"

"Hi, me!" Dad called out from the kitchen in response.

I laughed and waited for Teresa to join me in the foyer before closing the door. I hooked my suit coat on the newel post of the stairs and started toward the kitchen.

"There he is." Mom dried her hands before opening her arms.

I walked over to give her a hug and kiss her cheek. "Hi, Mom. Aunt Deb told you I was bringing a friend, right?"

Mom stepped back and turned to Teresa. "Of course she did. It's lovely to meet you, Teresa. How are you enjoying staying at my sister's?"

"It's a lovely room. And house." She cleared her throat. "Your house is wonderful, too."

Dad chuckled. "Linda tried to convince Deb to make you move over here. We have the room, no question, but ultimately sanity won."

Teresa glanced at me, looking lost.

"Gramps just moved in with them, too. He'd talk your ear off." I looked around. Gramps wasn't in his usual spot at the kitchen table. "Where is Gramps?"

"Deb fussed at him about his clothes at church, so he went to his room to change." Mom eyed my outfit. "Where's your jacket? She told me the guys would all be in suits for the photos, although I don't understand why we have to do pictures today. Honestly, sometimes my sister gets ideas and then locks on to them and nothing can change her mind. She's so stubborn."

"It's a family trait." Dad stepped out of the range of the kitchen towel Mom flicked at him.

"The grill should be ready for the chicken. Why don't you go make yourself useful, hon?" Mom shooed Dad toward the door that led out to the deck. "In fact, take your son with you."

"Can I get you something to drink first, Teresa?" I started toward the fridge.

"Oh, no. I'm good. Thank you though."

I pulled open the door and snagged a Coke for myself. I held it up. "Sure?"

"Yeah."

"All right, let's go help Dad grill chicken." I looked at Mom. "Is the chicken already out there?"

"No. It's in the fridge marinating. Your father seems to have forgotten that." She shook her head. "Maybe he was in too big of a hurry to get out of towel range."

"Probably." I grinned and opened the fridge back up. I quickly spotted the bowl holding chicken and a dark marinade and pulled it out. "Anything else need to go out?"

"Not yet." Mom hesitated.

I jumped in before she could find a way to get Teresa to stay. "Then we'll get out of your way."

Teresa followed me onto the deck. I set the bowl of chicken on the table beside the grill. "Mom was amused you forgot this."

Dad laughed. "I figured you'd bring it. And I was right. Why don't the two of you have a seat and relax. Everyone else should be here soon and then it'll be chaos, as usual."

I pulled a chair out from the big glass table and waved Teresa toward it, then grabbed the one beside it for myself. "You sure you don't need help with the grill?"

Dad shot me an annoyed look. "Boy, I've been grilling since before you were a twinkle in your mother's eye."

Teresa choked out a laugh.

I grinned. "Just checking."

Before long, the rest of the family arrived in little clumps. First Gramps, along with Bennett and Jericho. Then Aunt Deb and Uncle Rob along with Travis, Grady, and Austin. Ryan was only a few minutes behind them. My younger brother, Evan, was the last to arrive. He came out on the deck with two huge bowls clutched to his chest and Mom bustling out behind him with more.

Ryan popped up out of his chair. "Is there more, Aunt Linda? I can help."

"Would you?" Mom beamed at him. "You're a darling. It's all out on the counter, for anyone who wants to jump in."

I got to my feet, as did my brothers, and we followed Ryan into the kitchen.

"Nice going, suck up." Bennett drilled a finger into Ryan's ribs.

Ryan squirmed away. "C'mon man. Are you twelve?"

Bennett laughed.

I chuckled. "You're the only one of us who's still ticklish like that. You really think anyone's going to stop?"

Ryan glowered and picked up the salad bowl before stalking toward the deck.

Evan hurried in. He glanced at Ryan and his eyebrows shot up as he looked between Bennett and me. "Who tickled him?"

I pointed at Bennett before picking up the stack of plates. After a moment's hesitation, I put them back down and stacked some salad dressing bottles on the top plate, then picked them up again.

"Oh, sure. Throw me under the bus." Bennett muttered as he scooped up the cutlery and grabbed the pitcher of what was sure to be sweet tea.

"No bus. Just telling it like it is." I headed back out onto the deck, missing Bennett's retort.

When everyone was seated again, Dad stood from his seat at the head of the table and looked around. "Let's pray."

I smiled as I bowed my head.

Teresa's hand slid over to rest against mine. I flipped mine over, and closed it around hers as Dad started to speak.

"Heavenly Father, thank you. Thank you for this family and all the blessings you've poured out on us over the generations. Thank you for the newcomers to our table and for the joy they bring with them. Bless this food and the hands that prepared it. Amen." Dad sat back down. "Dig in, folks."

I squeezed Teresa's hand and released it before pulling the closest bowl over and offering it to her.

The meal was the chaos I'd come to expect. I kept glancing over at Teresa, but it was hard to read her expression. She didn't seem put off, which was good, but she didn't join in with the conversation—even when it touched on topics that she'd presumably have something to contribute to.

As people were finishing, I leaned over. "Are you all right?"

She nodded. "I like your family."

I grinned. "Me too. Most of the time."

She chuckled.

Down the table, a shriek split the air. I glanced down, wincing. Travis was taking his phone back from Grady, who was trying to hold onto it.

"Daaaad!" Grady pulled on Travis's arm.

"That's enough, Grady." Travis held his phone out of his son's reach. He shot an apologetic glance at the rest of us. "Sorry."

"Don't be." Aunt Deb sighed then sent Grady a perky smile. "Why don't we go down to the beach, kiddo? If we get the pictures taken fast, then you can change out of your suit and maybe we can swim a little."

Grady hesitated, his hand still clinging to Travis's arm, then he nodded. He pushed his chair back and darted for the stairs from the deck to the beach.

Deb scooted back her chair and hurried after him. She waved Travis back. "I've got him. You finish your lunch."

Travis frowned down at his plate and shook his head. He scooted his own chair back and stood. "Can I help clear the table, Aunt Linda?"

Mom nodded. "Everyone can. Then we can all get down for photos faster and give Grady a break."

"I'm really sorry—"

"Stop." Jericho cut Travis off. "We all love Grady. And if I had to guess, it's the suit causing the issue today."

Travis sighed and scrubbed a hand over his face. "Probably, yeah. Getting him into it this morning wasn't pretty."

"You two are excused." Mom pointed at Teresa and me. "Help Gramps down to the beach and keep your aunt company."

"I don't need help." Gramps grunted as he stood and scowled at Mom. "You'd think I was an old man."

Mom hurried over and took Gramps's arm to steady him. She pressed a kiss to his cheek. "You are an old man, Daddy. But you're my old man."

He chortled and patted her hand. "You're a good girl, Lin. Bossy. But good."

Mom jerked her head at me.

I stood and came around to offer Gramps my arm. "Come on, Gramps. You know it's better to do what Mom says rather than try to fight her."

He laughed this time. "You've always been a smart one, Christian. Introduce me to your girl."

I stopped myself from objecting to the term "your girl." Everyone was probably thinking it—when was the last time I'd brought anyone to a family meal? And it was better to have them assuming Teresa and I were an item than thinking she was some kind of charity project.

I'd certainly prefer the former to be true.

And she'd hate it if she thought we considered her the latter.

I crooked a finger at Teresa. She hesitated a moment, then joined Gramps and me.

"Teresa, this is Gramps. Gramps, Teresa."

"It's lovely to meet you, Mr. Loring." Teresa held out her hand.

Gramps took it and brought it to his lips to kiss her knuckles. "Call me Gramps, Teresa, if you would. Everyone does. Mr. Loring was my dad."

"All right, Gramps." She smiled at him.

Gramps offered Teresa his other elbow. She slipped her arm through and we walked slowly—more of a shuffle where Gramps was concerned—over to the steps leading down to the beach.

The stairs weren't wide enough for us to go down three-across. Gramps glanced at me. "Teresa and I have this. Why don't you grab me a chair to sit on down there? Standing on sand isn't so easy at my age."

"All right." I sent Teresa a questioning look. She nodded. So I let go of Gramps's arm and stepped out of the way, relieved to see him reach for the railing on the side where I'd been. I watched them start slowly down the stairs, then turned to consider the chair options.

Dad came over and slung his arm over my shoulders. "She's a keeper."

"We'll see. We're just friends right now, Dad." And I wasn't even sure friends was the right word for it. It was definitely what I wanted, but did our relationship qualify? I couldn't tell. Not really.

"That's how a lot of long-lasting love stories start." He squeezed me in a half-hug. "Take one of the chairs from the table for Dad. I don't think the others would do very well in the sand. I wish I understood why Deb got in such an all-fired hurry about photos. And on the beach? If she'd been willing to wait, we could have hired a professional and gone out in the reserve to get some varied scenery. And firmer paths for Dad."

"You know how Aunt Deb gets." It was the best I could come up with as a response. I didn't want to lie, nor did I want to spill the beans. Although, the big reveal would be happening any moment now. It still wasn't my surprise to spring.

I turned to get a chair.

Mom came back on the deck and held out my suit jacket. "Put this on before you forget. You're not going to be the only under-dressed man in these photos."

"Darn." I winked at Mom. "I was hoping you'd forget."

I took the jacket and shrugged it on.

Mom stepped close and fussed with the collar and lapels. She ran her hands over my shoulders and smiled. "Such a handsome man. I'm very blessed."

"One out of three isn't bad."

Mom laughed and patted my cheek with slightly more force than necessary. "Your brothers are also handsome."

"In their way." I grinned.

Dad roared with laughter.

"Don't encourage him, David." Mom shook her head.

Dad poked out his elbow for Mom. She took it. The two of them started down to the beach. I grabbed a chair and followed.

After a few minutes, everyone was milling around on the beach.

Evan cleared his throat. "All right, everyone. Let's get this started. Austin, you come stand here."

Evan pointed to a spot where Austin's back would be to the ocean and Austin moved that way. Evan nodded. "Bennett and Jericho, why don't you stand here."

Bennett and Jericho moved to stand in front of Austin, facing each other.

"The rest of you? Come stand over here." Evan made a circling gesture with his hand to indicate the area facing the bride and groom.

"What are you—" Mom broke off. She looked at Austin, Bennett, and Jericho. Then she narrowed her eyes at her sister. "Deb?"

Aunt Deb crossed to Mom and slid her arm around Mom's waist. "Now you can plan a party as big as you want whenever you want. And they don't have to wait to be together until then. Everyone wins."

Mom blinked rapidly, then swiped at her eyes. She looked at Bennett and Jericho. "This is what you want?"

"It really is." Jericho took Bennett's hands. "Is it okay?"

"Of course. Of course it is." Mom beamed and brushed another errant tear from the corner of her eye. "Of course."

"Then let's get this party started, shall we?" Austin took his hands out of his pockets and held his phone in front of him.

"I think you're supposed to say 'Dearly Beloved." Evan called out as he snapped a photo with his fancy camera.

Everyone chuckled as Austin sent Evan a sour look. "Who's performing this ceremony? You or me?"

"So far? Neither of us." Evan grinned and took another photo, this time including the gathered family. "Get on with it, man."

Austin cleared his throat, glared at Evan, and began, "Dearly beloved."

I stood with Teresa and watched my older brother make his vows to love, honor, and cherish this childhood sweetheart, longing to have that same thing for myself filling me. They were both beaming. And when Austin said they could kiss, I couldn't help but cheer along with the rest of my family.

"Before we get to those pictures—because I know Linda and Deb really will want them—will you humor an old man?" Gramps pushed himself up out of his chair and wobbled a moment before Mom hurried over and grabbed his arm.

"Dad. Sit down."

He patted Mom's hand. "I'm all right. Let's gather around Bennett and Jericho."

Gramps, with Mom's help, crossed the short distance to where the newly married couple stood. He placed a hand on Jericho's shoulder and the other on Bennett's. Mom turned and beckoned to the rest of us, and we all moved—all but Grady, who was busy making a huge hill out of sand—to form a circle around them and reached out to put our hands on their shoulders.

Gramps looked from Bennett to Jericho and back before praying. "Father, bless this new couple. You brought them together again after trouble and separation. You have bound them together as one with your Spirit. Thank you for the start of another new generation in the Loring family. May we always seek to live out Your will for us. Bennett and Jericho, as Paul said in Romans fifteen, may the God of endurance and encouragement grant you to live in such harmony with one another, in accord with Christ Jesus, that together you may with one voice glorify the God and Father of our Lord Jesus Christ. Amen."

Everyone whispered an echo of Gramps's "Amen."

After a moment of quiet, broken only by the gentle lapping of waves, Deb clapped her hands. "Let's get those photos. And then, I believe we have cake."

"Cake?" Grady came barreling across the sand to slam into Deb's legs. "Cake?"

She ruffled his hair. "In just a few minutes. Pictures first."

Grady's face morphed into a pout.

Before he could erupt, Travis scooped him up and paced a few steps away from the group, whispering sternly.

Evan took charge of arranging us for the big group photo. Then he took a moment to set up a tripod and get the camera situated on it. He spent several minutes adjusting its position, then nodded and called to Travis. "Trav? You and Grady ready?"

"As we're going to be." Travis sounded defeated. He and Grady trudged over. Grady wore a mutinous expression.

Evan gave Travis a sympathetic smile and took them over to position them near Aunt Deb and Uncle Rob. Then Evan took his place on the other side of the group where he'd arranged our immediate family.

"On three, everyone say 'cheese.' One...two...three."

"Cheese!"

The camera clicked. I realized Evan must have a remote. Clever. He took a few more with the big group, then with a glance at Grady and Travis, shifted to the smaller family unit photos for Aunt Deb.

I kept looking over at Teresa. I'd tried to get her to be in at least one of the pictures—she was here, after all—but she'd refused. I hadn't pushed too hard. It seemed to me that she was too used to being coerced into things she didn't want to do.

I didn't want to do that to her.

Maybe, though, she'd let me get a picture of the two of us.

It was something I found myself wanting more than I could explain.

Bennett sidled over to me while Evan was taking pictures of Gramps with Grady. "Does she know you're in love with her?"

"What?" I jolted back. "It's not like that."

"Ah. Sorry." Bennett shook his head, looking at me like I was an idiot. "You don't even know it yet. My bad."

"Bennett! You and Jericho with Gramps now." Evan called.

I stared at him as he walked away. I wasn't in love with Teresa.

Couldn't be.

Could I?

12

TERESA

Nerves jumped in my belly as I got out of Deb's car in front of the family law office in town.

"You're going to be great." Deb sent me a bolstering smile. "Bennett's an easy-going guy."

I managed a weak smile. "Thanks."

"I'll pick you up at five, okay?"

"You really don't have to do that. I can figure it out." I wasn't sure how I'd figure it out, but if I was going to be a grownup on my own, then that's what I needed to start doing. I needed to stop letting the disaster that was Nashville ruin my ability to stand on my own two feet.

Deb studied me a moment. "You have my number. If you end up with another way home, you text me. Okay? Otherwise, I'll be here at five."

"All right." I nodded. That was a reasonable compromise. And I was going to figure something out at lunch. She was already doing so much for her grandson, Grady. I didn't want to be an additional burden. "Thank you."

"You're welcome. Now you have a wonderful day, you hear me?"

"Yes, ma'am." As if I could just control such things. But this was day three of a new start, and I was going to make it count. Steeling myself, I turned toward the door and marched in.

The entry area was friendly and welcoming. There was a big, dark wood desk centered in front of an enormous painting of a beach house with the ocean behind it. The leather chairs with their shiny brass studs for waiting clients looked comfortably worn, as if waiting for a few minutes wouldn't be an awful thing with them to sit in. One corner held a tall potted plant—was it a ficus? I didn't know about plants—trees? —but something in the back of my mind came up with that as the identification. Either way, I'd ask if I was supposed to water it. And if so, how often. The opposite corner had a little coffee bar in the same dark wood of the reception desk.

"Hey. Good morning." Bennett appeared from down the hall and grinned. "I thought I heard the door buzzer. You're prompt."

"I try." I gestured to the room. "This is cozy."

"That's the goal." He pointed to the coffee pod machine. "Do you want some coffee before I show you around?"

"Not right now." Putting anything in my stomach right now seemed like the worst possible idea.

Bennett nodded. "Well, help yourself whenever. And if we don't have pods for what you like, I'll show you where we order from. Keeping that stocked will be part of your job. I think I remember seeing they have hot tea and cocoa in addition to coffee, if you're one of those people who doesn't like bean juice."

"Oh, no. I like coffee. Just not when I'm nervous." I blurted out the last part and winced. Great. So smooth.

He laughed. "I'm going to tell you not to be nervous, but I will also acknowledge that it's nearly impossible when starting a new job. But I promise you, I'm very happy you're here. Let's start with the tour."

"All right."

"That'll be your desk." Bennett pointed. "I'll run you through the computer and phone system in a bit. First, come on this way."

I followed him down the short hall to the left. He pointed out the bathroom—noting that he hired a cleaner to come in every-other night, so that wasn't part of my job—then the supply closet, which also contained the copy machine and a small fridge plus table and chairs. Finally, he pointed out the offices of his mom and dad, then his own.

"Mom and Dad come in when they want. You'll probably get a few calls a week for them, just let callers know that they check their voicemail daily and put them through for that. You don't have to write out messages. If they say it's urgent, you can definitely get a callback number and text. Unless they're out of town —which is unusual, and they'll keep you posted—they'll get right on it." Bennett gestured to one of the guest chairs in his office. "Why don't you have a seat?"

I perched on the edge of the chair.

Bennett went around and sat behind his desk. "How are you feeling about it so far?"

"It seems doable." I was still nervous. My track record with jobs of any sort wasn't great, but I'd do my best.

"I hope it is." He smiled. "When you run into something that I haven't explained, just ask. And feel free to bring in a book to read or whatever to keep you busy if we're slow. Because we definitely have slow times. A lot of them. I think that's some of why Angela left. Well, that and she was following her boyfriend."

I nodded. Maybe I'd go to the library and find a book during my lunch break. That would be a nice walk, and as much as I might enjoy owning the book, right now that definitely fell into the category of "things I can't afford."

That category pretty much encompassed everything.

"Do you have any questions?"

"No. I'm sure I will, but like I said, so far it seems doable."

"Great. Ask when you find something." He stood. "Let's head to the front desk and I'll walk you through the phone system and the appointment calendar. I had Ryan—you remember Ryan from yesterday? He's Deb's second son?"

"Yeah. Pretty sure."

Bennett grinned. "We're a lot. I get that. You'll figure it out. Anyway, he does all kinds of computer stuff, and as a favor to me handles all our IT needs. He set you up an email account and access to what you need. I made you a list of important numbers —his is on it."

I followed him back out of his office and down the hall to the front room.

Bennett picked up a folder from the middle of the desk and handed it to me. "This has everyone's contact info, as well as a kind of cheat sheet for some of the daily and weekly tasks that need doing. It's also on the computer, so you can add to it and make a new print out whenever you want."

I flipped the folder open. Stapled to the left flap was a list of names, numbers, and emails. More papers were loose inside. The top sheet was a W2 form.

Bennett was watching me and seemed to spot that as well. "Right. I put your HR paperwork in there. You can fill that out today and get it to me. That way I can make sure you're set up for payroll. We pay on the first and fifteenth, but if you need me to get you a check at the end of this week to bootstrap expenses, let me know. I'm happy to do it."

My eyebrows lifted. "That's kind of you. I think I'd like that if it's really not a problem."

"Sure thing. Can you put a sticky note on your paperwork to remind me?"

I nodded.

I didn't have a lot of expenses right now, but I also didn't have much money in my bank account. I bit my lip. My bank account. The one my parents insisted they be allowed access to as well.

"What's up?"

I shook my head. "I'll figure it out."

Bennett just waited.

He had that in common with Christian. Both of them knew how to use silence to their advantage. I sighed. "I probably need to set up a local bank account. The one I have is... complicated."

"Ah." He nodded and checked his watch. "The bank's just a block over. Why don't you go over and do that now? Then you'll have the account info for the paperwork. I can hold the fort until you're back."

"It can wait." I didn't have any money to put into an account to open one. I had some spending money that my parents gave me, but I wasn't going to use that. I didn't want them to think I'd taken something that wasn't mine. And they'd been very clear that any money they gave me was theirs and I only got to use it because they were being kind.

Bennett studied me a moment, then reached into his pocket. He pulled out his wallet and took out a stack of bills. "Use this."

"Oh. No. I couldn't—"

"I'll take it out of your paycheck on Friday."

I frowned at the money, then at him. "You promise?"

Now he frowned. "If I have to."

"You do. Your family is already doing so much. I don't—I'm not—"

He pushed the money into my hand. "I get it. Go open an account."

I hesitated, then closed my hand around the cash. "All right. Thank you."

"No thanks necessary. When you get back, we can go over

the computer stuff." He paused and glanced at the cast on my arm. "Are you allowed to use that arm?"

"Yeah. It just makes things a little slower and clunkier." The doctor hadn't said to keep it in a sling or still or anything like that. I wasn't going to be running around waving my arm in the air, but normal use ought to be okay.

"Okay. See you in a bit. The bank is to the left."

Right. I took that for the dismissal it was and headed back out onto the street. I turned left and started walking. The bank was easy to spot. It had a digital sign out front showing the time and temperature under the words "Loring Island Savings and Loan."

The air was already warming up, but the gentle breeze kept the humidity down and brought the pleasant scent of the ocean with it. I walked slowly, taking in my surroundings. Still, I found myself in front of the glass doors looking into the bank lobby before I was ready.

I took a steadying breath and pulled open a door. I stepped inside the over-airconditioned space and started toward the tall counter where a lone woman sat, waiting.

"Good morning. Can I help you?"

"Yes." I cleared my throat. "I'd like to open a checking account."

The process was simple enough, and if the bank teller thought it was odd to open an account with three hundred dollars in twenties, she didn't say anything. Within half an hour, I was on my way back to the office with a debit card in my wallet, their banking app installed on my phone, and my login credentials saved.

The app had been a relief.

As had the instant issue debit card.

They might be a small-town bank, but they were up-to-date with technology. Even more than some of the national bank chains. My parents' bank—and my old bank—didn't do instant issue cards in a branch. They were mailed and took a bit of time to arrive.

Back at the office, I went down the hall and tapped on Bennett's open door.

He looked up. "All set?"

"Yeah, thanks again."

"No problem." He glanced at his watch. "I have a Zoom meeting in about five minutes with some lawyers in Oregon. When that's done, I'll come out and show you the ropes with the computer and phones, but feel free to poke around and get a feel."

"Okay." I hesitated. "Should I close your door?"

"If you would."

I grabbed the doorknob and pulled the door shut, then went back out to the front desk. Maybe I could prove my usefulness and figure out the computer and phones on my own. I sat behind the desk, tucked my purse into one of the drawers, and flipped open the folder of information.

HR paperwork. Right. That first, then exploring.

Pleased to have something to do, I got to work.

The morning passed quickly. I found things to keep myself busy and had been pleased by Bennett's reaction to my progress when he got out of his meeting. There were a couple of features on the phone system I hadn't figured out, but he said I had the gist of everything else.

Go me.

As I was getting ready to take a short break for lunch, the door opened and Christian came in, followed by—I searched my memory—Travis? I was pretty sure it was Travis. I smiled. "Hi. Are you here to see Bennett?"

"I'm not." Christian smiled, then jerked a thumb at Travis. "He is."

I held up a finger. "Let me let him know you're here."

I clenched my hand into a fist as I studied the phone system, took a deep breath, and poked the buttons I was reasonably sure were the intercom.

"Yes?"

I grinned when Bennett's voice came through the speaker. "Travis is here to see you."

"Great. Send him back. Nice job on the intercom."

I gave a short laugh and hit the button to end the intercom session, then looked up at Travis. "You can head on back. It's good to see you again."

"Thanks." Travis's smile seemed distracted.

What was that about? Not my business. Not really. I looked up at Christian. "Checking up on me?"

He waggled a hand from side to side. "More wondering if you'd like to grab some lunch."

"I was going to go to the library." I had a little money, but spending it on food wasn't the smart choice. I'd learned that in Tennessee. Takeout and delivery were convenient and easy, but they added up fast. A loaf of bread and some cheese at the grocery store would be smarter. I could probably stash them in the office fridge.

"We can do that, too." One corner of Christian's mouth poked up. "My treat. As a celebration of your new job."

"I—" Everything in me said I should turn him down. He'd done so much. His family was doing so much already. I wasn't blind to the fact that he seemed interested in me. Attracted. I felt the same. But I wasn't in a place for that. Not right now. I couldn't drag him into the mess that was my life.

Except...I basically already had.

Spending more time with him might be a subtle form of torture, a lot like putting a huge bowl of ice cream on the table and then saying it was off limits.

But I found I couldn't say no.

"I'd like that."

Christian grinned and every part of him seemed to light up. "Excellent. You ready?"

I grabbed my purse out of the drawer where I'd stashed it and stood. "Sure."

"Why don't you text Bennett and let him know you're hitting the diner and the library? That way he can gauge how long you'll be gone. I assume Travis will have told him I stopped by too, so he probably can figure it out, but it's nice to keep the boss in the loop. Right?"

"Right." I smiled at the teasing tone in Christian's voice even as I wondered if that meant he'd already cleared it with Bennett. Still, it sounded like I was going to be gone longer than I'd originally anticipated, so it was definitely better to let Bennett know. Getting fired my first day on the job was not the plan.

I took my phone out of my purse and pulled up Bennett's contact, thankful I'd taken the time to put him and his parents in at the start of the morning. I tapped in our plans and sent it, then put the phone away. "Lead on, Macduff."

"I think it's actually 'Lay on.' And I hope we're not about to duel." Christian smirked.

"Hmm. I'll take your word for it. My Shakespeare is lacking."

He laughed and held the door for me.

On the sidewalk, Christian gestured to the right, then tucked his hands in his pockets. "How has the morning been?"

I tipped my face up to let the sun warm it before falling into step beside him. "Good. Slow-ish. But that means more time to figure everything out. Bennett said slow is usual?"

"Yeah, the island isn't a hot bed of legal wrangling usually. He takes some cases from the mainland, too. Some farther afield in the state, depending on what they need. But it's a lot like my work at the clinic, he does it because he loves it and wants the service to be available, not because he needs to make a killing."

I nodded. That seemed to be a common theme I was picking up from the whole of Christian's family. They had money—lots of it—but they still worked, doing things they loved and that could provide a benefit to the people around them. It was nice. And such a contrast to my own family. We had money, too, but Dad was focused on one-upping the people who had come before. He wanted to be able to say he'd earned more and left a bigger pile behind. Everything with him—and Mom—was about the money.

If I was honest with myself, right now I was that way, too. But only because I didn't *have* any. Six more months and I would have the financial safety net that meant every decision didn't have to revolve around dollar signs.

"The clinic is slow today?" It was a subtle change in conversation, but I'd rather get him talking and listen than have him continue to focus on me.

He shrugged. "Pretty usual, but yeah. A sunburned toddler who spiked a fever and the first-time mom panicked. Two stitches in a foot that found the sharp edge of a seashell. That kind of thing. Here we are."

I looked across the street at the old timey building. "I'm excited to eat here. Mom and Dad have mostly stuck to the country club for eating out. They're not big on diners."

"Their loss. I'll actually be eating here twice today, since my family has dinner here together on Monday evenings. Best thing about diners is you could eat every meal in one and never have to eat the same thing."

We hurried across the street, despite there being no traffic, and to the entrance. Christian opened the door for me. I walked in and grinned. It was perfect. From the mixed aromas of bacon and bread to the red vinyl and chrome stools at the counter—it was everything a diner should be.

"Two?" The girl at the hostess stand smiled at Christian.

He nodded.

"You can sit anywhere. We're not crowded today."

"Thanks." Christian glanced left, then pointed to a booth and looked at me. "That work?"

"Sure." Part of me wanted to sit at the counter, but I could do that another day. I could come down here on my own now and then on my lunch break. A tiny laugh bubbled up. Lunch break! Because I had a job. One I could maybe even come to enjoy. And if it stayed slow, maybe I could work on lyrics while I was there.

I missed songwriting. And playing. I missed music, in general. Mom and Dad had put their foot down when I came crawling home from Nashville. I'd failed to make a career out of it, so they expected me to put it completely away. It had taken a lot of wheedling to get them to let me keep my guitar—they'd gotten rid of everything else. I could replace it though, when I got my trust.

Or maybe sooner, now that I was gainfully employed.

I reached for the menus that were stacked behind the little jukebox by the wall. "What do you like here?"

Christian also took a menu and flipped it open. "Honestly? I've liked everything I ever tried. I don't think you can go wrong. But I'm getting a Reuben. With fries. Because who doesn't like fries?"

"Fries are good." I liked them, certainly, but I wasn't going to get any. The salads looked nice. That would be a good mid-day meal. Something lighter. Deb seemed determined to put enough food in front of me at dinner that I was going to end up packing on the pounds if I wasn't careful.

It didn't take long for a server to stop at our table. "Hey Christian. Ma'am. What can I get y'all to drink?"

"Hi Chrissy. I'll have sweet tea. This is my friend Teresa. She's just signed on to take over for Angela at the law firm."

"I heard she followed Jimmy over to Charlotte." Chrissy shook her head. "No ring yet. I tell you what, I wouldn't leave this island with a man who hasn't put a diamond on my finger. Better yet if he followed up with the actual wedding first. But Angela was always a lot more forgiving when it came to Jimmy than I ever would have been. Still, it's real nice to meet you, Teresa. Welcome to Loring Island."

It took me a second to parse through the rambling monologue to realize the woman was speaking to me. "Oh. Thanks. I love it here."

"Easy to do. What can I get you to drink?"

Right. Drinks. "Can I get a Coke?"

"Sure can. You need a minute or are you ready to order?"

"I'm ready." I looked over at Christian. "You are, right?"

"Your usual?" Chrissy was already writing on her pad.

"Yeah. Who's cooking today? If it's Ron, can you see about getting the fries extra crisp?"

Chrissy laughed. "It is Ron. I'll tell him. And you, ma'am?"

"The fried chicken salad with the honey mustard dressing, please."

She nodded. "I'll get those in and be right back with your drinks."

"So today you're getting a Reuben?" I grinned. "As opposed to another day when you would also get a Reuben?"

Christian's cheeks reddened. "Busted. I have tried a lot on the menu though. But once I found the sandwich? I don't see the need to branch out."

"But if you eat dinner here on Mondays with your family, what will you get tonight?"

He shrugged. "A Reuben. Maybe I'll switch it up and get a side salad instead of fries. But probably not."

I shook my head. "It must be amazing."

"I think so." He took our menus and slipped them back into their place. "How's the job going so far?"

"So far, so good. But it's day one. And there hasn't been a lot asked of me." I didn't necessarily get the idea that would change a lot. In some ways, it didn't seem like Bennett needed a receptionist. I wasn't going to be the one who pointed that out.

"Good. How's your face?"

"It's fine." I'd spent a little extra time on makeup this morning, but the bruising wasn't super obvious anymore. "I'm not convinced Dad even meant to hit me."

Christian frowned. "And yet he did."

"Yeah." I waited while Chrissy delivered our drinks. "I'm not excusing it."

"That's good. I hope you won't talk yourself into going back there. It's not safe." He reached across the table to rest his fingers lightly on top of mine, right by the edge of my cast. "I like knowing you're safe."

He was just being friendly. And concerned. He was a nurse, after all, so he had to care about his patients. I wasn't going to read anything else into that, no matter what sensations were charging through me at his gentle touch.

When I didn't respond, he moved his hand back. "How are you settling in with Aunt Deb and Uncle Rob?"

"Perfectly. They make that easy. They treat me like a daughter. Or, well, like I imagine a good family treats their daughters. How do I get them to let me pay rent?"

He laughed. "You don't."

"But—"

"Stop. They don't need it and you do. You need to be able to save up. They understand that. If they were in a place where they needed something, they'd tell you, but they just aren't."

I scowled. "I don't like feeling like a mooch."

Christian's head tipped to the side and he studied me. "Can you cook?"

I waggled a hand from side to side. "If it's simple. I'm not Gordon Ramsay, but no one will get poisoned."

"Offer to make dinner one night a week. Or breakfast. That's your best bet if you're determined to do something to help out."

"I can do that." I nodded. I could. And I'd get my own groceries when I did. "Do you think if I just show up and start cooking it'll be easier than trying to convince them?"

"One hundred percent."

"All right." I grinned. "That makes me feel a little better."

"If they push back, tell them that. They want you to be comfortable and feel at home. Let them know this is part of that."

I laughed.

Chrissy showed up with our food and, after assuring her that we didn't need anything else, Christian took my good hand and said a quick prayer over our food before we dug in. He'd made it through half of his sandwich when his phone rang.

"Sorry." He dug the phone out and sighed before he answered. "This is Christian."

After a brief conversation that I didn't really follow, he ended the call and slid out of his side of the booth. "I have to run, sorry. I'm going to grab a box for my food and pay the bill. I'll touch base with you tonight to hear how the rest of your day went."

I fought to keep the disappointment from showing on my face. I must have been semi-successful, because Christian sent me a warm smile before he strode to the counter. Very quickly, he was back at the table sliding his sandwich and fries into the box.

"I have a tab here, so if you decide you want pie or something—and their pie is amazing—please go ahead and get it."

"Thanks." I had no intention of getting pie, but it was a nice thought.

"Talk to you tonight." He knocked on the table and then hurried off.

I sighed. It was fine. Really. Maybe even good. Hadn't I wanted to have lunch on my own? So, now I was.

I picked through the salad, eating the fried chicken and croutons as well as the cheese and other yummy bits, avoiding the lettuce.

Chrissy must have been waiting tables a long time, because she showed up just as I was deciding I was finished. "Can I get you anything else? Another Coke? Some pie? We have French Silk today."

I shook my head. "It sounds good, but I'm stuffed."

"All right. You have a nice day. I'm sure we'll see you around." She beamed and headed off to another of her tables.

I dug in my purse for my wallet. I'd kept a little cash when I'd gone to the bank this morning. Christian may have covered the tip, but I couldn't walk off without leaving something. My choices were limited though. I didn't want to leave a whole twenty. Nor did I want to ask about getting change. That left the two singles I'd already had and a ten. The ten won. I dropped it on the table, then slid out of the booth.

A quick glance at the time revealed that I could still squeeze in a trip to the library before I needed to be back at work. Besides which, Bennett didn't strike me as someone who would quibble about me showing up a few minutes past my lunch break. I paused at the hostess stand.

"Can I help you?"

"I was wondering if you could point me in the direction of the library?"

"That's easy. It's basically across the street. Diagonal that way a bit." She pointed.

"Oh, great. Thanks." I crossed the little lobby and then pushed through the doors to the parking lot where I angled in the direction she'd indicated. The library was obvious.

I grinned and stepped off the curb so I could cross the parking lot. I'd made it to the street and was checking that it was clear so I could cross when I spotted Dad's car. Maybe he wouldn't see me?

I darted across the street and slipped between two parked cars. I kept my head down as I hurried toward the library steps. I had my foot on the first step, when I heard my name.

"Teresa!"

I started to climb the steps. I wasn't going to acknowledge Dad. If he wanted to talk to me about something, he could call me. He had my number.

"Teresa Duvall, turn around this minute."

His tone made my blood boil. I wasn't some misbehaving pre-teen. I turned and crossed my arms, scowling at him.

"Get in the car."

"No." I shook my head.

"I said, get in the car."

"I didn't say I couldn't hear you. I said no." I turned and started back up the library steps.

A car door slammed and as I reached for the library door, someone grabbed my arm and pulled me back. "Get in the car, young lady."

I yanked my arm, but Dad's grip was iron. "Let go of me."

"We put up with your little music thing. To no one's surprise, it didn't work out. Now it's time for you to do something useful for the family."

"No." I yanked on my arm again, trying to get free. "That's not a requirement for anyone in the family. Grandma and Grandpa made that clear to me from the beginning."

"Well. Grandma and Grandpa aren't the trustees, are they?

Your mother and I are. With that in mind, you will come back to the house and apologize to James and make nice, or we'll see to it that your trust disappears."

My jaw dropped. "You can't do that."

"Watch me." Dad tugged my arm so hard I cried out. He scowled. "Don't be a baby. Get in the car."

"Is there a problem here?"

I hadn't seen the man approaching and it took me a moment to realize he wore a uniform

"Yes."

"No." Dad replied at the same time I did.

I yanked my arm again and this time got free. I took a step backwards, nearly tripping up the library steps. I looked back at the man—Sheriff? —and nodded. "Yes. There is a problem. He's trying to force me into his car."

"Sir. I'm going to have to ask you to come with me."

"It's not like that. I'm her father. She ran away from home and I'm just trying to get her back to safety."

I snorted derisively. "Home is not safe. And I'm twenty-nine years old."

The Sheriff nodded once. "You don't look like a minor. You prefer not to go with him?"

"That's right." I glared at my dad even though my insides were quaking and my knees wanted to give out. I was going to stand firm. I could have a breakdown once Dad wasn't around to see it.

"Come with me, sir." The Sheriff gestured to the police cruiser that was double-parked on the street.

"You'll regret this, Teresa." Dad turned and stormed back to his car. He got in and tore off down the street.

The Sheriff scowled after him before looking at me. "Are you all right?"

"Yes. Thank you." I hesitated, looking down the street toward the receding view of Dad's car. "If you don't have to follow up with him, I'd as soon it was left alone."

"Hmm." The Sheriff tucked his hands in his pockets.

The door to the library opened and Deb stepped out to join me on the top step. "Morning, Carl. Thanks for the quick response."

"It's my job, after all Deb." He flashed a grin, then nudged his chin toward me. "Seems it was her father and she'd like me to leave it. I have grounds to go after him—speeding, if nothing else—but I'll take your advice into consideration."

Deb put her hand on my shoulder. "Honey, are you sure? Between your arm and this..."

"The arm wasn't him." I muttered. Although he was complicit. Definitely. But if I pushed this, it would just make it worse. And his threat about the money...well, I wouldn't put it past him to at least try to take it. That was, at the heart of every-thing, his primary concern. At least as far as I could tell. I sent Deb a pleading look, hoping against hope she'd let it go. "I'm sure."

Deb's lips thinned, but she nodded once and looked at Carl. "Maybe you could just write it all up so there's a report in place if he escalates?"

"I was going to do that anyway." Carl shook his head. "If you change your mind, you come on down to the station."

"Thank you."

I waited until Carl got back to his cruiser before sinking to sit on the step.

Deb came and sat beside me. "I wish you would have chosen differently."

"I know." My stomach churned and my limbs were quiver-ing. Part of me agreed with Deb. The smart thing—the strong thing—would have been to let the man haul Dad down to the station. Did they still use rubber hoses? The mental image put the ghost of a smile on my lips. "I can't though."

"Why not?" Deb rubbed small, light circles on my back. It was soothing.

I shook my head. "It's a lot to get into."

"All right. Maybe you'll tell us tonight at dinner."

Since her inflection had made it a statement, not a question, I decided the "maybe" at the start was simply out of politeness. Or the inherent phrasing moms used to make sure kids knew they were in trouble.

"Maybe."

Deb gave a short laugh and stood, her knees creaking as she did. "I should get back to Grady. Jericho is amazing with him, but you just never know what might set him off. Are you coming inside?"

I bit my lip. I wanted a book. I wanted to spend a few minutes wandering in the library—maybe chatting with Jericho if she had some time. I liked her. Shopping with her on Saturday had been the first time in a while that I'd spent with another woman my age.

I missed it.

But I shook my head. "I should get back to work."

"All right." Deb waited while I got to my feet then pulled me in for a tight hug. "We'll see you tonight. I'm making spaghetti."

I opened my mouth to object, but closed it when I caught her look. I could make dinner another night. "All right. Can't wait."

"That's the way. Enjoy the rest of your afternoon." Deb patted my shoulder then turned and pulled open the library door.

I sighed and gave the book-filled interior a wistful glance before starting down the steps and heading toward the law offices. I concentrated on enjoying the warm summer air and the ocean breeze while I walked. I dodged groups of tourists, and every time my mind tried to veer back to the altercation with my dad, I forced myself to say the alphabet backwards.

I was terrible at it.

But at least it kept me focused.

When I got back, Bennett was sitting on the edge of my desk.

"Am I late? I am, aren't I?" I reached for my phone.

"No. You're fine." He waved that off. "I wanted to see if you were okay."

"If I'm..." Light dawned. "Deb called you."

He nodded. "She's worried. And from what she said, it sounds like she should be. So...are you okay?"

"Yeah." I didn't bother sighing. Deb meant well. Maybe, in some ways, it was nice of her to care enough to let Bennett know.

He didn't speak for a moment, then cleared his throat. "I guess my aunt was listening from inside the library. She heard some of what your dad said about your trust."

Of course she did. My face heated and I looked away.

"I just thought I'd let you know that I am a lawyer with some experience handling trusts and disputes surrounding them. In case that was information that you found useful."

I looked back at him. "What do you mean?"

Bennett shrugged one shoulder. "I guess, in your place, I'd want to know if my parents could really take my trust away."

Right. That.

I'd been avoiding thinking about that. Everything in me rebelled at it being a viable possibility. It wasn't as if Dad was the one who set up the trust in the first place. "Would it be hard for you to find out?"

"I don't think so. What can you tell me about it?"

I crossed the room and sat in one of the guest chairs, then dug out my phone. I spent a minute searching through my email folders until I finally located what I was looking for. "I have the email that Dad's lawyers sent me when I turned eighteen and got the first installment of my money. I can forward it to you."

"That's a good place to start. Are your parents really the trustees?"

I frowned. "I thought it was my grandparents. But they're getting up there, so maybe they made a change while I was in Nashville."

"Hm."

I hit forward on the email and tapped in Bennett's name. I'd already added him as a phone contact, thankfully, so it could populate the email. I looked up. "What?"

"You should have been notified. As a courtesy, if nothing else."

Had I been told? It was entirely possible. I hadn't paid a lot of attention—I was too busy chasing the career I was sure I could have. I didn't honestly start taking notice until the money ran out.

Too little, too late.

"I'll look into it and let you know what I find out."

"Thanks." I stayed in the chair while Bennett headed back to his office. He hadn't said anything about how much it would cost. The reality was that I couldn't afford anything. He could charge me a dollar and I'd have to pay him from the money he'd given me this morning. Should I follow him and ask?

I closed my eyes briefly. No. That would be too much extra embarrassment. I'd figure it out when I got the bill.

13

CHRISTIAN

"Hang on, Teresa. Can I call you right back? Someone's at the door."

"Sure."

I ended the call, then dragged myself out of my recliner and strode through the great room to the front door. I didn't really want a visitor, honestly, I couldn't think of anyone who would stop by on a Monday evening, but it was exactly that that had me getting up to check. My immediate family had all had dinner at the diner after work. If it was one of them, it was probably some kind of emergency. And since they made up the bulk of my social connections these days—and I'd worry about what that said about me later—they were likely to be the only ones popping by.

I pulled open the door.

"Hi." Teresa's sheepish smile didn't reach her eyes. She looked...defeated. That was the word that came to mind.

"Hey." I stepped back and waved her in. "I'm not going to call you back. Just to be clear."

She managed a short laugh.

"Can I get you a drink? Something to snack on?"

She shook her head. "Your aunt is going to see to it that I gain twenty pounds, if I'm not careful. She's a really good cook. And she doesn't take no very well when I say I don't want thirds."

I grinned and led the way back to the great room. I resumed my seat in the recliner. "That sounds like Aunt Deb. Make yourself at home."

Teresa sat primly on the edge of the sofa. Her fingers twisted together in her lap.

I frowned slightly. "How was your first day?"

"You haven't already heard?"

My eyebrows lifted. "All Bennett said at dinner was that you got a handle on your duties quickly and that he was sure you were going to be a fabulous employee."

She relaxed slightly. "He didn't say anything else? Your aunt didn't call you?"

"It's not like he was silent the whole meal, but he didn't say anything about you. He talked a little about Travis and that whole situation." I tipped my head to the side. "Should my aunt have called me?"

"What's the Travis situation? Or is that a family thing?"

I spotted her conversational delay tactic, but I let it slide. "It's a family thing, but it's not super-secret. The whole island probably knows most of it. Long story short, Travis's wife left him in January. She wants a divorce. Bennett had a call with her attorney in Portland today, since she's nearing the six-month residency she needs in order to try and have the divorce granted in Oregon instead of here. But she's delusional."

"What makes her delusional?"

"She seems to think Travis is going to give her all of the family money to fund her lifestyle and she gets off without any responsibility for Grady." That was maybe too much of a nutshell, but the whole situation made my blood boil. Caroline didn't appear to care about Grady at all. From what Travis and Bennett had said, she'd barely asked after him. And what she did say was ranting about Travis's decision to have Grady evaluated for Autism and ADHD and then, when both were diagnosed, start figuring out what kind of treatment would help him most. Those were all things Caroline had staunchly opposed when she was here, even though she railed against Grady's tendency to melt down and hyper focus. She thought they were behavior issues.

"Oh."

I couldn't quite decide what she meant. I also wasn't sure I wanted to know. I liked Teresa. A lot. More than I'd liked a woman in a very long time. But if she was going to end up being someone who thought it was a good idea for a mother to abandon her child and her marriage because it was harder than she expected...that would be a problem.

I cleared my throat. "Anyway, that was the bulk of the dinner conversation. So. Why did you think my aunt would call me?"

Teresa sighed and sagged back into the couch. "Dad saw me after lunch. He tried to make me go home."

I waited, but she didn't add to it. "That doesn't sound too bad. Why would Aunt Deb have called me? You didn't go. He left. Right?"

"Not really. I mean, I didn't go. Ultimately, he left, but only after your aunt called the Sheriff. It was loud and a whole thing." She shrugged. "I'm glad Deb was at the library. But also mortified."

"I'm so sorry." I fought the urge to change seats so I could offer some sort of tactile comfort. Would she be receptive to it? I didn't want to find out that she wasn't. "I'm glad Aunt Deb was there, too. How did Bennett find out about it?"

"Deb called him while I was walking back to work. Dad made some threats about my trust. Bennett looked into them for me. It didn't take him too long, so hopefully I can afford the bill when he gets it to me."

I waved that away. "Bennett isn't going to charge you for something like that. What did he find out? If that's not over-stepping."

Teresa looked down at her hands clasped in her lap. "Turns out, Dad can revoke the trust until my thirtieth birthday. Or until I get married. Basically, I'm hosed if he decides that's what he's going to do. My birthday isn't until December, and I'm not exactly swimming in fiancés."

"Well, you'd only need one." My attempt at lightening the atmosphere fell flat. I cringed. "Sorry."

"No. It's fine." She rubbed her hands on her thighs. "Most people make it through life without a trust fund. I could figure it out if that was all."

"What do you mean?"

"Bennett found that there's also a clause in there that if my trust gets revoked, then I have to repay the first payout. And that..." Teresa trailed off and looked at me, hopelessness oozing from every feature. "There's no way. I guess Dad wins."

If it was just going back to her parents, I could maybe believe it would be all right. But... "What about James?"

She shrugged. "He wins, too, I guess. Maybe Mom can help me find some kind of alcohol that doesn't taste disgusting so I can live in a stupor like she does. It seems to work for her."

"Teresa." Apparently, the tone that parents used when they heard something completely ridiculous come out of someone's mouth was innate and could happen to anyone.

"What?"

I got out of the recliner and moved over to sit beside her on the couch. I took both of her hands in mine. "There have to be other solutions. We just have to look for them."

"We?" She looked up and her tear-filled gaze latched onto mine.

"We." I squeezed her hands. "I want to help. I know my family will want to help. Maybe..."

She tipped her head to the side. "Maybe what?"

I took a deep breath. I knew the words forming in my brain weren't likely to land well. Especially coming from me. "Maybe you just give up the trust?"

Teresa snorted. "Oh, sure. Because I have so much going for me and can totally support myself for the rest of my life."

I ignored the sarcasm. "Bennett pays well. I know that for a fact. And I also am pretty sure you could live with my aunt and uncle for as long as you wanted. Or, if you didn't want to keep doing that, we can probably find you an affordable apartment on the mainland."

Affordable and Loring Island didn't always go together. We didn't have many apartments on the island. There were some above shops in town, but those tended to stay rented year-round.

"Are you throwing an affordable car into that mix? Because I don't have my car here with me, and I guarantee when my parents realize I'm not coming home, they won't let me have it."

"Whose name is on the title?"

"Like that matters." She shook her head. "They gave it to me. Sure, it's registered to me, but I don't want to spend my entire salary on having Bennett threaten my parents with legal action. That's what it would take. And I'm not convinced they wouldn't try to get it to court just to drag things out. I've always given in. Or failed. Same result either way though—me, running back home."

I frowned slightly. My mind was racing trying to come up with alternatives. "Bennett didn't find any other way for you to get your money then? It's just your birthday? No one else in your family would be able to help you?"

"I guess I could reach out to my grandparents, but they always take Dad's side in things. He's their golden boy who took over the family business and is making it grow. I'm just the disappointing granddaughter who has ridiculous dreams of singing for a living. Even though they're the ones who pushed me into music in the first place." Everything about her seemed to deflate. "The only other way I get access to the money is if I'm married. And since I'm not going to marry James, I don't really see any viable options there."

"What am I? Chopped liver?" I blurted out the words without thinking.

"What?" Her jaw dropped. She shook her head. "I don't think I heard you right."

I might have initially been kidding—although I also wasn't positive that was the case—but now that I'd said it, the idea was solidifying. "It's the perfect answer."

"How? Because I'm not following. You want to marry me? You don't really know me. Maybe we're kind of on the way to being friends, possibly even dating...but skipping straight to marriage?"

My stomach clenched. Was marrying me that horrible of a prospect? I swallowed. "I was just offering an option. But it's fine. You're right."

I realized I was still holding her hands and quickly let them go, then scooted over on the sofa to put more space between us. I cleared my throat. "Maybe Bennett can do something legal that makes it harder for your parents to take the trust away. He always says the law has a ton of tricks if you know where to look for them."

She shook her head and twisted her hands together in her lap. "I think he would have said something this afternoon. He told me he'd done enough digging to be confident that my parents had the right to follow through."

"Okay." I blew out a breath. "That stinks. I guess we should just pray you figure out what God wants you to do."

That was, of course, the right answer. And it should have been the first thing I offered to do. But saying, "Let's pray about it." Always seemed like such an empty pile of words. I believed in prayer, absolutely, but I also figured God wanted us to use our brains, too.

"Right." She sounded resigned as she scooted to the edge of the couch and stood. "I'll do that."

I stood and tucked my hands in my pockets. "I can pray, too. I'd like to."

"Okay. Obviously the more the merrier there." She paused. "You really think I'd have to find an apartment on the mainland? There's nothing on the island?"

"I can ask Travis. Or you could ask Uncle Rob. He'd know, too."

"Okay. I'll ask him when I get back. Which...I guess I'll do now. Maybe tomorrow afternoon we could go over to the mainland and look around? I guess I'll need to find a car, too. Hopefully there's something cheap available nearby."

At least she wasn't cutting me out completely. I nodded. "I want to help you however you'll let me."

"Do you know anything about cars?"

"A little. Want me to poke around online and see what I can find?"

"Would you?" She smiled slightly. "That'd be one less thing for me to try to do tonight."

"Absolutely." I pushed away the hurt her flat rejection of the idea of marrying me caused and closed the distance between us, then held open my arms. "Need a hug?"

She stepped into my embrace and burrowed her face into my

chest. I wrapped my arms around her and rested my cheek on the top of her head. I let my eyes close and just breathed in the appley scent of her shampoo. We stood like that for a long time, then her hands slid to my sides and she stepped back.

She swallowed. "Thanks."

"Any time." My arms felt empty without her in them, but I forced what I hoped was an encouraging smile. "Let me know what time tomorrow. I'll pick you up at Bennett's office."

Teresa nodded.

We crossed to the front door in silence and a stood on the porch watching her walk the short distance back to my aunt and uncle's house.

When she disappeared, I stepped back into my house and closed the door, then leaned forward and rested my forehead on its cold surface. Thoughts and emotions swirled in my brain and I couldn't get a handle on any of them.

I closed my eyes and huffed out a breath.

Wasn't it supposed to get easier when you were older? Because that sure didn't seem to be my experience.

I straightened and headed back into the living room. I could, at least, spend a little time looking at what was available in the used car world around Loring Island and Bennett. We'd probably have to travel a little farther than either of them, but that didn't matter. At least not to me.

I'd spend whatever time with Teresa I could.

In my mind, at least, we were definitely friends.

What would it take to get her to see things my way?

14

TERESA

"You're sure you don't mind me leaving a little early?" I clasped my hands behind my back as I hovered in the doorway to Bennett's office.

He laughed. "Not at all. I know it's only your second day here, but you've surely noticed it's not exactly a job that keeps you going all day. I should be just fine managing the last couple of hours on my own."

"Thanks."

"It's no problem. Especially since you looking for a place to live means I don't have to hold my breath to see if you stick around."

I nodded. Of course he'd be worried about that. "I have no plans to leave the area. I like it here."

"I'm glad to hear it." Bennett paused. "I imagine Christian's pretty glad, too."

I shrugged. After some of the things I said last night—the words that had left me tossing and turning for most of last night —he might not be. He'd still seemed happy to pick me up and help with finding a place to live, but maybe that was simply because he'd been raised to keep his commitments.

Bennett studied me. For a moment, it seemed like he was going to say more, but he didn't.

"Should I lock the door?"

"Would you? That makes it even easier for me." He grinned.

"Yeah. No problem. I'll see you tomorrow."

Bennett offered an absent nod, having already returned his attention to whatever he was doing on his computer.

I slipped back down the hall to the reception area and checked that everything was tidy and ready for tomorrow morning. When I was sure I wasn't leaving a mess, I grabbed my purse and went out onto the sidewalk. I took the time to lock the door behind me, then moved a few steps over so I could lean against the side of the building and wait for Christian.

In a matter of minutes, Christian pulled up to the curb.

I hurried to the passenger door and pulled it open. "Thanks. I really appreciate this."

"I'm happy to do it. Uncle Rob didn't know of anything in town?"

I shook my head. "No. He said he'd keep an ear out for me, but he also said the apartments in town tended not to even hit the open rental market. It's all word of mouth."

"I thought it might be. Sorry." Christian looked around, then pulled away from the curb into a U-turn. He aimed the car toward the bridge over to the mainland. "I did find a couple of cars to look at while we're in Bennett. I just have to text the owners when we're ready. I wasn't sure how much you wanted to spend, so I focused on reliable."

I winced. I didn't want to spend anything. Obviously, that was unrealistic. If I was going to live on the mainland and commute to the island every day, I was going to need a car. But I probably couldn't afford anything remotely resembling reliable. Used or new.

I cleared my throat. "Well. We can take a look and see what we see."

"Exactly." Christian sent a smile my way. "Did you have an apartment complex you want to hit up first?"

There weren't thousands to consider. Bennett was a bigger town than the island, but it wasn't exactly a bustling city. And it still ran more toward homes than apartments. "I made a list."

I dug my cellphone out of my purse and pulled up the draft email where I'd made notes. I gave him the address of my first choice. That choice was based solely on price for a one-bedroom apartment. If I had to learn to live completely on my salary, it was what I could afford. Barely.

"Really?" Christian frowned. "That's on the far side of town. You don't want to be near the beach?"

Of course I'd rather be near the beach, but the apartments on the beach that weren't timeshares or condos were close to twice the rent. "I have some of those on the list. They're just... probably out of my reach right now."

Pink stained his cheeks. "Right. Sorry. I know you're doing this on your salary. I just forgot for a minute."

I gave a mirthless laugh. I would love to forget for even a second, but I'd done that in Tennessee and now I was in this position. I couldn't afford—literally—to ever do that again.

We spent the rest of the drive chatting about our day and other inconsequential things. Something about it felt different than any of the conversations we'd had previously. What had changed?

Was it possible to get it back?

I turned to look out the window as Christian wound his way through town and finally turned into a parking lot in front of an apartment complex that had seen better days. There was no other way to put it. My insides tightened. I didn't want to live here.

"Is it even safe?"

"What was that?"

I flinched. Had I said that aloud? I shook my head. "Nothing."

I unbuckled my seatbelt and reached for the door handle.

Christian took a deep breath, like he was going to say something, then he pressed his lips together and got out of the car.

I got out and stood for a moment looking at the building before closing the car door and concentrating on not letting my shoulders sag. "The office is on the main floor. According to the website at least."

He nodded and fell into step beside me.

Grass was growing between cracks in the sidewalk and the odor of an over-full dumpster teased the edges of the air. I couldn't see the trash when I looked around, but it didn't inspire confidence.

Christian pulled open the door and I stepped into the dimly lit, dingy lobby. The floor was cracked and the edges of the vinyl were curling slightly in places. A door stood open under a sign declaring it the office. Cigarette smoke billowed out.

I took a deep breath, steeled myself, and crossed to the door. I knocked and fought a cough.

"Help ya, hon?" The woman manning the desk had a cigarette dangling from between her lips as she spoke. Her voice betrayed years of smoking. Cat-eye glasses were perched on the edge of her nose and a gold chain dangled down on either side of them.

"Yeah, hi. I saw online that you had some one-bedrooms available? I was hoping I could look at one?"

"Sure thing." The woman swiveled in her chair and pulled a key off a board filled with hooks behind her. "It's unit 320. Use the stairs on the far side of the building. It'll be closer."

Stairs?

I took the key and headed out of the office as quickly as possible. It didn't do much about the overwhelming cigarette smoke, but at least my eyes stopped watering. I glanced around the lobby area. I'd been expecting an elevator. But instead, it was just a bank of mailboxes and doors to what were presumably first floor apartments.

"There are stairs here." Christian pointed to the door marked "STAIRS." "Or we can figure out what she meant by the far side of the building."

"Let's just go up here." I crossed to the door and pulled. It stuck. I pulled harder. It finally came loose and I stumbled backward. A new smell mixed with the smoky smell of the lobby. I swallowed and refused to look at Christian. I couldn't deal with whatever expression he might have.

We climbed the stairs without talking, but it wasn't silent by any stretch. The sound of TVs and yelling—though muffled—made their way into the stairwell. We finally reached the third floor and I stopped to take a deep breath before opening the door and stepping into the hall.

Someone had cooked—and burnt—onions recently. The carpet had dark splotches close to the wall. I glanced up to see brown stains on the ceiling above them. Seeing that, I realized one of the mingling scents in the stairwell had been mold.

Resolute, I started down the hall, checking apartment numbers as I passed them, until I reached 320. I put the key in the lock and opened the front door. The wave of smell that rolled out and over me made me turn aside.

"Okay. Just no." Christian had one arm over his nose and mouth as he reached to pull the door closed again. He turned the key to relock it and stepped away. "You're not living here."

"It's all I can afford." I wanted to curl into a ball and sob, but there was no way I was going to touch the wall or floor in this building.

"You'll stay with my aunt." Christian took my hand and tugged me back down the hall to the stairwell. He kept hold of me as he hurried down the stairs and I struggled to keep up. Back in the lobby, he marched over to the office and set the key on the desk.

"Well?" The woman snatched up the key and turned to hang it back on its hook.

"We're going to think about it." Christian smiled slightly. "Thanks for letting us have a look."

"Course. Don't wait too long. These places go fast." The woman tapped her cigarette in the overflowing ashtray on her desk.

"I'll keep that in mind." Christian turned and headed for the front door.

I should say something. Shouldn't I? This was my apartment search, after all. Except Christian was pulling me out of the building. And he also wasn't wrong. I couldn't live here. I couldn't fathom what we would have found if we'd actually gone in to see what was causing the stench.

At the car, Christian opened my door and held it. He locked his gaze with mine. "There have to be better options."

I hunched my shoulders. "This was my first choice."

He stared at me, unblinking, as seconds ticked by. Then he finally said, "Why?"

I managed half a laugh. "I can afford the rent. And a car loan —if it's not huge—and still have money for groceries."

He nodded slowly. "Did you ask Aunt Deb about staying there? I'm reasonably sure she'd let you—"

"Of course she would." I cut him off, holding up my hands. "But that's not exactly learning to live on my salary. And if that's the rest of my life, because I'm walking away from the trust and my parents and any possibility of school to help me figure out some kind of career, this is what I have. Your brother is paying me really well. I can't complain about that. But this is a tourist town, and everything is more expensive."

I got into the car and reached for the door. "Let's go look at the next one on the list, okay? Maybe it won't be so bad."

"I don't think it's possible to be worse." Christian muttered it mostly under his breath, but I still heard it.

One corner of my mouth poked up as he shut the car door and went around to get in on his side. He wasn't wrong.

When he was settled behind the wheel, I told him the next address.

"Nope. I know that one. Just no." He shook his head emphatically. "It might not reek of cigarettes like this place, but instead, you get clouds of weed."

My eyebrows lifted. "You know this how?"

"Not from my own experience. Austin had a friend in high school who tried to get him into all kinds of stuff. Those apartments were often the host to his illegal escapades."

I sagged back against the seat as my eyes filled. I turned to look out the window and swallowed against the lump in my throat. Now what? "I guess I have to reconsider."

"Teresa." He reached out and squeezed my hand. "You can't go back to your parents. Just stay at Aunt Deb's. Work for Bennett. Take some time to save up since you won't have expenses and then maybe you can afford one of the condos near the bridge. I could help you with a down payment."

"No. I don't want your money. And I don't want to spend my whole life mooching off your aunt and uncle, either. Even though I know they'd let me." I dashed the tears off my cheeks with my good arm. "I wasn't thinking of reconsidering going back to my parents. I know I can't do that."

"Then what?"

"What if we did get married?"

Christian froze. "I thought..."

"I know. But I don't think I have to stay married for too long. Maybe just a month after my birthday, to be safe? So, seven months? And if we don't tell anyone, and I still live with your aunt and uncle, then we can quietly get it annulled at the end and I'll have my money—legally—from both conditions. Then I can get a cottage or something on the island and keep working for Bennett while I figure out what I'm supposed to do with my life. But with a safety net." Once I started talking, the words tumbled out. I didn't know how hard an annulment would be to come by, but surely Bennett could help us out. Especially since we wouldn't have lived together or anything else married people did.

I took a deep breath and held it a moment while I tried to read Christian's expression. "Well? What do you think? Will you marry me?"

15

CHRISTIAN

I blinked.

I wanted to pinch myself, because this wasn't real. Was it?

Last night, I'd pitched the idea of getting married and she'd shut it down unequivocally. Or, at least that's how it had seemed at the time. Obviously, that was no longer the case. But a marriage just on paper? That hadn't been exactly what I'd been hoping for. Although I couldn't have said exactly what I was hoping for beyond a chance to help Teresa out and a way to keep her on the island so we could explore our relationship.

And this was still exactly that.

"Bad idea. I'm sorry. I just thought—"

"No." I held up a hand as I cut her off. "Let's do it."

The smile that broke slowly over her face left me breathless. I wanted to pull her into my arms and kiss her, but we weren't at that stage of our relationship yet. I almost laughed. We were getting married, but I couldn't kiss her?

What was I doing?

I started the car and glanced at the clock. "If we hurry, we can probably make it to the county offices and get our marriage license. Maybe even have them do the ceremony, too, if there's someone available."

"That's fast."

I shot a look her way as I navigated out of the apartment parking lot and onto the street. "Too fast?"

She shook her head immediately. "No. No, I'm sure Dad is already working on whatever it is he's going to do to try and steal my money. Meeting the terms of the trust before he can finalize something is important."

In the back of my mind, I could hear my mother's voice whispering something about fools rushing in, but I tuned it out. I was helping keep Teresa out of a dangerous situation. And keeping her from diving into a new one, if an apartment like the one we'd looked at was truly all she could afford.

Why wasn't there more affordable housing here? I made a mental note to talk to Uncle Rob about that. It seemed like something we ought to be doing as a family. And if not with the whole family's involvement, it was something I could do. I had, so far, stayed out of the family tendency toward owning at least one or two rental houses on Loring. Being a landlord for summer people wasn't something I wanted to make time for. But landlord for apartments that were affordable and not disgusting? I could get behind that.

It didn't take long to get to the building that served as city hall as well as the offices for various county departments. I pulled into a parking spot and turned off the car. "Ready?"

"Yeah." Teresa bit her lip as she nodded. "Are you?"

"Of course." The words popped out without any hesitation. I'd been trying to help her since I first met her in the clinic. That hadn't changed. And it didn't seem likely to ever go away.

I pushed open my car door and got out. Teresa followed suit and we met at the hood of the car. After a moment of waffling, I took her hand.

She glanced quickly up at me, but she didn't pull away. Instead, her fingers curled tightly around mine. Was she nervous? Of course she was. I was. Anyone in this situation would be stupid not to be. Marriage was a big step. Not something that people in our family took lightly.

Was her family the same?

Her parents were still together, even though their relationship didn't appear to be wonderful. That had to count for something, didn't it?

We crossed the parking lot and went into the building. I scanned the directory located on the wall. "Looks like it's on the second floor."

Teresa nodded mutely.

"Are you all right?" I stopped and looked at her. "We don't have to do this. We can figure something else out."

"No, we can't. I already tried that, remember?" She smiled weakly. "I'm worried, I guess, that you'll regret this."

"Not possible." I stepped closer and pulled her into a gentle hug. I didn't fully believe my words. There were tiny doubts in the back of my mind screaming for attention, but I squashed them mercilessly. Teresa needed help. I wanted to be the one who gave it to her.

After a moment, she relaxed and her arms slipped around me. She rested her head on my shoulder and let out a shuddering breath. I glanced down. Her eyes were closed. I smiled as the image burned itself into my memory and something in me shifted.

I pressed a quick kiss to the top of her head. "Come on. Let's go get that license."

With a slow nod, she stepped back. This time, she took my hand.

The process wasn't as difficult as I'd thought it might be. We only needed an ID and our Social Security Number. Since we were nearing the end of the workday, there was no line—not that our town was a bustling hub for elopements, so maybe there was never a line—and we were picking up our license after a thirty-minute wait.

"Congratulations." The woman handing me the paper smiled brightly.

"Thank you." I looked down. It was surreal to see my name on a marriage license. Surreal, but nice. I glanced back up at the woman—she looked somewhat familiar, but then, that was small-town living. "Is there someone who can perform the ceremony available?"

Her eyebrows lifted, but she didn't ask any of the questions I could see in her eyes. "Let me go check."

I turned to Teresa as the woman got up from behind the counter and disappeared through a doorway. "We're halfway there."

"Are you nervous?" She pressed a hand to her belly. "I'm a little nervous."

I held my thumb and forefinger a little way apart.

"Oh, good." She blew out a breath. "You seem so calm, it's hard to tell."

I chuckled. "It's a necessary skill in the medical field."

"I guess I can see that."

If she was going to say more, it was cut off by the return of the woman who had issued our license. "I'm so sorry. He left early today. I can make you an appointment for first thing tomorrow, if you like?"

I glanced at Teresa then back at the woman. "Can you give us a second?"

"Of course." She smiled and turned her attention back to her computer.

I stepped away from the desk and gestured for Teresa to follow. I lowered my voice. "What do you think? Can we wait?"

She bit her lip. "I'd rather not, but what choice do we have?"

"We might have one alternative. Give me a second." I dug my phone out of my pocket and tapped on my cousin Austin's contact. It rang. And rang. I was about to give up when he finally answered.

"Yo. What's up?"

"Are you on land?"

Austin laughed. "Just pulled in at the marina. Had a couple of guys out for a fishing tour today. Think it's a bachelor party, because one of them was green before we even set out this morning. Bonus for them, though, was him hanging over the side of the boat most of the day brought a lot of fish over to feed."

"Gross. Thanks for sharing."

"Anytime." Austin was unrepentant. "What's up?"

"Are you going to be on your boat for a bit?"

"Yeah. The engine's making a noise I don't love. I thought I'd poke at it for a while. Why?"

"I'll explain when we get there. We're in town, so give us an hour?"

"Who's we?"

"I'll explain in person. Just stick around, okay?"

"Yeah, all right. Hey, I got a nice mahi if you want to hang for supper. I can grill it on deck."

I looked at Teresa, eyebrows raised in query.

She nodded, her expression hopeful.

"That sounds good. Need me to pick up something in town to go with it?" We'd drive past any number of options on our way back to Loring Island. And a little food bribe was never a bad idea with Austin.

"I wouldn't say no to hush puppies from the Shack."

"All right. Need about ninety minutes if we're doing that."

"I'll be here, man. I'm curious, now."

"See you in a bit." I ended the call and looked at Teresa. "You followed that?"

"Yeah. He'll go along?"

I hesitated. I didn't doubt that Austin would marry us. Would he keep it secret though? That was the big question. He would try. He wasn't malicious. But Austin and secrets weren't always a good pair. "I think so."

"Okay."

I went back to the counter and waited until the woman looked up.

"Want that appointment?"

I shook my head. "I think we've got it. We can come back as walk-ins tomorrow if not though, right?"

"Sure can. Or you can look online for an appointment. I don't think we'll be busy on a Wednesday, but it's June now, so you never know."

"Thanks."

"Of course. Congratulations again."

I nodded in acknowledgment, then took Teresa's hand as we headed out into the hall toward the elevator.

We didn't talk much on our way back to the car, or out to the Shack for the sides—I got a pint of coleslaw, too. Might as well try to add a vegetable, even if the health benefit was dubious when it was slathered in mayo.

Half-way across the bridge on our way back to the island, Teresa finally spoke. "Are you sure about this?"

She was asking me? I glanced over quickly. "Aren't you?"

"I am. For me. I just...I guess I feel bad about dragging you into this whole mess. I should have just sucked it up back at Easter. Or on Memorial Day. Or with the whole arm thing."

Was she serious? "No, you shouldn't have. It's good that you didn't. You deserve to be safe."

Everyone deserved to be safe. If I had an opportunity to help,

I was going to take it. Maybe this wasn't how I pictured myself getting married—because really, who imagines this? —but it would work out. One way or another.

"Does that mean you're sure?"

I hadn't answered the question, had I? "Yes. I'm sure."

"Okay."

We lapsed into silence again, but this time, at least, it didn't have the heavy, awkward feeling to it that it had before.

It wasn't too long before I was pulling into the marina parking lot and hunting for a spot to park. Most of the slips were empty—it was a beautiful day to be out on the water, so that wasn't too much of a surprise—but people would probably be coming back in shortly. When I finally found something to squeeze the car into, I parked and turned off the engine.

"Here we go."

She nodded and managed a weak smile.

I got out of the car and reached into the back seat for the bag of food from the Shack. I glanced over the hood at Teresa. "You have the license?"

She held up the paper.

"Great. He's this way." We wound through the parking lot and out onto one of the piers. It was good there weren't too many boats, because I wasn't actually sure which one was Austin's newest. I just assumed that he'd managed to wrangle a slip near the one that he already used for his other maritime adventures.

"Austin?" I hollered, trying to make sure my voice could be heard over the loud music blasting from one of the boats.

His head poked into view. "Hey. C'mon aboard."

I took Teresa's hand to steady her as she climbed aboard the boat and stepped up into an open seating area under a sun canopy.

"This is nice." I looked around and reached out to push on one of the cushions. "Fancy."

Austin laughed. "What's the point in a boat that's not comfortable?"

I shrugged. I wasn't big on boats, despite having grown up on the island. Not that I hadn't—and didn't—spend my time on them. The rest of the family were all at least somewhat boat people. But nobody more than Austin.

"You remember Teresa, right?" I gestured to her with a tight smile.

Austin reached out for her hand. "Of course. Good to see you again. Make yourself at home. I'll get the mahi on the grill now that you're here."

Teresa moved to one of the curving banquette seats and perched on the edge.

I carried the bag of sides over to what was clearly the kitchen area and set it on a counter. "Need any help?"

"Nah. Have a seat." Austin flipped the cover of the built-in grill up and fiddled with knobs before reaching into the fridge that was tucked below to pull out a wrapped plate. "Since I don't think you wanted to see my boat, want to tell me why you're here? Not that I mind sharing my fish. Especially since you brought hush puppies."

I glanced at Teresa then cleared my throat. "We need a favor."

"What? Are you eloping so you can avoid your mom's wedding mania?" Austin guffawed at what he clearly considered a joke.

I didn't answer.

Teresa shifted slightly on her seat.

His laugh trailed off and he frowned over at me. "C'mon, man. Have a sense of humor. I know it's ridiculous. Why do you think I said it?"

I took a deep breath. "Actually."

"What?" Austin straightened and looked at me, then Teresa, then back again. "No way."

Teresa lifted the marriage license off her lap and slid it across the small, triangular table toward Austin.

He picked it up. His eyebrows lifted and he fell back against the counter. "Huh."

"Will you do it?" I fought the urge to wring my hands. He didn't need to see my nerves. That would lead to questions. Questions I really didn't want to answer.

Austin set the paper aside, pausing to set a salt shaker on top of it so the breeze off the water didn't send it flying. "Maybe. Let's talk about it over dinner."

Beside me, Teresa stiffened.

I gave her leg what I hoped was an encouraging rub. We'd be able to convince him. And if we couldn't? We'd just have to go back across to the mainland tomorrow. One day hopefully wouldn't make the difference with her trust. I couldn't fathom that her father could move things along in less than a week.

"You want something to drink?" Austin pointed to the fridge. "I'm stocked."

I sent Teresa an inquiring glance. She nodded slightly.

I crossed the short space to the fridge and squatted to see what was in it. "Sparkling water or soda?"

"Water's fine. Thanks."

I grabbed two, then looked up at Austin. "You want?"

"Yeah, sure. See if there's any lemon-lime left."

I pushed the cans around until I found one, then stood and closed the fridge. I set Austin's beside the grill, then took the others back to where Teresa was sitting.

"So. Give me the scoop. Are we talking love at first sight? Do you two know each other from before like Bennett and Jericho?" He squinted at Teresa a moment before returning his attention to the grilling fish. "I don't remember seeing you before, but I'm the youngest, so I might not."

"Not exactly." Teresa spoke before I could.

I would have gone along with the love at first sight thing, personally. I wasn't sure—not one hundred percent—that I was in love with her. But if I wasn't yet, it was only a matter of time.

"Are you pregnant?" Austin scowled at me. "Didn't we all learn that lesson from Travis and Caroline? Dude."

"She's not pregnant." I held up my hands. "We're not sleeping together."

"Better not be." Austin muttered as he expertly flipped the fish. "So, what is it?"

I scrubbed a hand over my face. The truth was the way to go here, even if it was the last thing I wanted to get into. "She needs my help."

Austin drummed his fingers on his leg as he glared at me. "I never thought you were dumb before."

"Hey." Now it was my turn to scowl.

Austin turned to Teresa. "You can't get to his money. Not even if you marry him. The family money is all tied up and protected."

"I don't want his money!" Teresa leapt to her feet, her voice rising. "I want to keep mine."

"The fish is gonna burn." I nodded toward the grill. "Serve that up. We'll explain while we eat."

Austin huffed out a breath, but he turned his attention back to the food. Within a few short minutes, we each had a plate of fragrant grilled fish, coleslaw, and hush puppies in front of us.

I took a bite and chewed slowly so I could organize my thoughts. Then, with as little preamble as possible, I outlined the situation, beginning with Teresa's injury at Easter and ending with the confrontation with her father yesterday. When I finished, I looked at her. "Did I leave anything out?"

"Not really. Just the part about how if I hadn't been an idiot, I would have been able to stretch my money in Nashville and none of this would be happening." She looked up steadily at Austin. "I've learned my lesson there. Promise. I don't want Christian's money. Or your family's money. I want to work and live and know I have a cushion if something happens. And maybe that's enough of a cushion that I can keep writing songs in my free time. I can't walk completely away from music. Not yet."

Austin nodded slowly. "I don't love the idea of you divorcing in seven months."

"Annulment." Teresa quickly corrected him. "Surely, we can get an annulment. We're not going to live together. Or even tell anyone. It's all just on paper."

"Good luck with that." Austin shook his head.

I frowned. "What's that mean?"

"You know your mom. And you know my mom. You really don't think they're going to figure it out? Mom was talking about the style designs for this boat before I'd even decided for sure that I wanted to buy it."

"Because it's an easy guess. Is there a new way for Austin to be on the water, doing something marginally risky? He's going to do it." I popped the last bite of my final hush puppy into my mouth. "This is not in character for me."

"Eh." Austin wiggled a hand from side to side. "You're big on helping people. This might be the most extreme version you've undertaken, but if they figure out the whole situation? And then it goes away? They're gonna find out."

"You won't tell them, though. Right?" Teresa sent him an imploring glance.

He sighed. "No. No, I won't tell them. And when it does come out, you better back me up that I wasn't completely on board with the idea. No offense."

"None taken." Teresa smiled slightly. "I know it's unusual."

"That's one way of putting it." Austin wiped his fingers on his shorts, then reached for the marriage license. "You want words and vows and such, or do you just want me to sign this and file it for you?"

"Just sign it."

My heart lurched and I whipped my head to look at Teresa. She didn't want any sort of ceremony? "Are you sure?"

"Why not? It's not like we need to promise each other forever, right? You're helping me out. I appreciate it more than I can possibly explain. But I like the idea of not making it seem like it's more than it is." She looked across the table at Austin. "If you're okay with that."

I felt Austin's gaze and couldn't make myself meet it.

"Christian?" Austin was clearly giving me an out. It almost seemed like he was begging me to change my mind.

"She's right. Of course." I let my breath out slowly. "Just sign it."

I caught the barest flash of disappointment in Austin's expression before he stood. "All right. Gotta find a pen."

He was back quickly and made short work of signing the license, then folding it and putting it into his pocket. "I'll drop it off tomorrow to get it filed."

"With today's date, though, it's effective now?" Teresa bit her lower lip.

"Yeah. I have ten days to file them, but they're in force as soon as they're signed. Congratulations, I guess."

"Thanks, Austin. For this and dinner. And for not telling anyone." I held his gaze.

"I won't say anything. But you're taking the heat when it comes out."

"Deal." I stood and looked at Teresa. "I should get you back to Aunt Deb's. I have to be at the hospital in town tomorrow early, so I need to call it."

"Oh. Of course." She stood. "I really appreciate this. Both of you."

Austin shook his head.

I shot a glare in his direction, then followed Teresa to the back of the boat where we could step off to the pier.

I glanced over my shoulder and saw Austin watching us, a frown on his face. I turned away. This was the right thing. I was helping Teresa escape an impossible situation. Maybe it didn't make immediate sense, but hopefully, once Austin sat with it for a while, he'd understand.

And maybe Austin wasn't the only one who needed to do that.

I should have asked him to say some words. We should have said the vows. Something to make it seem more...more. Instead of the empty let down that it felt like now.

16

TERESA

"Hey." Bennett came down the hallway from his office and pulled one of the visitor chairs closer to my desk, then sat. "Heard from Aunt Deb that the house hunting expedition yesterday was a bust."

"That's putting it mildly. You pay me really well, but beach towns are apparently not cheap." I shrugged. "I'll figure something out eventually. Deb and Rob are insisting that I stay with them until either something opens up above a shop here in town or I can save up enough of a cushion to buy a condo in Bennett. They wouldn't listen to any of my objections."

Bennett laughed. "That sounds like them. Honestly, I think they're enjoying having someone there. But I might have another solution, if you're interested?"

"I'm at least interested in hearing it." Finding a place to live was less of a priority for me now that I'd met the terms of my trust. But when Dad figured that out, he was going to have a royal fit, so it might be better to live somewhere that other people didn't get caught in the crossfire.

"Little backstory. When Jericho moved here in January, she rented a beach house I own. I wasn't living in Gramps's place yet.

I had a house down closer to the lighthouse. Not in the homes near the public beach, but that general area. Now, though, I have both of those houses sitting empty. I'd planned to get them cleaned and fixed up for the rental market, but there's no reason you couldn't live in one of them."

I blinked. "I'm sure I couldn't afford whatever you'd want to charge."

"Ah. See, that's where you're wrong." Bennett grinned at me. "Since I happen to know your salary and I'm also not looking to meet any particular threshold with the rent—I'm positive we can work something out."

I stared at him. What was I supposed to say to that? "I..."

Bennett's smile softened. "You're not used to catching a break, are you?"

"I'm really not." I pressed fingers to my eyes as thoughts jumbled around in my head. Would I have been able to make walking away from the trust work if I'd just waited a little? The money...it mattered. But maybe it shouldn't matter quite as much as it did. And now I'd dragged Christian into a fake marriage and maybe I didn't need to. Maybe I could get a hold of Austin and have him not file the license.

My belly clutched.

All that money.

I looked at Bennett who was just watching me steadily. "You're sure?"

"Yeah. It's way easier to have a long-term tenant than deal with the summer rental season. Plus, then one of them gets lived in year-round. Everyone wins." He stood and moved the chair back to its position against the wall. "If you're not busy after work, why don't I take you over to see them and you can figure out which you prefer."

"That would be amazing. I'm going to insist on rent that's reasonable though. Not pity rent." I was firm on that.

He nodded once. "That's fair enough. I'll get Travis to suggest reasonable numbers. Then you can take that into consideration when you're looking at them."

"Thanks. Really."

"Glad to help." Bennett checked his watch. "I have another call with Caroline's attorney in ten. Travis may come, if he's not busy. Just send him through."

"Will do." I waited while Bennett strode back down the hall to his office, then covered my face with my hands. What should I do? I tried to pray, but my mind wouldn't quiet enough for words to form. Instead, I pulled out my phone and opened my texts with Christian.

Hey – you busy?

It took a few seconds, but before long, Christian responded.

Nope, what's up?

Bennett is offering one of his empty houses for me to rent.

That's great!

I shook my head. Did he not understand what that meant?

Should I ask Austin not to file the license? This would mean I could let Dad do what he wants.

The dots started and stopped several times before his reply finally came.

What do you want to do?

I scowled at my phone. If I knew what I wanted, I wouldn't have had to ask Christian what to do.

Except...that wasn't completely true.

I wanted my money. Because it was *my* money. My grandparents and great-grandparents had set it up so that every generation knew what to expect. It wasn't as if Mom and Dad were hurting for money. They had their own family wealth. In addition to the money Dad made with his company. He was only going after my trust to try to force me to keep doing what he wanted. And I was so tired of that. It was about time I had the ability to make something hard for him for a change.

Before I could type another reply, the front door opened. I looked up with a smile. "Welcome to Thomas and Thomas. Oh, hi Travis. Bennett said to go on back."

He managed a weak smile. "Thanks. Hey, before I do…"

I shot him an expectant glance. "What can I get you?"

"Oh, nothing like that." He waved that off. "I just wondered if Mom and Dad have said anything to you about Grady?"

My eyebrows drew together. "You mean like how much they love him and enjoy spending time with him? Because they say that. A lot. Your mom especially."

"Does she?" Travis bit his lip, then nodded slowly. "All right. I worry that I'm asking them to do too much. Grady can be a lot."

I shook my head. "I don't think they feel that way. Deb, especially, always lights up when she's sharing stories from their day."

"Okay." He blew out a breath. "Would you…if you're comfortable…let me know if that changes? You haven't lived there long, so maybe Mom's keeping it cheerful and upbeat."

"I guess. Although, Bennett mentioned he has some houses sitting empty, so I might be moving."

"Ha. Well, okay. Not a bad idea on Bennett's part. Forget I asked." He smiled slightly. "See ya."

I watched him walk down the hall and frowned. Travis looked like he was carrying something heavy on his shoulders. I didn't imagine divorce was ever easy, but if everyone was unhappy in the marriage, wasn't it better to stop pretending? I certainly felt that way about my parents. Mom would probably be so much better off without Dad in her life.

Well, maybe not anymore. Not now that she was effectively an alcoholic. Would she be able to dry herself out and live a normal life if she got away? Would she even want to?

My phone buzzed.

I unlocked it.

You still there?

Sorry, Travis came in to see Bennett. I want the trust.

Then leave it.

But what about you?

I agreed to this. It's all good. Can I take you to dinner tonight?

I blinked at my phone. He wanted to take me out to dinner? Why did the way he asked sound like more than any of the meals we'd shared together before? Would it be so bad if it was? I'd liked holding his hand yesterday. And just being together.

I'd like that. After Bennett shows me the houses?

Sure. Gotta run.

I laughed and tucked my phone back in the top drawer of my desk, then returned my attention to the list of tasks Bennett had emailed me.

The day passed relatively quickly, but I'd also had plenty of downtime. I was just shutting down my computer when the door opened and Christian walked in, grinning. My breath caught as I saw him. Why did he have to look so good?

"Hey. Did you need to see Bennett?"

"Nope. I'm here for you."

I frowned slightly. "I thought we were having dinner after I looked at the houses?"

"We are."

Bennett came down the hall into the waiting room, clearly ready to leave for the evening. "Oh great, you're here."

"You said not to be late. I can follow directions."

"Ha. Sometimes." Bennett dug in his pocket and pulled out a key ring. He tossed it to Christian. "Just send that back with Teresa tomorrow. Night, you two."

"Night." I turned my attention back to Christian. "I'm confused."

"After we texted, I asked Bennett if I could show you the houses. He said sure." Christian tipped his head to the side. "Is that all right?"

"Yeah. Of course." I grabbed my purse and scooted my chair back from the desk. "I'm ready when you are."

He held out a hand. I hesitated a moment before taking it. He squeezed gently as we crossed to the door. He held it open for me to exit and waited while I locked up.

"I parked just down there." He nodded down the street.

I followed his gaze and spotted his car. "How was your day?"

"I was at the ER in Bennett today. Busy. But nothing crazy, thankfully. How about you?"

I shrugged. "Bennett had some stuff for me to do, but I also had time to play with some lyrics I've been working on."

"Yeah?" He grinned and we slowed as we approached his car. He opened the passenger door for me. "Can I hear them?"

"What?" I froze in the process of getting into the car. "The lyrics? Not yet. They're just—I'm just playing right now."

"Okay." He smiled, as if it didn't matter, and waited until I was in the car before closing the door.

I watched him come around to his side of the car. Why would he want to hear the lyrics? We'd never talked about music. Not really.

"Houses first?" Christian started the car and looked over at me.

"Do you mind?"

"Nope." He waited for a break in the traffic before pulling away from the curb and heading out of town toward the beach. "What kind of songs do you write?"

My shoulders hunched. "Different kinds. I think the fact that I never settled firmly into one particular genre is part of why

Nashville was so tough. When I went, I thought I was committed to country."

"But you weren't?"

I shook my head. "It's not that. I like country well enough, but it's hard to stand out. So I played with other types and, I don't know, I couldn't settle. Then when I became a Christian, I wondered if I should be writing Christian music. But it seemed even more difficult to break into than country."

"That sounds frustrating."

I laughed. "That's an understatement."

"Sorry."

"Don't be." I watched out the window for a moment. "Now, I'm trying to figure out how I keep music in my life. I was hoping I'd let go of the dream when everything crashed and burned in Nashville."

"But you haven't?"

I shook my head. "Not yet, anyway."

"You're praying about it?"

"Of course." Except...was I? I did a lot of praying for God to show me what to do. To open a door. To make it clear. But I never felt like any of that happened. So, I kept doing what seemed like the right thing and asking God to bless it. The church I'd attended in Nashville had been big on saying that God's will would always be done, so if it's what we did, it was God's will. I couldn't honestly wrap my head around how that worked in conjunction with humans having free will, but I tried to let it go as something I had to take on faith.

I didn't know if I was doing that right, either.

"I'll pray too."

"Really?"

"Sure." Christian turned off the main road into the eastern side of the houses near the public beach. "That's what friends do."

"Not all friends. Which makes me value your friendship even more." Did that sound as cheesy to him as it did to me? Did that matter? The sentiment, at least, was true. Which was somewhat startling, since two days ago I'd told him I didn't think we were friends. Because I was lashing out, I guess.

He reached over and squeezed my hand.

A few minutes later, he pulled into the driveway of the most adorable little beach cottage I'd ever seen.

"Seriously?" I hurried to unbuckle my seatbelt and get out of the car. "This is amazing."

Christian chuckled and moved toward the porch.

I turned in a circle, stopping as I faced the street. The beach was right there. No walking. No obstruction of the view. And sure, it wasn't a private beach like my parents had, but that didn't matter. It didn't look like too many people came down this way from the number of umbrellas and other setups on the sand. Just the folks in the houses close by.

I could absolutely deal with that.

I turned and hurried to catch up with Christian.

"This is Heron Cottage. It's the first one Bennett bought. He did the usual short-term rentals for a bit, then did a long-term lease with Jericho in January. But obviously she doesn't need that now."

"Most married people do tend to live together." I nudged him with my elbow. "Not everyone is unconventional like us."

"True enough." His laugh sounded a little forced.

I glanced his way, but nothing in his expression encouraged me to explore further, so I let it go. I was grateful he'd done this for me. I wasn't going to poke at him if it was a sore spot. Although, if he regretted it, I wish he'd let me try and hold his cousin off this morning when there was a chance to keep it all from being legal.

Christian pushed open the door and waved me in. "It's

smaller than the next one. Two bedrooms. Two baths. Pretty small living area and kitchen."

I moved through the living room into the kitchen, poking into closets and cabinets. "I don't need a lot of space. Less to keep clean. And it's not as if I'm bringing much with me. More than likely, I can write off anything of mine that my parents still have."

He frowned. "You really think so?"

I shrugged, hoping it looked casual and unbothered. "I didn't cave, this time. And I still got the money. So yeah, I think they're going to be angry and write me off. Completely."

I lengthened my stride as I moved down the short hall toward the primary bedroom so Christian wouldn't see my eyes fill. I could act nonchalant, but it hurt. It hurt a lot. If my time at home after Nashville had proven anything to me, it was that my parents valued money over anything and everything else.

Including me.

Then again, was I that different?

I squashed that thought and the tendril of guilt it brought along. I had reasons for needing my money. And Christian had volunteered. It wasn't as if I tricked him into something he didn't want to do. I hadn't pretended that I was in love with him and led him into some false hope for a happy ending together.

I wiped the tear that I hadn't managed to will back under control and blew out a breath.

"All the furniture is included."

I jolted slightly when Christian spoke from directly behind me. "Good. That saves me trying to find stuff. Although I did see there are a couple of thrift stores in Bennett, so I could probably have made it work."

"Questions about anything?"

I turned and finally met his gaze, then quickly looked away.

"Nope. I like this one a lot. I'm not even sure I need to see the other."

"Might as well. It's not far. Come on." Christian took my hand and we walked down the hall to the door.

I waited on the porch while he locked up, then followed him down to his car and got in.

The drive was very short—as promised. As he pulled into the car port, I knew it was too much. It wasn't huge like Deb and Rob's house. Or Linda and David's. Or Christian's, for that matter. But it was still at least half-again as big as Heron Cottage.

"This one has a private beach out back and three bedrooms. The kitchen and living room are larger overall, as well." Christian climbed the stairs to the front door as he spoke. "Bennett lived here while he was trying to decide what to build on the lot Gramps gave him when he turned eighteen. All of us—the cousins—got one. Most went ahead and built, because why wouldn't you?"

I nodded.

"Worked out, though. Bennett bought Gramps out of his house earlier in the year when Gramps moved in with Mom and Dad. Everyone was happier not to see Gramps' house leave the family. Or sit vacant, which isn't good for houses."

"You wouldn't have rented it?" I went in when Christian pushed the door open. The difference between the two houses was immediately apparent. This one was furnished, too, but in a more comfortable, lived-in way, not the designed-for-rental feel of the things at Heron. And everything felt more designed for daily, long-term use. If there was more than me, I could see choosing this over the other, but it really was too much space.

"Doubt it. We're all protective of our privacy. It's why we own all the property that isn't part of the science station or nature preserve on that end of the island."

Right. It was easy to forget that Christian's family had

founded the island. That they were at least as rich as my parents —probably more. A lot more. Because none of them acted as if wealth was their most important characteristic.

Did he think I was obsessed with money?

I pushed that thought away. It didn't matter. Not really.

But something deep in my heart ached at the concept that he thought badly of me.

I swallowed and headed down the hall to look in each of the bedrooms.

When I returned to the main living area, Christian was leaning against the kitchen island. "What do you think?"

"It's wonderful. Really. But also, too much space. I could be very happy in Heron Cottage, I think."

He nodded. "All right. Why don't you let Bennett know? That way he can get Travis working on whatever contracts you need. Maybe we can meet up with him after dinner."

"That fast? You think?" I dug out my phone and tapped a quick text to Bennett.

"I don't see why not. Unless either you or Bennett want something that isn't pretty standard. Travis writes rental contracts in his sleep."

I laughed and sent the text, then tucked my phone back into my purse. "All right. We'll see what happens. Where did you want to eat?"

"Have you eaten at The Yacht Club yet?"

I frowned. There was a yacht club? How had Dad missed that? He'd spent quite a bit of time grumbling about the fact that the golf club was the only truly elite option on the island, and even it allowed anyone to come in and eat or hit some balls if they were willing to pay the prices. "No. I didn't even realize there was one."

Christian grinned. "It's not a real yacht club. That's the name of the restaurant. The family of one of my high school friends runs it now. They classed it up some when they took it over, oh, three years ago? Maybe four? It's a nice change from the diner."

Well, that explained it. And it probably is one of the reasons Dad went ahead with buying a house here. Knowing him, he simply saw the name and decided that's what it was without doing any research. "Sure. That sounds great. You said it was classed up though. Do I need to change?"

"Nah. On the island, classy means no shorts, no swimsuits and coverups, and no flip flops. You look great."

My cheeks heated.

He opened the front door and waited for me to step onto the porch before he followed and locked up behind me.

When we were back in the car, my phone chimed. I checked it and saw Bennett had responded. "You were right?"

"About Travis?"

"Yeah. Bennett said to get in touch with him and let him know where to meet us." I paused. "Should we invite him to join us for dinner?"

Christian shook his head. "Best not. Grady isn't big on the kind of atmosphere there. Trav and Caroline tried to make it a weekly family night place and it was a disaster from the beginning. It took entirely too long for Caroline to finally let it go."

I had questions. Many of them. But it wasn't my place to ask any of them. Christian's whole family had rallied around Travis and Grady—and that made sense, and it was lovely to see—but none of them had much positive to say about Caroline. They all tried to spin it as if they were giving her the benefit of the doubt. At the same time, it didn't really fly.

Was that how they'd talk about me in January?

That stupid ache in my heart returned, stronger now. I rubbed at it. It was silly to have even a small regret. I was letting Christian help me. I'd figure out how to pay him back eventually.

"Are you all right?"

"Me?" I followed his gaze to where I was pressing and shifted to scratch my collarbone. "Of course. Itchy. I think I need to switch detergents."

He nodded.

Was he convinced? It was hard to tell. At least he let it go, though.

Christian found a parking spot a block down from The Yacht Club. He came around and opened the door for me just as I reached for the handle. I flashed a quick grin in his direction and took his outstretched hand.

The warmth in his touch soothed all my jagged edges and stirred up childhood dreams of happy endings.

All the things that could never really be.

17

CHRISTIAN

Even in the middle of peak tourist season, it wasn't possible to go somewhere in town without seeing people I knew. Eating at the fanciest place on the island, well, other than the Golf Club, didn't change that. There were plenty of tables filled with visitors, but Teresa and I had had to pause plenty as the hostess took us to our table. Hopefully, Teresa hadn't noticed the speculative looks like I had. But they'd been pretty hard to miss.

Despite all of that, I'd enjoyed every second of our dinner.

I liked spending time with Teresa.

I just plain liked Teresa.

Good thing, really, since she was my wife.

I snickered.

"What's funny?" Teresa set her spoon down on the edge of the plate holding the last scrapes of sticky toffee pudding that we'd shared.

"Just a random thought." I tried to play it off. I certainly wasn't going to get into that—we'd been having a nice, easy conversation. I'd like that to continue.

She eyed me a moment before nodding. "All right. Did you hear back from Travis?"

"Let me check." I dug out my phone and tapped my texts. Sure enough, Travis had a rental contract ready to go. "He says it's easiest for him if we swing by his place. That work?"

Teresa shrugged. "Sure. I don't have anywhere pressing to be."

I lifted my hand slightly to signal the server.

Within a few minutes, I'd handled the check—over Teresa's argument—and we were back in the car on our way out to Travis's.

Teresa sighed quietly.

I glanced over. She looked...happy? Content? I wasn't used to seeing her that way. It made her even more beautiful.

Before I could stop myself, I reached over and took her hand. I'd intended a quick squeeze, but she wrapped her fingers around mine and seemed content to leave them there.

I certainly wasn't going to complain.

We made the drive in companionable silence, letting the soft music of the radio fill the space for us. Now and then, Teresa hummed along, her fingers tapping on her leg to the beat.

It was as if everything around me seemed to click into place. I wanted this. I wanted her in my life, like this, forever. Now I just had to figure out how to convince her she wanted it, too.

"Here we are." I slowed, then turned into Travis's driveway.

"Your family has such beautiful homes." Teresa unhooked her seatbelt as I put the car in park. "I see why you stay instead of moving away, off the island."

"Most of us left for a little bit—school, that kind of thing. But the island is home. It always draws us back." I pushed open my car door and got out. That had sounded sappier than I'd intended, but it was still true. Loring Island was special. I was blessed—and most of the time I knew it—to have a place and a family that made it easy to know where I was supposed to be.

Teresa fell into step beside me as we crossed the driveway and made our way up the stairs to Travis's front door. I knocked, then turned the handle and poked my head in.

"Trav? It's us."

"Come on in, we're in the kitchen!"

I pushed the door the rest of the way open and gestured for Teresa to enter. I followed behind, making sure the door was firmly closed behind me, then pointed across the living room to the doorway that leads to the kitchen.

Teresa and I crossed the space, and paused as we reached the kitchen.

"Uncle Christian!" Grady popped out of his seat at the table with such force that his chair clattered to the ground and the tub of sensory sand he'd been playing with teetered precariously.

I strode quickly over and pulled the tub back from the brink before scooping Grady up and giving him the tight bear hug that he craved. "Oof. You keep getting bigger. Pretty soon, you're going to have to pick me up."

Grady giggled and squirmed out of my arms.

"You remember Ms. Teresa?"

Grady nodded but his eyes squinted. "Bees."

"There were bees." Teresa gave an exaggerated shudder. "But not here. What are you building with your sand?"

Grady's tremulous expression morphed quickly to delight and he scampered back to his seat at the table and the tub of sand. He picked up a Matchbox-sized bulldozer, sand dripping off of it. "Diggers! You want to dig?"

Teresa shot Travis a questioning glance. He nodded and flipped the dishtowel back over his shoulder before returning to the sink full of soapy water.

Teresa pulled out the chair beside Grady and took the

offered vehicle. She pushed it into the sand and grinned. "It's squishy."

Grady nodded vigorously, then took another of the vehicles in the tub and began to drive it around.

I crossed to where Travis stood and leaned on the counter. "Thanks for whipping up this contract for her tonight."

Travis slowly turned to face me; his expression stony. His voice was low, almost a hiss. "What do you think you're doing?"

I leaned back, startled. I glanced back at Teresa and Grady, then returned my gaze to Travis. "What do you mean?"

Travis crossed his arms. "You know what I do, right?"

"You're a real estate agent?" My words were slow, like I was clarifying the obvious.

"Correct. Well done." Travis scowled. "Shall we go to round two?"

"What is this, Travis?"

"I'll take that as a yes." He stabbed a finger at me. "As a real estate agent, can you think of a county building where I might know, oh, let's call it, conservatively, ninety percent of the staff?"

I opened my mouth to ask where this was going, then slowly closed it. I pressed my lips together as I began to realize what he was getting at.

"There's that big brain that got you through nursing school." Sarcasm dripped from each word. "I'll ask again. What do you think you're doing?"

I tried to swallow, but my mouth was a desert. I cleared my throat. "Helping a friend."

"Helping a friend." Travis snorted. "I see."

I was pretty sure he did not, in fact, see anything. Except red. He was definitely seeing red. "Look. I think I see what you're thinking, but I've got this under control. There were—are— extenuating circumstances."

"Is she pregnant?"

"What? No. How could you think..." I let the question trail off as I remembered exactly why Travis and Caroline had gotten married. "Sorry. But this isn't like that."

"What is it like? Be specific."

I shook my head. "I can't. Seriously. It's not my story to tell, and it's handled. We'll fix it in January."

"Fix it." Travis cocked his head to the side, his voice dry as dust. "No big deal, just fix the glitch?"

I winced.

Travis shook his head.

I looked back at Teresa and Grady who were still playing in the sensory sand and blissfully unaware of our conversation. For that I was grateful. Travis had never been one to raise his voice, and it was good that seemed to be continuing.

"Look." I took a deep breath and let it out. "She needed help. This was the way for me to help. That's it. It's going to be fine."

"Oh, sure. Because divorce is always a walk in the park. No big deal. Everyone's doing it, I guess."

"Travis." I took another breath. Given his current situation, his reaction was understandable. But still. "Annulment. Not divorce. It's not like with Caroline. I'm not going to be blindsided and we don't have a kid."

For several heartbeats, Travis stared at me with a mixture of pity and incredulity. "Did you take even, oh, let's be generous, ten seconds to investigate how likely an annulment was going to be?"

"No." My heart sped up slightly. "But Teresa said—"

"Then she didn't research it either." Rather than raising his voice, Travis's voice dipped low, coming out almost like a hiss. "Because it's basically impossible. Especially after seven months."

My insides turned to solid ice. *Basically impossible?* That couldn't be right. Could it? I'd thought...I flicked a glance over at Teresa again.

This time, she seemed to sense it. She looked up with a grin that slowly faded as she caught my glance. She tipped her head slightly to the side, eyebrows raised.

I shook my head and tried for a reassuring smile. Hopefully, it didn't look ill. Because that's how I felt. Absolutely, one-hundred percent, ill. I looked back at Travis. "You're sure?"

Travis snorted. "Of course I am. After the third person congratulated me on having two weddings in the family one right after the other, I did some digging. Then a little more."

"Can I get a glass of water?" My voice came out in a rasp.

Travis laughed mirthlessly. "Help yourself, man."

I moved robotically to the cabinet where Travis kept his glassware and got a tumbler down. After a moment of thought, I turned back and raised my voice slightly. "Teresa? Would you like a drink?"

She glanced up from the sand and shrugged. "If you're getting something, water would be great."

I nodded and got another glass down. I filled them with crushed ice and water from the dispenser in the fridge, then carried them over to the table. I set Teresa's down in front of her.

"Thanks." She gave me a searching look. "Everything okay?"

"What? Yeah. Of course." I took a sip of my water and nearly choked on a piece of ice.

Something in the situation must have returned Travis's sense of humor, because he began to laugh. The scathing look I sent his way only made him laugh harder. When he finally pulled himself together, he cleared his throat. "Five minutes, Grady, then it's bath and bed."

"But Dad!" Grady clutched his cars to his chest, oblivious to the sensory sand dripping onto him.

"I know. But the sand will be there in the morning. Don't you want to find out what happens next with Mole and Rat in the Wild Wood? I think something exciting is about to go down." Travis's voice took on an enticing note. "I know I want to find out."

Grady hesitated, then nodded once and dropped his cars back into the sand. He pried the truck Teresa had been driving out of her fingers, then grabbed the tub and dragged it along the table to the end. He picked up a lid off the floor, snapped it in place, then hefted the tub and slid it onto the shelf of the credenza that anchored the far end of the kitchen. Then he dusted his hands off, sending sand flying and scampered out of the room yelling, "Bath time!"

Travis winced. "Let me go get him set up before he dumps a whole bottle of bubbles in, and then I'll get that contract for you."

"Okay." I took another drink of water, my thoughts still racing. Should I tell Teresa? What would be the point? Sure, we could get an annulment now, probably, but then she'd still risk losing her trust fund.

I really didn't want her to have to give that up. It seemed so important to her.

Teresa stood and crossed to the sink where she washed the sand off her hands. "Do you know where he keeps his broom? I can sweep up the sand before it gets scattered even more."

"I'll get it." That was at least something productive to do. Because trying to unravel the right course of action right now made zero sense.

I put my water down and moved through the kitchen to the walk-in pantry. The shelves were stocked with easy-to-make kid food by quality makers like Chef Boyardee and Kraft. Blue boxes only. There were also cans of green beans—cut, not French cut

—and taco shells. I added running bloodwork for Travis to my to-do list. If he was eating like this, too, his cholesterol might have a thing or two to say.

I grabbed the broom and dustpan from their hooks and went back to the kitchen. Teresa had grabbed the dishcloth and was wiping down the table. I started on the far end of the dining space and began to methodically sweep the sand—and a lot of other random bits and pieces like dried up noodles—into a pile.

By the time Travis came back into the kitchen, Teresa and I had done a pretty decent job of cleaning not only the eating area, but the counters as well.

"All right. Rental contract." Travis held up a file folder, then he paused and looked around. "Y'all didn't have to clean up."

I shrugged. "It was the least we could do."

"You seem to have your hands full." Teresa smiled. "And this was easy enough."

Travis hesitated, then nodded. "Well, thanks. Have a seat."

Teresa took a moment to rinse her dishcloth and drape it over the kitchen faucet and then dry her hands before she went back to the kitchen table and pulled out a chair. I looked around for something else to clean, but there wasn't anything left that could be reasonably considered helping out without crossing the line into intrusive, so I joined them at the table.

Travis flipped open the folder and quickly walked Teresa through the terms of the rental, pointing to the areas where she'd need to initial and then sign. "Take your time to read it through first, though. If you have questions, I'm happy to answer them."

Teresa pulled the papers closer and began to read.

Travis jerked his head toward the living room. "Can I speak to you out here a sec?"

My stomach sank, but I stood and shoved my hands into my pockets. "Sure. Of course."

Travis crossed to the side of the room that was farthest from the kitchen. He kept his voice low. "You know you have to tell your parents, right?"

"I know no such thing." Telling Mom and Dad was so far down the list of things I planned to do, it might as well not exist.

Travis snorted. "You'd rather they find out with no warning? Are you insane?"

"They might not find out." I sounded defensive and I hated it.

Travis just looked at me.

I hunched my shoulders. "It's possible."

"Seriously?"

I scrubbed my hands over my face as reality finally hit. Asking Austin to keep the secret had made sense, but Travis was right. We lived in a small community. And it wasn't as if our family was unknown within that community. "Crud."

"At least." Travis glanced over toward the kitchen. "In my opinion? You need to come clean before she signs that rental contract."

"What? Why? They're completely unrelated issues."

"No, man. No, they are not. You. Are. Married." He tipped his head to the side. "You really think your parents—heck, my parents—are going to be okay with the two of you living apart?"

"But it's not like that. It's just to help her out with some stuff." I paced a few steps away and then back. "It's short term and then annulment. Period."

"You're okay with that? You don't want more?"

I pressed my lips together. I could lie to myself, but I wasn't going to lie to someone else. Not aloud. "It's not about what I want."

"Do you know anything about marriage? At all?" Travis shook his head. "Because you sure aren't acting like it."

I threw my hands in the air and my voice came out louder

than I intended. "What do you want, man? She needed help to keep her trust fund. Her parents are...words I really try not to even think. I couldn't make it her birthday faster, which would have solidified her claim on the money, but I could do this. So, I did."

"Everything all right?" Teresa's voice was quiet, almost timid.

"Yes." I frowned at Travis before moving over to stand by her. "It's fine. The people at the courthouse have big mouths."

"Oh." She bit her lip and closed her eyes. "I should have thought of that."

"Why? Why would you have thought of it? I've lived here my whole life and it didn't occur to me." I took her hand and squeezed. "It'll be okay."

The look Teresa gave me made it clear she wanted to believe me but couldn't quite get there.

I knew the feeling. Still, I tried to project confidence. "Travis pointed out, and he's probably not wrong, that we maybe ought to fill in the rest of the family before someone in town does."

Teresa looked at me, then shifted her gaze to Travis. She flinched.

I looked over at him and lifted my eyebrows at his stony stare. "What?"

Travis just shook his head. "I'm going up to check on Grady. You're welcome to invite everyone over here. Consider it neutral territory."

"Is it though?" I blurted the words before thinking.

Travis shot me a cool look. "It's a lot more neutral than anywhere else I can think of."

Oof.

The awful thing was? He was probably right.

I swallowed. "I guess that's my cue to send some texts."

"Christian..." Teresa trailed off when I met her gaze. She shook her head and looked away. "Never mind."

I crossed to the couch and flopped down before getting out my phone and opening the family group text.

Can y'all come to Trav's? It's probably urgent.

18

TERESA

"Are you sure about this?" I leaned closer to Christian and whispered close to his ear.

"Not in the slightest." He shrugged. "But we don't really have a choice. If people are saying something to Travis in under twenty-four hours, the rest of my family is going to find out. And I wouldn't put it past Travis to be the one to tell them."

I stiffened. "Really? He'd do that?"

Christian nodded. "Travis...has opinions."

"Everyone does." I crossed my arms, more to try and ward off the sudden internal chill than as an act of defiance. "Not everyone decides to blab other people's business because of them. Austin was willing to keep it quiet."

"More than likely because he already figured out he wouldn't have to stay silent for long." Christian ran a hand through his hair. "I should have thought it through more."

"We can probably still just get it undone." My gut twisted as I said the words, but I wasn't trying to trap him into something. He was clearly unhappy, and that was my fault. I'd let him help me when I should have kept saying no. It would mean kissing my trust fund goodbye, but I had a place to live now. And a job.

I froze. I had those right now. After his family found out what we'd done, would I still?

Christian's family arrived very quickly in little family groups. Everyone paused and shot Christian curious glances when they saw I was here. Had they thought they were coming because of Travis? We were at his house, so that would make sense. Boy were they in for a surprise.

Bennett and Jericho were the last to arrive. Jericho's smile was warm. She honestly looked happy to see me. I clung to that while everyone settled in their seats. Before Christian could start talking, Grady barreled down the stairs in pajamas, hair glistening with water.

"Grammie!" Grady launched himself at Deb, who caught him with a laugh.

Deb made a production of sniffing his hair. "You smell like bubblegum."

"Bubbles." Grady's eyes danced as he wiggled out of Deb's lap and threw himself at Rob.

Rob gave Grady a tight hug. "Bedtime for you, kiddo. Isn't it?"

"It is." Travis hovered by the stairs. "But I promised he could come down and see you first, since we're missing our chapter of *The Wind in the Willows* tonight."

"Two tomorrow." Grady frowned at his dad.

Travis nodded. "That's the deal."

Grady looked like he wanted to object, but Travis's calm, steady presence seemed to keep him under control. Finally, he trudged back toward the stairs. Travis scooped him up.

"I'll just be a couple of minutes. Go ahead and start. I know the gist."

I tried to sink further into the cushions of the couch as everyone shifted their attention to Christian. And me.

I worked hard to avoid everyone's gaze—especially Austin's smug one—as Christian started to explain the situation with my parents. He gave them more detail than I would have liked, but with the cast on my arm and the fix I'd put him in, I didn't really have room to object.

When he reached the end of the background, including my dad's threats to revoke the trust, Christian paused, then cleared his throat. "So, we got married."

"You did what?" Christian's mom leapt to her feet, hands fisted on her hips.

His dad tugged on one of her arms and, after a moment, she returned to her seat. He studied Christian before he spoke. "I'd appreciate if you'd walk us through your thought process."

Christian shifted in his seat. "I basically just did. Teresa tried to find a place to live that would work if she only had the money she earned at the law firm, but have you seen those places?"

Rob sighed. "Is this behind your call earlier today about making some affordable housing?"

"Yeah." Christian rubbed his hands on his legs. "I still want to do that."

"It's a good idea." Rob glanced over at Travis as he came down the last steps and joined the family in the living room. "We talked about it this afternoon. Both of us wondered why it wasn't something we'd talked about before."

Travis laughed. "Because we have talked about the slum-like conditions of the apartment buildings that pass for affordable on the outskirts of town. I have a call in to the property owners. I suspect we can start by buying them out. We should still look into building new, but getting those units up to actually habitable would be a really good start."

I had to work to keep my expression neutral as I listened. This family really was incredible. Of course, that realization just piled the guilt that was swamping me even higher. How had I allowed myself to suck this generous man into my problems? I ignored the whisper at the back of my mind that reminded me he hadn't exactly run screaming. Just because he didn't have the ability to turn away from a woman in need of help didn't mean that I had to take advantage.

This was on me.

Which meant it had to be on me to fix it.

I cleared my throat. "We can probably file for an annulment. Right?"

"What? No." Christian reached over and gripped my hand so hard I winced. "Then you'd be back in the same place."

"Not really." I tugged my hand free and crossed my arms. "At least, not unless I no longer have a job and the offer of Bennett's beach house to rent."

Bennett and Jericho exchanged a look before Bennett spoke. "The job and the house are yours for as long as you need or want them. I realize you haven't been working for me long, but I'm already impressed with your efficiency and work ethic. And the house needs to be rented by someone. I've grown to appreciate the long-term rental over the weekly turnovers."

"And," Jericho took Bennett's hand, "it sounds like you really need to be away from your family. I understand challenging family a bit more than the rest of the people in here. Mine isn't as bad as yours, but we have our issues. I get needing to be out on your own. If there's a way to help with that, I'm going to be behind it firmly."

I sagged back against the cushions in relief. "Thank you."

"What about your trust?" Christian's father frowned slightly at me. In that moment, I could see the older version of Christian in so many little ways. He was already a handsome man. It was a blessing that his genes suggested he'd just keep getting better looking as he aged.

Not that looks were everything. But they didn't hurt.

It wasn't my business though. He wasn't mine to keep.

He couldn't be.

I shrugged, hoping it came across as casual. "Dad will revoke it. I'll have to figure out a plan for my life that doesn't include that cushion. Like ninety-nine percent of the people in the world."

"There are probably legal actions you could take." Bennett leaned forward and glanced over at his father. "I only took a cursory glance when I initially looked into things. You should go over it, Dad. You know more about trusts from that end than I do."

"I'm happy to do that, if it's all right with Teresa." He sent a questioning look my way.

I shook my head. "I can't ask you to do that. I can't pay you. Your son is a generous employer, but even still, my salary doesn't run to legal fees."

"I wouldn't charge you." Bennett and Christian's dad looked affronted.

"I don't want—I don't need—"

"To accept help?" Deb cut me off, one eyebrow raised. "Is that why you started looking for a place to stay without talking to us about it? Because neither Rob nor I expected you to move out unless you wanted to. We were—are—perfectly happy to have you as long as you care to be with us."

I looked from face to face, trying to find anyone who looked like they could understand where I was coming from. There was no one. Christian came the closest, and look where that had gotten him.

I sighed. Time to push the situation back on track. "The annulment. Can we focus on that?"

Bennett shook his head. "The words 'intent to defraud' might not mean anything to you, but they should."

I stiffened. "What do you mean?"

Bennett's dad gave a short laugh. "You have to give reasons for an annulment. Changing your mind about a fake marriage in order to fraudulently meet the terms of a trust fund aren't going to fly. And will probably end up with the two of you in hot water."

"We can just say I was impaired!" I threw up my hands.

"But you weren't." Austin shrugged. "I'm not going to lie about that. Plus, it could have repercussions for me, which I'd rather avoid."

I squeezed my eyes shut. Why were they making this so hard?

"No. I think the only thing to do, really, is accept that you've married my son and live accordingly." Christian's mother leaned back in her chair, a wry smile on her lips. "It can't be that bad of a thought. Can it?"

"Mom." Christian scowled at her.

"Don't even go there." She held up a hand and sent him a look that had probably been cowing him since he was a toddler. "You were *not* raised to take marriage lightly. Because marriage isn't something that you play at. It's a promise—a covenant—between a man, a woman, and God. It's not something you throw away because it's no longer convenient."

Travis snorted.

She sent him an apologetic grimace. "Sorry, Travis. But you weren't the one doing the tossing. And there's still hope that Caroline will come around and mend things. It's certainly what I'm praying for."

"Thanks, Aunt Linda. I'm not sure that's the right thing anymore. But then, I don't know what the right thing is. I guess it's whatever God wants to happen." Travis sighed. "I just wish

He'd hurry up and make it obvious so it would stop hurting Grady."

Deb closed her eyes briefly and nodded.

Linda turned her piercing gaze back on me. "I realize your upbringing is different, and I'm trying to make allowances for that, but I thought Christian mentioned you were a believer?"

I nodded.

Something in my expression made her pause. She closed her eyes and took a deep breath, then let it slowly out. "I won't lecture. It's not my place. You're both adults. But as a mother and as someone who has loved Jesus for a lot of years, I'm going to say, now that you've made this decision, you need to commit to it."

"I guess that's my cue to say the house is off the table." Bennett sent a rueful smile. "Sorry."

I opened my mouth to object, but snapped it shut when I saw just how unyielding all the family's faces were. I turned to Christian, imploring him silently to do or say something.

He just sat there. Silent. His expression blank.

"All right." Linda stood and clapped her hands together once. "That's settled. We'll be on our way and let everyone get back to their evenings. I'll expect to see you all on Sunday after church for lunch as usual. Come on, David."

David stood and grabbed his wife's hand to keep her from leaving. "Before we go, I think we should say a prayer over the new couple."

I couldn't quite stop the wince. This was never what was supposed to happen. We weren't supposed to be a couple, new or otherwise. His family was never supposed to find out. I shot another glance at Christian, but his expression hadn't changed.

The family all stood and gathered around us, holding hands.

David bowed his head and began to pray. "Heavenly Father, thank You for Christian and Teresa. We ask Your blessing on their union. They came to marriage in an unconventional way, and one that is likely to bring more than the usual challenges with it. We ask that You would guide them, individually and now as the new couple that they are. Give them strength, patience, and grace for each other as they work to establish their marriage into a union that is pleasing to You. In Jesus name, amen."

Linda gave us a long look before her own quiet "Amen."

Bennett and Jericho waved awkwardly as they followed David and Linda through the front door.

Rob and Deb came over. Deb took my hand and pulled me gently to my feet before enveloping me in her arms. She whispered, "Congratulations. Welcome to the family."

Rob was next in line for a hug when Deb finally stepped back. "Come get your things whenever you want. There's no hurry, but we also have a peach pie and vanilla ice cream if you want to come tonight. It's one of Christian's favorites."

Christian nodded. "Thanks. We might do that."

Might we? I shot Christian a look. Maybe we were, on paper, married. And maybe his family was pressuring us to make it a real thing. But if he thought he got to start unilaterally making decisions for us, he had another think coming. Fast.

Austin sidled over when Deb and Rob headed for the door. "Sorry. Wasn't me."

"No. I know. Someone at the county building told Travis." Christian's shoulders were slumped. "Should have figured it."

Austin punched his arm. "Yeah. You should've."

Christian's younger brother Evan just shook his head as he looked at me. "Things must be bad if you're settling for this guy."

"Hey." Christian scowled.

Evan laughed. "Seriously though, welcome to the family. I'd like to tell you we aren't always this meddlesome and overbearing, but I don't want to start your marriage off with another lie."

I winced.

"Really?" Christian pushed Evan's shoulder. "Just leave, bro."

Evan grinned and waved before turning and heading for the door.

Christian looked toward where another man was chatting with Travis. They were definitely brothers, but I couldn't quite place his name.

"No more commentary from the peanut gallery, Ry?" Christian crossed his arms.

"Nah. I think it's been covered. And honestly, I might be the only one who gets it. I think you were trying to do a good thing. The right thing. You just bungled it."

"For a minute there, I thought you were going to be nice. But, since you're imparting your great wisdom, how did I bungle it?"

"Not just you. Teresa too. Sorry."

I gave a short laugh. "Whatever."

"I'm serious." Ryan squeezed Travis's shoulder and crossed the room to stand in front of us. "Aunt Linda pretty well covered it, but I'll reiterate it. One, no one ever truly solves big problems like this alone. You have this huge, loving family, man. Why didn't you ask for advice? Or help? And two? Which kind of ties in to the first one, did you spend any time praying this through, or did you panic and jump into solutions? Because I'm pretty sure you grew up with the same lectures I did about how God doesn't expect us to solve our problems in our flesh."

Christian blew out a breath.

"Still. Your heart was in the right place." Ryan turned to me. "Welcome to the family. I promise, it'll get better with time."

That was an easy promise to make. It couldn't possibly get worse.

19

CHRISTIAN

fter a quick stop at Aunt Deb's to get her things, Teresa and I pulled into the garage at my house. Our house, I guess.

I swallowed and put the car in park, then cut the engine. I turned to look at Teresa. "Welcome home."

Her eyebrows lifted.

"What?"

She shook her head. "Nothing."

"Come on."

"No. I mean...do you really think we'd get in trouble for calling the whole thing off now? I don't understand the intent to defraud thing. I get that your Dad seemed pretty sure, but maybe he was making a point?"

"Dad's not big on saying things to make a point if they aren't real." I shrugged. "We could always find another lawyer and have them look into it, but..."

"You trust your dad."

"I do." I couldn't quite stop a wince. If she noticed, she let it slide. Nice of her, given the whole situation we had going on right now. "Come on. Let's get you in and settled."

I pushed open my door and climbed out, then moved around to the trunk to gather up the small collection of belongings Teresa had at my aunt and uncle's. She joined me, reaching to take her guitar case before I could get to it.

She closed the trunk and followed me as I went up the stairs that opened into the kitchen.

I paused. "I have four bedrooms. You get your choice. Even the primary, if that's the one you want. I can move to a different one."

"I'm not doing that to you." She hugged her guitar case. "Just tell me which one you want me to have."

Seriously? I didn't want to make that choice for her. Maybe caution was finally kicking in. That said, might as well give her the biggest one. After one more brief moment of hesitation, I started through the kitchen to the stairs. My bedroom was on the main floor, a choice the architect and my parents had steered me to when I'd first designed the place. I hadn't cared one way or the other, but had certainly grown used to not going up to the third floor. Basically ever.

At the top of the stairs, I turned right and went the few short steps to the larger of the three extra bedrooms and pushed open the door. "Will this do?"

Teresa brushed against me as she walked into the room. My breath caught in my lungs and I fought to ignore the warmth at each touchpoint. That wouldn't do. At all.

"It's wonderful." She set her guitar down and turned, a slow grin splitting her face. "Who decorated it?"

I looked at the room, trying to see what made it special. It was done in what I always considered "standard beach house" blues and whites. The thick, whitewashed horizontal planks of wood that covered the wall where the bed stood were accented with wicker—though that wasn't the word Mom had used. Those same warm browns were picked up in the woven headboard. A mixture of light and dark blues contrasted with white bedding and all the tones were echoed in the ottomans at the foot of the bed, the desk and chair pushed against the window, and the sea-chest inspired dresser.

"Mom." I returned her smile. "She helped with basically all of my house. And my brothers' places. Probably because we'd all default to leather recliners and big TVs if no one stepped in."

Teresa laughed. "I doubt that."

She wasn't wrong. I did love a comfy leather recliner, but I didn't spend a lot of time watching TV. "Anyway. I'm glad you like it. Feel free to change whatever you need. There's different furniture in the other rooms—I can swap things around. Or we can buy something else. Make it your home. Whatever you need."

"Thanks."

I carried her things over and set them on the foot of the bed, then eased back toward the doorway. "I'll leave you to get settled. Let me know if you need anything. There's a bathroom through there."

I nodded toward the door on the far wall.

"Yeah? Even better."

"It's shared with the bedroom next door. But, obviously, it's just you up here. And the other rooms—you can spread out if you want. Be at home." I managed an awkward wave before hightailing it out of the room and back downstairs.

Be at home? Ugh. I sounded like some kind of alien welcoming a new species to my planet.

I crossed the living room to my bedroom and shut the door behind me. I leaned against it, my head hitting the door with a thump.

What a disaster.

Maybe it would have been possible for things to turn out worse, but if so, I couldn't quite put my finger on how. I stared up at the ceiling. *Why, God? I was trying to help out—shouldn't You have made it not work if it wasn't what You wanted to happen?*

If I stuck with that line of thinking, then...what? This *was* what He wanted to happen? He wanted me actually married to Teresa? Living in the same house? For...all eternity?

I snickered.

All eternity was a little dramatic. It wasn't as if we'd be ghosts haunting the place long after we died. But she wasn't quite thirty and I was only thirty-two. That left us what, fifty years, anyway. Give or take a handful.

Fifty years was a long time.

I didn't hate the idea. Deep down, in the parts of my mind that I tried to ignore, I'd been okay with the idea of being married—really married—to Teresa. But she wasn't there. She just wanted a solution to her problems. She'd been vocal and open about this being temporary.

And I'd gone along with it.

Why?

I shook my head. Still no answer I could put words to.

With a sigh, I pushed away from the door and crossed the room to the big walk-in closet. I took off my shoes and stored them, then went through the motions of changing into sleep pants and a t-shirt before moving into the bathroom to brush my teeth.

I caught the sound of my phone ringing as I dried my face. I tossed the towel on the counter and hurried back out. Thankfully, habit had kicked in and my phone was on its charger on my nightstand. I grabbed it up without looking at the display.

"This is Christian."

"Hey, man. It's Ryan."

"Hey." I sank onto the side of my bed. "What's up?"

"I just thought I'd see how you're doing. I imagine this evening was a little much."

That qualified as the understatement of the year. Even if it was only June, I was ready to call it. "A little. Nothing to do about it though."

"True enough. You made some choices."

"I did. Shockingly, I don't need you to call and remind me of that. I'm very well aware."

"Sorry. I really am not trying to pile on." Ryan blew out a breath. "Look. I made a couple of calls—you said Teresa's family is from the DC area."

Had I said that? I didn't really remember a lot of the conversation. Then again, he might not mean tonight. Didn't matter, really. "Yeah. They are. Why?"

"I know people up there. I'm starting a big consulting gig with Robinson Enterprises in August."

"Did I know that?"

Ryan grunted. "No idea. Most of y'all's eyes glaze over when I start talking tech."

"No, we don't."

"Please." I could practically hear Ry's eyes roll. "It's fine. I don't understand why I ended up being the only person in our family who sees the beauty of computers, but it's fine. It's like how Evan is the only one in your family who gets science like Mom."

"Computers are science." It seemed like I should remind him of that. "You and your mom have a lot in common."

"Eh. Maybe." Ryan cleared his throat. "That's not why I called. I chatted with a guy at Robinson—Christopher Ward. He's in charge of a lot of the government contracts they do. You don't care. Anyway, he's familiar with the Duvalls. Teresa's dad particularly. The man's not a good guy."

"Well aware." I scowled. "Did y'all think I jumped into marrying Teresa because her dad was just kind of annoying?"

There was silence for several moments. "No. I guess not. Maybe."

"Gee. Thanks for the overwhelming vote of confidence."

"Yeah, well. After talking to Chris and doing a little digging, I just wanted to say I think you did the right thing."

My eyebrows lifted. "You do?"

Ryan backpedaled a little. "There were probably other options. Like talking to your family about things. I still stand by that. But I also get why you maybe felt like you needed to act first, think later."

"I didn't—" I broke off, unable to honestly finish the statement. Maybe I'd done some thinking, but obviously not nearly enough. And, as everyone had pointed out earlier, I clearly hadn't prayed about it enough.

But seriously, how long was I supposed to have waited for God to answer? I wasn't a big proponent of the whole "God helps those who help themselves" nonsense, but there was also the ubiquitous joke about the guy on a roof in a flood not taking any of the rescues God sent because he was waiting for God to intervene. How was I supposed to know when it was time to act and when it was time to wait?

Wise council.

Deep in my soul, those were the words that I felt bubble up.

I closed my eyes. I had wise council available in spades, and I'd studiously avoided seeking it out.

"You're quiet. You okay?" Ryan's voice dragged me back to reality.

"Yeah. I guess." I sighed. "What do I do now, Ry?"

"You make a life." He was so matter of fact about it and laughed.

"Just like that?"

"Well, yeah. What choice do you have? You're married. You need to stay married at least until the new year, right? So, seven months? And you and I both know that no one in our family is going to be on board with you deciding to walk away like nothing happened when you get there. You make a life. And you figure out how you get Teresa on board with it. I'm not going to ask if you're in love with her, because you've known her what, two weeks?"

I hunched my shoulders. "A little longer than that, if you count from when we first met."

"When was that?"

"You remember the clinic call at Easter? That was Teresa."

"Hm."

I waited, but he didn't seem inclined to continue. I wasn't sure I wanted to know what he meant by it. "But it's not like we got to know one another all that well then. We can go with two weeks."

"Is she at least someone you could love?"

I heard Mom telling me over and over in high school that love was a choice. "Yeah."

"Do you think she can love you?"

That was the big question. I had no way to answer it. "I hope so."

"Don't sell yourself short, man. You're loveable, in a 'wow, he needs help' kind of way."

I snickered. "Thanks. I can always count on my cousins, can't I?"

"Of course. Your brothers, too. I'm sure Bennett would admit that he's now at least a little glad Aunt Linda found you under whatever box you were found under."

"Har. You're so funny."

"Oh. You'd rather think about your parents having sex?"

"Ew. No." I made an exaggerated retching noise. "Cardboard box it is."

"That's what I thought." Ryan paused. "Speaking of sex."

"No, man. Don't go there."

"That's what I was going to say to you. At least not for a while."

I cringed. "Yeah, I didn't need that suggestion."

"Just figured I'd put it out there. You *are* married. So, it's not like it'd be wrong."

Maybe not technically, but it felt wrong to even be having this conversation. Because for good or for ill, our relationship wasn't like that.

If we were staying married, it would need to get there.

But there was time.

"I'm not sure I want to continue this conversation."

It was Ryan's turn to laugh. "Fair. I'm pretty done, too. Don't run away from your family, okay? We're all here for you. And for her, now, too."

"I know it. I appreciate it." I sighed. "I honestly do. Thanks, Ry."

"Don't mention it. Also, though? Watch your back with her family."

With those ominous words, he ended the call and I stared at my phone for a moment before setting it back on its charger.

I hadn't planned to go out of my way to interact with her family again. Her father would figure out that he couldn't yank her trust fund sooner or later—probably sooner. If I knew Bennett at all, he'd already put in a call to the trust management people and let them know about Teresa's change in status.

But should she let her father know before he found out from them?

I bit my lip and glanced up at the ceiling. After a moment's hesitation, I stood and padded out into the living room. I stood at the bottom of the stairs and called up, "Teresa?"

For a minute, I didn't think she was going to answer, then the hinges on her door squeaked quietly. A couple of seconds later, she appeared at the top of the stairs. "Yeah?"

It took me a moment to find my words. She had on shorts that showed off miles of leg and a tank top that clung in all the right places. *Don't go there.*

I had to remind myself of that a couple more times before I cleared my throat. "Should we let your parents know? If word's getting around town...is it going to be better coming from you?"

She crossed her arms like she was hugging herself and puffed out her cheeks, then slowly let out her breath. "I don't want to."

I smiled slightly. "I get that. Hundred percent. But should we anyway?"

Teresa groaned.

I held up my hands. "Just a thought. I'm not going to push."

"No. You're probably right. I'm just...I had this all planned out, you know? And now it's all messed up and I ruined your life and—"

"Whoa whoa whoa." I shook my head. "You didn't ruin my life."

She just stared at me, eyebrows raised.

"You didn't."

"How can you say that?" Teresa threw her arms up in the air. "You agreed to a paper marriage purely out of a desire to be a helpful person and now your family has pushed you into trying to make something real out of it? What part of any of that isn't ruining your life?"

I stared at her a moment. "Why don't you come downstairs and I'll make us hot chocolate? This feels like a conversation that maybe shouldn't be had on two different floors of the house."

"Now he wants to make hot chocolate." Her mutter was just barely audible.

I grinned. "I probably have whipped cream."

"Of course you do." Teresa heaved a sigh and stomped down the stairs. "I didn't think nurses went for things like hot chocolate and whipped cream?"

"Well, now you know some of us do." I waited for her to join me at the bottom of the stairs before pulling her into my arms. Maybe she didn't need the contact, but I sure did. Even still, she stayed wooden long enough that I was about to let her go and apologize when she finally sagged into the hug and rested her head on my shoulder.

Without thinking, I kissed her forehead.

"I'm really sorry about all this." Her breath was warm on my neck.

I swallowed. I was having a hard time being sorry about anything at that precise moment. "We're going to make it work."

She tipped her head back and her eyes met mine. "You think?"

I held her gaze. The only response—the *right* response—popped out before I could think better of it. "I do."

20

TERESA

Nerves jangled in my belly as I pulled open the door to Bennett's law offices. Last night, he'd said I still had a job, but I wasn't going to blame him if he'd changed his mind. He probably wished me far, far away from anything having to do with his family.

"Morning." Bennett looked over from where he was fixing some coffee.

"Hi." I hesitated by the door. He didn't look angry. Or disappointed. Or anything outside of his usual, friendly self.

"Can I fix you a cup?" He nodded toward the coffee.

"I can get it." I eased the rest of the way into the room and crossed to stow my things in my desk first.

Bennett took his mug with him and settled into one of the guest chairs. "Shouldn't be anything huge on the schedule for today. At least, not so far. I'm thinking we might hear from your parents before long though."

I nodded. That was a given.

I cleared my throat. "I—we—I called them last night. Christian thought it was the smart thing to do."

Bennett chuckled. "Once he starts to really think, he's intelligent. Better to let them know than to wait for the gossip mill to fill them in."

"Or to have Dad think he was pulling a fast one and have his lawyer explain that he'd missed." I crossed to the coffee. I didn't want coffee, but having something hot to hold in my suddenly icy hands seemed like a good idea. "Dad is displeased."

Bennett sat quietly for a moment.

I filled my mug and turned to go back to my desk, trying to avoid meeting his gaze.

"Are you all right?" His voice was quiet and calm.

"Not really." Which continued to be a surprise. After all the abuse—and I couldn't escape calling it what it was now—I'd endured from my parents, I hadn't honestly believed there was a way for them to hurt me more. I'd learned otherwise last night.

"I'm sorry."

I shrugged. I was, too. I was sorry for having roped Christian into my mess. Sorry for dragging the rest of his family into it. I was sorry that I couldn't quite shake the feeling that having my money still made it all worthwhile.

"Should I reach out to the trust people for you?"

I flashed a grateful smile at him. Christian had told me Bennett wouldn't pry, but I'd been skeptical. Looks like the brothers knew each other well. Or had Christian warned Bennett? I could see that happening. Part of me might find that annoying. The other part called it what it probably was: considerate.

I swallowed. "Probably. They need to be told. Dad said something about declaring me unfit. I don't know if he meant in terms of being able to choose to marry or something else, but he's clearly not giving up on getting his hands on my money. Not yet."

"All right. Leave it with me." Bennett stood. He crossed to the front door and flipped the lock. "We'll keep that locked today. Just in case."

"Oh. I don't think—"

Bennett shook his head. "It's a few extra seconds for legitimate clients to wait, and it keeps everyone safe from other possibilities."

"If you're sure." I didn't like the change in routine, but I couldn't deny that I appreciated the extra layer of security.

"I'm sure." He lifted his mug in a toast before turning and heading down toward his office.

I got myself settled behind my desk and had just started working through the email, when the door clicked and then opened.

"Morning." Linda called out as she bustled through the door. She shot me a toothy grin as she turned to flip the lock once the door was shut. "I thought I might spend a few hours in the office today. Got a call from an old friend this morning who just had a new grandbaby. She wants to make a few changes to her will."

"Oh. That's lovely." Was lovely the right choice of word? I didn't even know. "Do you have a photo?"

Linda beamed and set her briefcase on a chair so she could get her phone out of her purse. She tapped a few times before offering me the phone. "I had her text me some immediately. Isn't she the sweetest?"

I reached for the phone and looked at the photo of the wrinkly baby wrapped tightly in a hospital standard blanket, a pink knit cap covering her head. Honestly, she looked just like every baby ever born, but I gave the expected answer. "She's adorable."

I handed the phone back.

Linda laughed. "I've always thought babies look the same for the first few months. Unless they're yours. Then they're special."

I managed a sheepish smile.

"Did you sleep well?" Linda tossed the question out like it was the most natural thing to ask.

I froze. She wasn't...was she implying...? I cleared my throat. "Yes? Christian said you helped a lot with setting up his upstairs rooms. You did a great job."

"The upstairs rooms?" Her poker face couldn't quite hold out. "Well. I'm glad you were comfortable."

"Very much so." I moistened my lips. Was she ever going to actually go to her office? "Let me know if you have anything for me to do. We don't have any appointments on the books for today."

"I'll do that." She gathered her briefcase and headed down the hallway.

I barely had time to blow out a breath before the door was clicking and opening again. This time, Christian's dad breezed in.

"Did I see my wife's car out there?" He paused and flipped the lock before turning his attention to me.

"She's in her office." I gestured toward the hallway. "Can I get you some coffee?"

"Hm? Oh, no, thanks." He smiled absently. "I'll go see what she's up to."

I watched him stride down the hallway and shook my head. At least there were only three lawyers in the family. Surely the rest of them wouldn't find a reason to pop by. Right?

I opened a browser and put on some quiet music in the background while I returned to processing email. Most of the inquiries were simple enough. Bennett's previous receptionist had a standard response with rates and areas of specialty— although it honestly seemed like the Thomases took whatever sounded interesting at the time—so it took very little effort to handle. Other messages were probably spam, but Bennett said to do a little investigation before deleting them just in case.

It was actually kind of fun.

Obviously, I didn't click any of the links in the email, but searching up the supposed companies or offers proved amusing. I'd yet to determine any were legit, but that made it more interesting. Were there people who actually fell for these scams? Obviously there had to be, or the folks who sent them would quit bothering.

With the email finished, I glanced down the hallway. All the office doors were still shut. I dug out the blank journal I'd decided to use for song writing, and took a deep breath. Last night, while I'd been curled in bed with my mind racing, words had played a sneaky game of tag with one another. I hadn't been able to corral them into anything useful, not when I'd been busy reliving one of the most awkward nights of my life.

And that hug.

Man. Christian could hug.

I absently jotted down some of the adjectives that came to mind when I let myself remember relaxing into his embrace at the bottom of the stairs. And when he'd said he believed we would make it work?

He'd sounded so sure.

I wanted him to be right.

Wait.

I frowned slightly and focused on the notebook in front of me. Little hearts decorated the edges of the page and trailed in chains between words like "cherished" and "seen" and "known."

When was the last time I'd felt like someone knew who I was and liked me because of it? That would be just about never.

Could Christian and I really make this work, despite how things had started?

The thought sparked an idea, so I bent my attention to my notebook and scribbled words as quickly as I could get them down, pausing only when a little burst of tune suggested itself in the back of my mind. Then I'd take a second to note down chords. I'd have to revise those when I got to my guitar—I had a decent ear, but not the perfect pitch I'd always wished for.

It was too bad Christian didn't have a piano.

But, when Bennett got the access to my trust worked out, I could buy myself a keyboard. And that would be almost as good. Better, in some ways, since it would mean I could play with headphones on and not bother Christian if he was around.

Not that he'd mind me playing.

He just didn't seem the type. He was entirely too accommodating. And caring. And just plain kind. And I'd completely taken advantage of him.

All the excuses I'd made about how it would work out in the end when we got our marriage annulled had been rendered moot. Now he was stuck. I was, too, but I was definitely getting the better end of the deal. I'd married an incredible man. And he'd ended up with me.

Was there any way to make it up to him?

The sound of a door closing and quiet conversation had me flipping my notebook shut and quickly wiggling the computer's mouse. I wasn't doing anything wrong. Bennett had told me it was fine to fill my time with whatever I wanted if I wasn't doing something for him. But it still felt like I was being sneaky.

Linda stopped in front of my desk with a smile. "Why don't you come to lunch with us?"

"Oh. I was just going to eat a sandwich at my desk." Christian had left a packed lunch for me beside the coffee machine this morning. Apparently it had been an early shift at the clinic this morning. Or something. Whatever it was, the vague plans she'd had for coffee in the kitchen with him as part of a new morning routine had been thwarted.

Which was fine, of course. He had his own life.

"Pfft." Linda waved that off. "Go stick it in the fridge for tomorrow. It'll keep."

"Honey, she might not want to eat lunch with her in-laws." David patted Linda's arm. "Which would be fine. How many meals have you had with my folks?"

Linda scowled at her husband. "That's completely different, and you know it."

He wiggled a hand from side-to-side. "Not completely."

Linda sighed. "Fine. All right. Though I wish you'd reconsider. We do come in peace, you know. I realize maybe after last night it doesn't seem like it, but we do."

I managed a weak smile. "You care about your sons. It's a good thing."

"We care about more than just Christian, but I can see why you'd stop there. I'll allow it. For now." Linda slipped her hand into her husband's. "The offer stands, any time. We're never too busy to go out for lunch. And I hope you'll join us on Monday nights at the diner for family dinner."

"And Sundays." David chuckled. "Christian will keep you posted and drag you along. We're a tight family. You get used to it."

I wasn't sure about that part.

I hadn't factored any of the family meals into my plans, because this marriage was never supposed to be more than a chance for me to get back on my feet with minimal imposition to Christian.

Thankfully, they turned and headed out of the office before the silence got awkward and I had to drum up some kind of reply. I waited until they disappeared from view before burying my face in my hands.

"Are you all right?"

I jumped and looked up. How had I not heard Bennett approaching? "Yeah. I'm okay."

He shook his head. "I don't believe you, but we can let it slide. Why don't you come back to my office for a few?"

It was phrased like a question, but it also very clearly wasn't one. "Sure. Of course."

I stood and grabbed a notebook and pen before following Bennett back down the hallway to his office. He gestured to a chair as he moved behind his desk.

" I spoke to the firm that handles your trust to let them know your change of marital status." He flashed a quick grin. "There was some consternation, as it appears that they've been busy prepping paperwork to take to a judge this week to get the revocation process started. I called over to the courthouse and got a friend there to do me a favor and pull an official copy of your license, so I'll drive over this afternoon to get it. I sent along a scan, but they want a copy with the official seal."

I winced. "You don't have to go do that. I can—"

"It's not a problem. Part of my job." Bennett tented his fingers. "And I convinced Jericho that we should go out to dinner. She's going to close the library a little early so we get over there before everything closes."

"That's a lot of hassle." I didn't realize a library could close early. "Won't people mind if she's not there?"

Bennett shook his head. "Nah. It's a beautiful summer day. She said the only people who had been in so far today were Aunt Deb and Grady as well as the older gentlemen who play chess there most mornings. Since they left, it's been dead. She went ahead and called up one of the council members who's a big fan though and double-checked that it would be all right. She got the okay."

Small towns. I couldn't fathom a library in Northern Virginia just closing early because the librarian needed to go somewhere. Then again, there weren't any libraries small enough to only have one staff member near home, either.

Not home.

This was home now.

"Well. Thank you." I started to stand.

Bennett held up a hand. "I got the impression that your father is going to be more than mildly put out when he gets this news. He might have, already. I suspect one of the attorneys left the meeting to make a call—no proof, but I tend to have a feel. I think you should get Christian to come pick you up after work."

I blinked and tried to take that information in. "You really think that's necessary?"

"You rode over this morning, right? That's Christian's bike locked up out front?"

I nodded. We'd talked about that briefly last night and since I was currently without a car, riding in seemed reasonable enough. It had been long enough since I'd been on one that I was worried about making it this far, but apparently the cliché has some basis in fact.

"That's a lot of road between here and home for your dad to find you on. And on a bike, you can't exactly lock the doors and wait him out."

I sighed. "I'll text him and see if he's free."

Bennett frowned. "If he can't make it, let me know, okay? I'll get someone else to come by."

I opened my mouth to object, but snapped it closed at the look on Bennett's face.

He nodded. "Now. I may have overstepped slightly, but I consider you my client at this point—so I let the other firm know, in no uncertain terms—that any attempts to harm you or your reputation would be met with vigorous defense. They acted amazed that I'd think it was a possibility, but there were subtle nods. Hopefully, they'll give your father the message and he'll cut his losses."

My lips twitched. Good luck with that. "Dad doesn't like to lose."

"In this case, that's too bad for him." Bennett smiled. "Now. Why didn't you want to go to lunch with my folks?"

"I didn't—I packed a sandwich."

He tipped his head to the side and studied me.

My face heated.

"We can be a lot. But I promise, you can't find better people to have on your side. You're family now."

Why did the underlying message of that statement feel like a double-edged sword? A lot less *Olive Garden* and a lot more *Godfather*. "I appreciate that."

"I'm not sure you do." He tapped his desk. "Hopefully, before long you will. If you're eating at your desk, be sure you tell Christian to be here around four. No sense in pretending you're taking a lunch break when you aren't."

"Oh, but—"

"Are you always this difficult?" Bennett cut off my excuse.

I hunched my shoulders. "Probably?"

He laughed. "You're going to fit right in. Enjoy your lunch."

"Thanks." I took it as a dismissal and stood. I paused by the break room on my way back to the front desk and grabbed the paper bag out of the fridge. Back in my seat, I shook out the contents and smiled slightly. Not only was there a ham and cheese sandwich—cut on the diagonal, which everyone knew tasted better—but also an apple, a soda, a bag of chips, and a napkin bearing instructions to have a wonderful day.

I arranged the food on my desk blotter and snapped a photo, then attached it to a text message.

> Thanks for lunch. Looks amazing. I'm supposed to ask you to pick me up at four.

I hesitated a moment, then hit send. What would Dad do?

What *could* he do? Track me down and scream at me from his car? He'd done that already. And sure, it was mortifying, but not dangerous. Did I believe he'd hurt me?

I bit my lip and reached for the sandwich.

He probably wouldn't hurt me himself. But he'd let it happen. He'd proven that. More than once. I frowned at the cast on my arm. Mostly it didn't make my life too much harder, which was a bonus, but every time I caught sight of it, I remembered just how far Dad was willing to let things go.

I sighed and took a bite.

As I was chewing, my phone buzzed. I tapped to open my messages.

> Is that where my sandwich went? I wondered.
> 😂😂😂😂

I laughed at the string of laughing emojis he'd added at the end before wiping my fingers on the napkin and tapping out a reply.

> Nice try. But you left me a note by the coffee about it. Remember? Also? Good coffee. Thank you.

> We aim to please.

The dots danced for a moment on the screen, then another message appeared.

> Four is no problem. I'm on island today. Could always get a call, but I'll lock the doors at three thirty so I'm not held up with a walk-in.

I stared at the words.

I was making everyone's life so much harder than it needed to be. First thing I was going to do when I got my money was buy a car. Then no one would have to pick me up or drive into Bennett to get things—and how had I been figuring I'd do that, if Bennett had taken me up on the offer? It was good he had a steadier head on his shoulders than I did.

> Thanks. Sorry.

>> Don't apologize. Guessing your dad is making noise?

> Not yet, but Bennett says it seems likely.

>> Bennett would know. He's got good instincts. I'll see you at four. Keep the front door locked.

I searched through the emojis until I found one of someone saluting and sent it, then set my phone aside.

Maybe that was snarky, but if so? Well, tough.

I hadn't expected a reply, but I had to laugh when he came back with an eyeroll emoji. Fair enough.

21

CHRISTIAN

I parked a block down from Bennett's office and got out of the car. I was a few minutes early, but that shouldn't be an issue. Early was probably better than late, if Bennett was worried. My steps slowed as I neared the office and spotted the woman banging on the door.

"Caroline?"

The woman turned, scowling. "The bimbo at the desk won't let me in."

"She's not a bimbo." I closed the distance between us. "Do you have an appointment?"

"I don't need an appointment to see my brother-in-law. Or my son, which is more to the point." Caroline banged on the door again.

I pushed the intercom button. "Teresa, is Bennett there?"

"No. She won't believe me. He left about thirty minutes ago to handle some business on the mainland." Teresa's voice was a little shaky, but the undertone was annoyed anger.

I looked at Caroline. "Bennett's not here. Does Travis know you're here?"

"No. I don't owe him a run-down of my comings and goings."

I bobbed my head from side-to-side. "I mean, you kind of do. You're his wife."

"For now."

I tucked my hands in my pockets. "Did you say you were here to see Grady?"

"Of course I am. I have a place in Portland now, so I'll pack him up and take him home."

Ah. Not a visit. This was probably on the advice of her attorney. "I don't think so."

"Like you care. Like any of you do." Caroline crossed her arms. "So where is he? I tried to get in at home but my key doesn't work anymore."

"I think it's good you came here. Let me make a call." I glanced through the door at Teresa and held up a finger before pulling out my phone and tapping Mom's contact.

"There's my baby. What's up?"

"Do you think you and Dad could come down to the office? It's probably urgent."

"Of course." All the teasing had drained out of Mom's voice. "Is it Teresa's family? Bennett mentioned he was concerned."

"No. Caroline's here."

There was a long pause. Mom's words dripped ice. "I see. We'll be right there."

"Thanks." I ended the call and debated with myself about making her wait on the street or getting Teresa to let us in. Probably better to go in. I pushed the intercom again. "Can you let us in? Mom and Dad are on the way."

Teresa pushed a button and there was a quiet buzz then a click. I pulled open the door and gestured for Caroline to go on in.

Caroline frowned as she brushed past.

"Have a seat." I slipped around and cut her off before she

could march down the hallway to the offices. "Would you like some coffee?"

"No."

"There's soda, if you'd rather?" Teresa offered hesitantly.

I sent her a bolstering smile before moving back to the front door to lock it. Then I took a seat across from Caroline. "I'd love a Coke."

"Sure." Teresa popped up from her seat and hurried off. She returned a minute later with a couple of Cokes. She handed me one, then crossed to offer the other to Caroline.

"Do you have diet?"

"I'll check." Teresa disappeared again.

"How long have you been back in town?" I popped the top on the can and took a short sip.

"Why do you care?"

"I'm just trying to make conversation." I took another sip.

"The only no calorie thing we have is this." Teresa offered a can of flavored seltzer water.

Caroline sighed and took it. "Fine. Thank you."

Teresa hurried back behind the desk.

"Are you enjoying Portland?"

"What is this, twenty questions?" Caroline opened her drink and took a swig. "It's okay. It'll be better when I get what I'm owed from your stupid brother. Then I'll be able to live somewhere better than a dinky one-bedroom apartment."

One bedroom? And she thought she was taking Grady back with her? There were a whole host of issues that meant that wasn't going to happen, but not having a place for him to sleep was icing on the cake.

I nodded slightly. "That's what your lawyer says?"

"Him?" Caroline shook her head. "He doesn't see the big picture. I know Travis will cave. He always did. I wanted us to sleep together? We slept together. I wanted a baby? We had a baby. The only time I couldn't convince him was the whole marriage thing. Would've been a lot easier if he'd gotten on board with living together."

My heart was breaking for Travis and Grady. Did she hear how she sounded? How had the poison gotten so rooted in her soul? "I think it was good for Grady to grow up with two parents who were committed to each other."

Teresa made a noise.

I looked her way. It was clear she disagreed. Given the situation with her parents, I kind of understood. But Travis and Caroline had, at the time at least, both professed faith in Jesus. Did Caroline still? "Have you found a church in Oregon?"

"What? No." She took a long drink. "I guess I'll have to when Grady goes back with me. Need to show the court that I'm willing to uphold some of what his dad wants."

A flash of movement caught my eye and I shifted my gaze to the front door. Dad had his key in the lock and a look that I'd learned to avoid when I was a kid. It was his no-nonsense, down to business, you done messed up look.

I felt a little pang of pity for Caroline.

Sure, she was making some terrible choices that were having horrible consequences, but she was still my sister-in-law. And she was still Grady's mom.

"Caroline." Mom came in and held out a hand. "What a surprise."

Caroline shrugged and shook Mom's hand.

"Why don't you come on back to my office. I see you've got a drink. Would you like some chips? Or a cookie?"

"I'm fine." Caroline stood. "I just want—"

"Oh, let's hold off on that 'til we're settled in back." Mom gestured down the hall.

Dad shook his head. "You two go ahead and go. I called

Travis and Bennett. We've got this under control. For now. She say anything useful?"

"She really hates your family." Teresa picked up her purse from the desk and held it to her chest.

"It sure seems that way." I took a long sip of Coke. "She says she wants to take Grady to Oregon with her. Back to her one-bedroom apartment."

"Ha. Good luck to her with that." Dad sighed. "You two go have fun."

I watched Dad start down the hallway then returned my attention to Teresa. "Ready?"

"Yeah." She came around the desk. "Can we just go home?"

I studied her for a moment before nodding and tossing out any half-baked plans to suggest going somewhere for supper. "Of course.

We made it down to my car and I was holding the passenger door open for her, when another car squealed to a stop beside mine. Teresa's father threw open the door, got out, and slammed it before storming over to us.

"What do you think you're playing at?" He bellowed loud enough that people on the street turned to stare.

"Just get in. I've got this." I murmured to Teresa, my hand on the door, ready to close it as soon as she was in.

"No. It's fine. He can't—" She broke off as she dodged a slap.

I nudged her into the seat and closed the car door, then leaned against it, arms crossed. "Don't ever try to hurt my wife again."

"Wife." Teresa's father spat the word. He shot me a pitying glance. "You really married her?"

"I really did."

Mr. Duvall stared at me and I fought to keep my face impassive. Finally, he shook his head. "Things don't work out? Don't come crying to me. I'm not taking her back. Not after this. You hear that, Teresa? We're done."

The door pushed against me. I glanced in and then stepped aside so Teresa could push the door open. She hesitantly stood, ducking back slightly behind my shoulder. "Do better by Mom."

Mr. Duvall snorted. "Your mother is fine. She knew what she was getting into. She made her choice."

Teresa nodded slightly. "If she changes her mind, my door's always open."

"I'll let her know." His expression suggested the opposite.

"Does this mean you're going to stop causing my wife trouble?" I blurted the words as Mr. Duvall began to turn.

He slowly faced me. "*I've* been causing *her* trouble?"

"You have." I held his gaze until he looked away.

"The lawyers say the money's gone. Unless that changes, and I have a few more things to look into, she's your problem now."

"If you knew we were married, why'd you come storming over here, Dad?" Teresa called after him.

He paused by his car. "People lie. Documents can be forged. I had to check."

She shook her head as he climbed into his car and drove away.

I slipped my arm around her and tugged her in close. "I'm sorry."

"No. You don't get to be sorry. Not for defending me." She drew in a shuddering breath. "But I can be sorry that you had to."

I chuckled. "All in all, that wasn't so bad. Not really. Bennett had me worried it was going to be like a shootout at the OK Corral."

Teresa tipped her head back and our eyes met. After a moment, one corner of her mouth quirked up. "Now that you've rescued this damsel in distress. Again. Can we go home?"

Going with instinct, I brushed a feather-light kiss across her lips. "Absolutely."

There were no more interruptions in our brief journey home. Teresa was quiet, mostly just looking out her window.

"I have some chicken in the freezer I could grill. And I think there are some potatoes in the pantry. It's simple, but I've never poisoned anyone yet."

She turned away from the view and smiled. "That sounds nice. Do you mind if I lay down a little before dinner? My head..."

"Not at all. It's going to be a couple of hours. You rest." I turned in at my—our—house, and pulled into the garage. "Maybe after dinner we can look at cars? I think you need something of your own. We can get you your own bike, too, though."

Teresa winced. "Your bike. It's still locked up at the office."

"That's fine. I'll text Dad and see if he can toss it in his car when they're finished meeting with Caroline. And if not, it'll be there tomorrow. I'll just run you in to work on my way."

"I don't want to be a bother."

"You're not. I'll let you know if it changes." I took her hand and squeezed it. "Let's go inside so you can rest."

I got out of the car and waited at the bottom of the stairs that led to the kitchen for her to join me. We climbed up and I unlocked the door, then pushed it open.

"Do you think he's really giving up?" Teresa looked at me as she slipped past into the house. She stopped when she was inside and turned to face me.

I shrugged and closed the door behind us. "If all he cared about was your trust, then maybe. Yeah. Bennett seems to think that the paper copy of our marriage license is just a formality at this point. He imagines by the end of next week, at the latest, you'll have free access to the rest of your money."

She drew her eyebrows together. "How do you know that? I don't know that."

"I called Bennett after we texted. I wanted to know how worried he was. What we were looking at. That kind of thing." I crossed the kitchen and got a glass out of the cupboard, then carried it to the fridge to fill it with water. I took a long drink, then slowly lowered it as I clued in on her expression. "What?"

"Why did he tell you all that and not me? It's not your money, it's mine. It's not your family, it's mine. None of this has anything to do with you!" Her voice raised to almost a shout at the end.

"Other than that last statement, I agree completely." I carefully set my glass on the counter. "I suspect he told me because I kept asking more questions. Did you ask him questions?"

Teresa hesitated, then shook her head.

"And everything he told me, he prefaced with his little spiel about how he wasn't guaranteeing anything and this was just his thoughts. Would you have wanted to hear his guesses?"

She looked away. "I don't know."

"I'm sorry if I overstepped."

"You did over step."

I flinched. "I'm sorry I overstepped. I truly am."

She gave a curt nod.

I pressed my lips together. We needed to talk about a lot of things now that this was a marriage we were going to keep. Or at least try to. I wasn't a big believer in "your money" and "my money." I'd always imagined marriage as the ultimate combination—where everything got mixed together and became "ours." That was certainly how Mom and Dad had managed things. And my aunt and uncle. And Gramps and Grammie. There were some Loring trusts that couldn't be considered communal property—and that was a good thing in Travis's case. But we all had residual income, and once that hit our accounts, it was meant to be shared. Wasn't it?

Maybe the right thing to do was ignore it. She could have her money and I'd have mine. But it didn't sit right.

I sighed and opened the freezer for the chicken. Now wasn't the time to worry about that. I glanced over my shoulder. "Why don't you go rest. We can talk over supper."

I took the frozen poultry to the sink and grabbed a big mixing bowl from one of the cabinets. I filled it with water and pulled the rock-hard chunks of bird out of the packaging and dropped them in the bowl. When I turned, trash in hand, Teresa was still standing there. Staring.

I raised my eyebrows in query.

"You didn't yell." Her voice was a whisper.

"I don't like yelling." I crossed to the trash can and dropped in the tray that had held the chicken, then went back to the sink to wash my hands, avoiding getting suds in the defrosting bowl. "I can, if I have to. But I've never liked it. It doesn't seem like the best way to get a point across. Most of the time."

A smile flirted with the corners of her lips. "My family likes to yell. Well. My parents do. I don't like it. I'm sorry. I'm not sure you understand how deeply sorry I am about this."

I dried my hands and crossed the room so we were closer and I held open my arms. After a moment, she stepped into them and I held her. "I'll say it as often as I have to. You don't need to be sorry. This was my idea, and it's going to be all right."

"How, Christian?" She pressed her face into my shoulder. "How is it all right that you're married to someone you don't love? Someone who used you because she couldn't walk away from money?"

"I don't feel used. And I'm not married to someone I don't love." I'd come to that conclusion in the middle of the sleepless night. It was fast, yes. And the circumstances were far from ideal.

But I loved Teresa. I don't think I could have gone through with the wedding if that wasn't true. "And I'd appreciate it if you could speak more kindly about my wife."

She went still. "You love me?"

"I do." I moistened my lips. "I understand it may take you a while to get there. That's all right. We have time. I don't want you to feel pressured."

When she didn't respond, I kissed her forehead gently and stepped back. "Go lay down. Do you need aspirin or something? There should be pain killers in the bathroom upstairs, but if there aren't, text me and I'll bring some up."

Mutely, she nodded, then started slowly up the stairs. She paused half-way, turned, and looked at me for a long moment before continuing on her way.

I blew out a breath and scrubbed a hand over my face before heading back into the kitchen to hunt up some sort of side to go with the chicken.

In a way, it was a relief to tell Teresa that I loved her. But now the ball was in her court.

What if she could never feel the same?

22

TERESA

"Relax."

I glared at Christian as we walked up the steps of his parents' home.

"What? You've been to Sunday lunch before."

"Not like this." I gripped the plate of cookies I was carrying so hard my knuckles turned white.

"Bennett says that Mom and Dad invited Caroline to join us. You have nothing to worry about."

Oh, great. Saved from whatever was going to happen by the first woman to push her way into their family. The woman who, at least from what I'd gathered, everyone hated now. "That isn't comforting."

Christian slid an arm around my shoulders and pulled me to his side. "I'm sorry. They like you. They're going to love you given some time. And seeing as how things seem to have worked out with your parents, everything should settle down."

"I hope so." I couldn't put much enthusiasm behind the words. Sure, it seemed like I'd achieved my end goal and had my trust, but at what cost to Christian? He said he loved me. Which was crazy fast. I liked him well enough. We were friends. And yes, I found him attractive. But love?

I had no idea how to even start to decide if I loved him.

Christian opened the front door and called out, "It's us!"

"Hi, Christian." Linda called from the kitchen. "Come on back. You're the first ones here."

We were? I shot a sidelong glance at Christian. "I thought you said there was no way we'd be the first ones here."

He shrugged. "Maybe no one wanted to be first today. We're half an hour past when people usually start showing up."

I followed him into the kitchen.

"Teresa made cookies. Where should we put them?"

Linda beamed at me. "What a treat. Thanks. Just there on the bar should be fine. I'll make sure to point them out when we get to dessert."

I slid the plate of cookies where she indicated. "Can I help you with anything?"

"We're basically ready. Everyone seems to be late today. I was about to call out the Marines to round people up, then y'all got here." Linda chuckled.

"We're here!" Bennet's voice came from the direction of the front door. "And the rest of them aren't far behind."

"Great." Linda called back, then turned to me. "Would you mind stepping out on the deck to let David know people are here? Then see if Gramps will let you fix him a plate. I'd just as soon he not do all that walking."

"I can do that, Mom." Christian started toward the door.

I grabbed his hand. "I'll do it. I'd like to."

He looked at me a moment before gesturing for me to go ahead. I smiled. Having his mom give me a task somehow eased a lot of the tension that had been building in my gut. It was almost as if it solidified that she was okay with me being part of the family.

Might not be true. But I was going to go with it for now.

I opened the door and stepped out onto the deck.

David looked up from where he lounged in a chair at the table. He grinned. "Everyone finally here?"

I nodded. "Linda asked me to let you know."

He set down his drink and pushed to his feet. "I'll get the burgers and dogs onto a platter and take them inside. It's good, I was about to starve."

Gramps, sitting in the chair beside the one David vacated, chortled. "I was about to ask you to nab me one of those hot dogs off the grill and I'd just eat it nekkid."

"Why didn't I think of that?" David glanced at his father-in-law with a laugh, then returned to the task of transferring the grilled meat to a big plate.

"Linda also asked me to see if you'd let me make you a plate."

Gramps eyed me. He shook his head. "She's worried about me falling again. Honestly, I think at my age I'm entitled to be a little unsteady, but that's fine. I'm not going to turn down a helping hand."

I made a show of dragging my hand across my forehead. "Phew. I'm not sure what she would have done if I failed in that mission."

Gramps laughed. "And I'm too old to protect you. Thank you, missy. For all I said I was going to eat a hot dog, I'd really rather have a burger. Load it up and don't skimp on the sides. Anyone in there can tell you what to put on a plate for me."

"All right. If I get it wrong, I'm going to remind you of that." I turned and hurried a few steps to open the door for David as he approached it with the meat.

"Thanks."

"I didn't want to risk it falling. I'm hungry, too."

David laughed as he stepped into the kitchen.

The rest of the family was hovering around the kitchen, clearly waiting on the food. David set the platter on the counter and clapped his hands together. "Let's pray so we can eat."

It only took a second for everyone to settle, then David bowed his head. I hurried to do the same.

"Heavenly Father, thank you for this big, late family. Thank you for your bountiful blessings and for this food. Bless it to our bodies and bless our bodies to your service. Amen."

A chorus of amens were muttered around the room.

"You know, Dad, calling us your late family sounds like you're planning to do away with us." Bennett took a plate from the stack and started moving down the line of dishes.

Jericho followed behind him. "To think yesterday I ordered the latest release from your favorite author, just for you."

David laughed. "For me? Or for Bennett? Because I seem to recall he's the one who got me hooked on that series."

"Busted." Travis took a plate and handed it to Grady, then took another for himself as they joined the line. "He got me hooked on the series, too."

"The whole island is hooked." Evan slid into line behind Travis. "That's what happens when the first book is featured in one of Bennett's picks at least three times. You need to figure out some new favorites, man."

"Maybe some romance, honey." Linda stood on the other side of the counter, smiling as everyone slid past filling their plates. "I like a legal thriller as much as the next person, but some diversity would be good."

"I'm not reading romance just to recommend it. Maybe Jericho can add her own picks." Bennett glared at his mom. "Or you and Aunt Deb could get your own section to make recommendations. You have an in with the librarian."

"Oh, I wouldn't want to take advantage." Deb got a plate and started adding food.

"Maybe I should just put out a box and everyone can submit recommendations. I'll switch them out more frequently if we get more than a handful." Jericho balanced her plate in one hand and dug through the cooler for a drink. She pulled out sparkling water, then turned to her husband. "Does that work?"

Bennett leaned in and kissed her. "Sounds perfect. Especially since it keeps me from reading romance."

"A little romance wouldn't hurt you." Jericho winked at him. "Let's go join Gramps on the deck."

I slid behind Christian at the end of the line for food. When we reached the plates, Christian took one then handed me two.

"You hold those and let me know what you want. I think I can guess what Gramps wants, but catch any mistakes."

"He said some of everything, basically. But hamburger, not hot dog. I'll go the hot dog route though." I waited while Christian put buns on our plates and then added the meat. We continued down the little buffet adding condiments and potato salad and pickled green beans that Christian assured me were amazing.

I didn't see how they could be, but I'd give them a try.

With full plates, we headed outside to join the rest of the family at the table.

I set Gramps' plate in front of him.

"Looks perfect. Thanks." Gramps shot me a wink.

"Any time." Did Christian—and the rest of them—know how blessed they were to still have their grandfather? And for their grandfather to be such a fabulous man? I loved my grandparents, but they were nowhere near as warm and real as Gramps.

I followed Christian to two empty chairs and sat beside him.

Grady stared at me from across the table.

"Hi, Grady." I gave a little wave. "Have you been playing more with your sand this week?"

He brightened. "Got new sand."

"Yeah? What color this time?" I picked up my fork and tucked some of the pickle relish that was trying to escape back onto my hotdog.

"Green." His lower lip poked out. "Mama says not to let it mix."

Travis frowned. "If you want to mix them, Grady, you can mix them. It's your sand."

Grady shook his head. "I'm not bad."

"Of course you're not." Travis turned to look at his son. "No one here thinks you are. And mixing sand colors isn't bad."

Grady just hunched his shoulders.

"Sorry." I picked up my hotdog and took a bite. I guess I shouldn't have brought up the sand, but I'd had a lot of fun playing with it—and with Grady—on Thursday. Before it turned into a big intervention at least.

"Don't be. Caroline—well, you know she's been in town."

I nodded.

Christian pointed his fork at Travis. "I thought Mom and Dad said she was coming to lunch."

"They invited her. But I can't see her showing up. She only spent about fifteen minutes with Grady on Saturday before she remembered something that she had to be doing." Travis sighed. "I don't know what to do."

I focused on my food. I was in no position to offer advice here, and, in reality, I didn't know the situation. Grady was a great kid, and if Caroline really didn't spend time with him after yelling about how she was there for her son at the office? Well, maybe I didn't have the full picture.

I'd certainly rather not believe that my husband's family were monsters who kept a child from his mom.

Husband. Weird.

I looked at Christian. He caught my eye and smiled. My lips curved in response, without thought.

Christian reached over and took my hand.

"Hi, honey." Deb rubbed Travis's shoulder as she moved to sit in the seat beside Grady. "Heya, Grady."

Grady glanced up; his mouth stuffed with food.

"Ooh. You need to chew, bud." Deb tapped his chipmunk cheek. "Be careful."

Rob sat down beside Deb. He smiled over at me. "You weren't a noisy houseguest, but it's eerily quiet again now that you're gone."

"Sorry?" What was I supposed to say to that?

He waved that off. "I'm just saying we miss you. But we're glad that you've landed as part of the family. Is Christian treating you right?"

"Uncle Rob." Christian spread his hands. "What kind of question is that?"

"An honest one." Rob winked. "Happy wife, happy life."

Deb elbowed Rob. "Happy spouse, happy house. It's a two-way street. And you know it."

"He's doing great. Thanks."

"See?" Christian practically beamed.

I felt a tiny little ping of guilt. Not because it wasn't true, but it seemed to imply more than I meant.

Deb and Rob laughed before turning to their food.

After several more minutes of conversation flying around the table as people ate and traded jabs, Gramps knocked his fist on the table.

"All right, everyone. I have something to say."

The family settled down and all eyes turned to where Gramps was sitting near the head of the table.

Gramps took a deep breath and pursed his lips. "Your Grammi

and I were married a lot of years before she went home to Jesus. And I hope every day that it won't be too many more years before I join her there. But it seems to me that maybe one of the reasons I'm still lingering here is to remind my grandchildren of the guiding principle of Grammi's and my marriage. You've seen the words on the art she hung all over our house, from Psalm 127."

He paused and looked over at Linda.

Linda nodded. "Unless the Lord builds the house, those who build it labor in vain."

Gramps shot a finger at her. "Exactly. And I think my daughters and their husbands have done a good job in their marriages. I'm grateful to God for that. But now I've got three married grandchildren, and I want those marriages to be strong and able to survive the trials life throws at them."

Travis cleared his throat and looked down.

Deb reached around Grady to rub Travis's shoulder.

Christian looked at me. I had a hard time holding his gaze.

"The three of you boys who aren't married yet, well, your time will come. You can start building that solid foundation now so you're ready when God drops His chosen woman in your path. Look how quickly things went for Christian." Gramps paused, his eyes sparkling. "You managed to beat Grammi and me, and everyone said we married too quickly at just under six weeks of knowing one another."

A quiet chuckle rippled around the table.

My face heated and I looked at my hands clasped in my lap. Gramps and Grammi had rushed to the altar because they were in love. Christian and I had gone there because I'd wanted my trust fund. I closed my eyes, shame washing over me. I'd done this for money. It was a horrible thing to realize how focused on wealth I'd become.

I was no different than my parents.

I started to scoot my chair back, my only thought to run... somewhere.

Christian put his hand on my arm, then slid down and took my hand. He gave a comforting squeeze. "Hey. You all right?"

I shook my head.

He frowned slightly. "Do we need to go?"

We. No, *we* didn't need to go. But I did.

Except I couldn't say that. Or do that.

I shook my head again.

Gramps was still talking. "...so, I want to encourage you—all of you—to find a Bible study to do together. Make it an addition to your personal study time, something designed to help the two of you grow closer to one another as you grow closer to Jesus. If you're not married yet, add in some reading about what makes a Christian marriage. Study the role of a husband. Be ready to be the man your future wife needs you to be. And, if you'll humor an old man who loves you, I'd appreciate an update now and then about what you're learning. That's it."

Gramps leaned back in his chair. He seemed slightly out of breath.

Linda popped out of her seat and moved closer to Gramps. She looked down the table, caught Christian's eye, and jerked her head.

"I'll be right back." Christian stood and made his way to Gramps's seat.

I watched as he and Linda put their heads together before Christian took Gramps's wrist in his hand.

Christian frowned slightly and squatted beside Gramps.

I bit my lip.

"He'll be fine."

I turned to Deb. "He will?"

She nodded, though signs of strain and worry were evident on her face. "Talking a lot taxes his lungs. He's stubborn enough that getting him to the doctor is an epic adventure, so we haven't managed to convince him. Yet. But we're wearing him down. Maybe this episode will push him into agreeing."

Rob rubbed Deb's arm. "He's feisty yet."

She nodded.

I looked back toward the head of the table in time to catch Christian helping Gramps to his feet and then supporting one side, with Linda on the other, as Gramps shuffled toward the house.

"That's just what he needs." Deb nodded to emphasize her words. "He'll have a little nap and be right as rain."

Rob smiled.

"So." Deb pushed her plate away from her. "Would you like some recommendations on studies you and Christian can do?"

"Oh. I...sure." I'd planned to talk to Christian about that, see if it was something he wanted to do. The whole idea made me uncomfortable, but I respected Gramps. And looking around the table at the collected years of Christian's family, it was probably a good suggestion. If a little awkward to consider in my current situation.

By the time Christian returned, I had a draft email with six links to books that Deb and Rob recommended for newlyweds.

"He's fine. Just tired." Christian said as he resumed his seat. "But I think I've finally convinced him to let me take him in and get checked out. We'll see if it lasts when he's rested, but I planted the seed of living long enough to hold another great-grandchild and that seemed to perk him up."

Deb's eyebrows rose.

My cheeks burned. We hadn't talked about kids. I wanted them, no question, but we had a long way to go before we got there.

"Jericho. I meant Bennett and Jericho." Christian reached for his drink and took a hasty swallow. "Not us. Geez."

"What about me and Bennett?" Jericho leaned forward.

Christian's face glowed red. "I might have mentioned to Gramps that he could have another great-grand before too long."

"Wow." Jericho shook her head. "Maybe you should work on that yourself if you're making those kinds of promises."

Christian's mouth opened, then snapped shut.

"Good choice, bro." Bennett pointed down the table, then his eyes met mine. "Did you know Christian's really good at putting his foot in his mouth?"

"Hey." Christian paused, then shrugged. "I guess you're right."

He pushed his chair back and stood, then picked up his plate. He glanced at me. "Are you finished?"

"Yeah. I can get it." I stood and picked up my plate.

"Teresa made cookies, if anyone wants something sweet." Christian paused and collected some plates as he walked down the length of the table. I gathered the ones he bypassed when his hands got full.

In the kitchen, I turned on the sink and started rinsing dishes and Christian put them in the dishwasher. Before I could figure out how to broach the awkward elephant in the room, most of the rest of the family came streaming through the door, heading straight for the cookies.

Linda appeared, apparently convinced that Gramps was settled and okay. "Oh, good. You found the cookies. Deb also made a peach pie. It's in the fridge if anyone wants it."

There were a few assents, so Linda started toward the fridge. The doorbell rang.

"I'll get it." David snagged another cookie off the plate, patted his wife's backside as he passed her, and disappeared into the foyer.

Linda grabbed the pie and turned as David and the newcomer reappeared. "Caroline."

The room went silent.

"I guess I missed lunch."

Linda hurried to put the pie down. "We still have plenty, if you're hungry. Or you can just have dessert."

"I don't want anything. I'm here for Grady." Caroline's gaze roamed the room, finally spotting him. "C'mon, Grady. Let's go."

"No." Grady slid behind Travis.

"Caroline." Travis reached around to lay a hand on Grady and held the other out. "You're not doing this. Didn't your lawyer—"

"Him? Pfft." She flicked that aside. "Once I'm back there with Grady, he'll get it figured out."

"I wouldn't be so sure." Bennett came to stand beside Travis, effectively blocking Grady from view. "But let's get him on the phone."

"I don't need to talk to him. Don't you want to come with Mommy, Grady? I'll buy you some Lego." Caroline moved closer, edging around the other side to try and reach for Grady.

Grady shrieked. He covered his ears with his hands as he screamed, then sort of folded to the floor and began to rock.

Travis got down on the floor beside Grady. "It's okay. You're okay."

"Ugh. Get up, Grady. Stop this. This is not how good boys behave." Caroline grabbed one of Grady's arms and pulled. It only made the screams louder.

"Caroline." Bennett shifted to block her access to Travis. The other family members finally jolting into action to assist. "This isn't why you were invited today."

"Like I want to sit around and talk with you people. I've had enough of that." She glared in the direction of Grady. "You know what, fine. If he doesn't want to come, fine. I don't want him. Hear that, Grady?"

"Caroline." Linda's voice held censure. "Why would you say that to anyone? Let alone your son."

"Whatever." Caroline turned and strode from the room.

I jolted when the front door slammed, then turned to look at Christian.

"I think it's time for y'all to go." David murmured just loudly enough to be heard over Grady's sobs. "Take some pie on your way, if you want."

The wall around Travis and Grady slowly broke apart. Christian paused at the food to slide my cookies onto one of his mom's plates, then grab his platter. He met my gaze and held out his hand.

I hurried to turn off the faucet, then dried my hands on a dishtowel before crossing the kitchen. I looked at Linda. "Thanks for lunch. It was delicious."

She managed a weak smile and patted my cheek. "We're glad you're here, Teresa. Family's messy, but it matters."

I let Christian take my hand as we left his parents' house and walked the short distance to his—our—place. My thoughts were jumbled and more confused than ever.

23

CHRISTIAN

"I appreciate you coming with me." Teresa slipped her arm through mine and clutched at it, clearly nervous. "I don't know why they want me to come over. Not after our conversation two weeks ago."

I had some ideas, but I was biting my tongue. Better to wait and see. Maybe it wouldn't be as awful as I imagined it was going to be.

Then again, knowing Teresa's parents, it could end up being worse.

I grabbed the door leading into the country club and held it for her as she went in, then took her hand as we crossed the ornate foyer to the restaurant entrance.

"Hey, Christian." The hostess' eyes darted quickly to Teresa. "Did I hear congratulations are in order?"

"You did." I nodded to Teresa. "This is my wife, Teresa."

"Hi." Her smile was tight. "We're meeting my parents. The Duvalls?"

"Nice to meet you, and welcome to Loring Island. They're already seated. Let me show you." The girl slipped from behind the hostess stand and led the way through the scantly populated dining room to a table by the windows looking out over the golf course.

"Thanks." I reached for Teresa's chair and held it while she sat, then took the seat beside her.

Mr. Duvall frowned. "I thought you'd come alone."

"Anything you have to say to me, you can say in front of Christian." Teresa's voice quavered slightly.

I took her hand under the table and gave it a quick squeeze.

"It's fine, Bernie. Maybe even better. That way everyone will know exactly what's going on." Mrs. Duvall sounded more sober than usual, though the tall glass of clear liquid and ice was probably not water. No matter that there was a lime slice adorning the lip. She must have caught my evaluation of her beverage, because she smiled. "Would you like one? They do a reasonable gin and tonic."

"No, thank you."

"Teresa?" Mrs. Duvall looked toward her daughter.

"No, I'm fine Mom. Thanks."

"Enough. Let's just get this over with. Then, if you want to stay for lunch, you can, but I suspect you'll decide you're not hungry." Mr. Duvall reached down beside him and brought up a file folder. He slid it across the table to Teresa. "Go ahead and open it up."

Teresa flipped open the top of the folder. Her eyebrows lifted. "What's this, Dad?"

"It's a document releasing your claim on any further funds or property from the family. I can't stop your trust. That's now been confirmed from the lawyers and you should be getting access completely next week. No more restrictions. But I can keep you from taking advantage of anything else." Mr. Duvall crossed his arms.

"Taking advantage." Teresa's voice was emotionless. "That's what you think this is?"

I rubbed Teresa's leg under the table and took a deep breath. "You couldn't just change your will and not make a spectacle out of things?"

"I wanted to make sure everyone understood where things stand. No confusion or miscommunication." Mr. Duvall's expression was stony. "You may have your own family money, but you're not getting your hands on the Duvall family business."

"I don't want it." I scowled. "I wouldn't have any idea what to do with it."

"Neither do I, Dad. And...maybe that's part of the problem." She tipped her head to the side. "You were hoping after I failed in Nashville that I'd come be your little minion. That's what the whole James thing was, too, wasn't it?"

"He would have been a far sight better than this one. He's a *nurse*. Not even a doctor. I mean, Teresa." Mrs. Duvall shook her head. "A *nurse*?"

I opened my mouth, but Teresa shook her head slightly, so I closed it.

"It's good that we were able to close the deal even with you leaving, so I don't have to see what would be involved in compensation for lost profits." Mr. Duvall sighed and sent Teresa a look that he probably thought was sorrowful. Hopefully Teresa saw through it.

"I guess it's also good that Christian's brother and parents are lawyers." Teresa flipped the folder shut and started to stand. "I'll of course want them to look this over before I sign anything."

"There's no need for that. It's just standard. Boilerplate." Mr. Duvall tried to reach for the folder.

"Do you think I didn't learn anything about business just because it's not what I wanted? What would you say to anyone— literally anyone—if they asked you about signing a contract without going over it with a lawyer?"

Mr. Duvall's face turned nearly puce.

Mrs. Duvall glanced over, winced, and quickly gulped down half of her drink before speaking in a soft, soothing voice. "Breathe, honey."

With obvious effort, Mr. Duvall took a deep breath. His eyes narrowed to slits as he breathed out. "Fine. Have your people call my people when you're ready to be reasonable."

I stood and pushed in both of our seats. After a moment, I reached into my pocket and pulled out my wallet, then removed a card from inside it. I put it down carefully in front of Mrs. Duvall. "This is my contact information. I know you have Teresa's. I hope that, if you ever need anything, you'll get in touch. We'd both be happy to help."

Mrs. Duvall's eyebrows lifted. "What could you possibly have to offer me that I don't already have?"

"I guess that's a question for you to answer." I looked at Teresa. "Are you ready? We could get our own table and stay for lunch, if you wanted."

"No." She shook her head sadly. "We can go. Bye, Mom. Bye, Dad. Believe it or not, I do love you."

She turned and I followed suit. I wanted to take her hand, but Teresa held herself so stiffly, I didn't think she'd appreciate it. Maybe it was a case of not wanting to show her parents that they'd gotten to her. Maybe it was something else. But my heartbreak for her warred with my desire to turn around and plow my fist into her father's face until he saw just how stupid he was being.

We crossed the foyer much faster than we had when we arrived. Every step Teresa took seemed to increase her speed until we were practically jogging. As she pushed through the doors to the outside, Teresa stopped and rounded on me. She smacked the folder into my chest, her eyes filling with tears.

"I can't believe this. Did you read this?" She jabbed the folder.

"Ow." I gingerly pried the folder away from her and pulled her into my arms. She stood there a moment, stiff as a board, before dissolving into heaving sobs.

I held her and just let her cry. I didn't know how much time passed before her sobs turned into wet snuffles mixed with an occasional hiccup.

"Sorry." She stepped back, swiping at her eyes. "I'm so sorry."

"Don't be sorry. Not about this." I clung to her hand as she tried to pull completely away. "You matter to me, Teresa. I will do whatever I can—whatever you need—to help you."

She looked up and swallowed. Her eyes filled again and she looked away. "Can you just take me back to work?"

My shoulders fell, but I nodded. "Of course. Do you want me to stay while you talk to Bennett about this?"

"Don't you need to get back to the clinic?" She started down the steps, past the valet station, and out to the parking lot. They didn't offer valet on weekdays. Maybe that was a good thing, today, since it was a little more time for her to collect herself as we crossed the asphalt.

"If I get a call, sure. But so far, it's a quiet Friday." Should I ask her to let me help her? I barely managed to swallow a short laugh. Forcing her to let me help her is why we ended up married. But at this point, I was in for the whole pound.

The last two weeks of nightly Bible study together had been changing something in my heart when it came to Teresa. I loved seeing the side of her that she showed, gradually, as we read the Bible and prayed every evening after dinner.

She'd been surprised when I came home the day after Gramps's speech at Sunday dinner with two of the books that Aunt Deb recommended, but I was pretty sure Gramps had called Sara at Books and Bites, because she had a whole new shelf loaded up with options when I'd gotten there.

I thought since she included me in this meeting with her parents, that her feelings were changing, too. Had I been wrong?

"If you're sure you have time, then yes. Please." Teresa wiped her eyes again and turned to me. "How bad do I look?"

"You look beautiful."

She scoffed. "Thank you. But seriously, how red and puffy?"

I shrugged. "You look like you had a good cry. The minute Bennett reads whatever your dad gave you, I'm guessing he'll understand that."

"You didn't read it?"

"No. I didn't get the impression that your parents wanted me to. And I figured I could take a look when we got home. But whatever it is, I'm glad you didn't sign it before consulting Bennett." We reached my car and I opened the passenger door for her, then went around to get behind the wheel.

"Dad's number one rule of contracts." She gave a mirthless laugh. "I didn't realize how little he thought of me that he expected me to just sign whatever he gave me."

I started the car. "That's on him for being stupid."

Teresa looked at me, mouth agape, then she laughed. "Oh boy. I don't think anyone has called Bernard Duvall stupid in a long, long time."

"Maybe not where he could hear it. But I'm guessing it happens more often than anyone knows."

"You could be right." She sighed and tipped her head back and let her eyes close. "It hurt when he did that drive by and said we were done. I didn't think there was anything worse he could do. Turns out, I was wrong."

"You love them. That's not bad. Or wrong. You should love your parents."

"Even if they're monsters?"

I winced and navigated the car out of the parking lot as I considered. Monsters felt at once a little too harsh and not harsh enough for her parents. They had to have some redeeming qualities though. Didn't they? "I think so. In the 'love your enemies' kind of way. Where you love them because they're made in God's image and you pray for them because you know what they're missing."

"I can do that." She let out a deep breath.

We passed the rest of the drive in silence. It wasn't long before I pulled into a spot near Bennett's offices and we got out and made our way there.

"Hey, you're back fast." Bennett stopped and frowned. "What happened?"

Teresa held out the folder. "Do you mind going over this for me and letting me know if I should sign it?"

Bennett's eyebrows lifted but he took the folder. "Sure. Are you okay?"

"No. But I will be. I'm going to see if I can do anything about my eyes." Teresa turned and headed toward the bathroom.

Bennett met my gaze. "Fill me in?"

"Yeah. Let's go down to your office."

Once we were there, and seated, I filled Bennett in on the meeting with the Duvalls. He didn't look like he believed me until he flipped open the file folder and begin to read the document inside.

After several minutes of silence, he looked up. "You've got to be joking."

"They're something special."

He snickered. "That's one way to put it. I'm glad you were there. Do you think she would've signed it if you hadn't been?"

"I doubt it. She said it's his number one business rule not to."

Bennett grinned. "It's a good rule. And I'm glad it's going to bite him in the butt this time."

Teresa knocked on the door frame, then came in and sat beside me. "Did you read it?"

"I did." Bennett shook his head. "And the first thing I want to say is that I'm sorry your father tried this. It's...I'm not sure I have words for what it is."

Teresa shrugged. "I'm not all that surprised. I wish I was."

"Second thing? You're family now. And I promise you, we'll never treat you this way."

"Even if we don't end up making this marriage work?" Teresa blurted out the words.

I stiffened. "Where did that come from?"

She huffed out a breath. "You can't tell me you're treating Caroline like family."

Bennett and I exchanged a look. He rubbed the back of his neck. "There are things I can't get into because of confidentiality. Hopefully you know that. But you were there two weeks ago."

Teresa nodded slowly. "But what pushed her to be like that?"

"I wish I knew. Or that Travis knew. Or anyone. She can't even tell us. Or she won't." Bennett spread his hands. "Travis has all but crawled over glass trying to get her to come home and do counseling and figure out how to fix whatever's broken. She refuses. And as soon as it was clear that Travis wasn't going to let her take their screaming little boy away from his safe place, she was on the first plane back to Oregon to continue pushing for a fast divorce."

Teresa looked away. "Sorry. I just..."

I waited, hoping she'd finish the sentence. But she didn't. I wet my lips. "I'm committed to you, Teresa. To us. But if you're not all in, too..."

"I am." She turned back to look at me. "I—it's been a rough day."

I chuckled and reached for her hand. "It has. Trust me. Please?"

Teresa nodded.

"You can trust all of us, for that matter." Bennett was looking at us with a measuring look. "And this? Don't sign this."

"That's kind of what I figured. Would it even stand up in court?"

Bennett wiggled a hand from side-to-side. "Maybe if you signed it. I can see how to make a case. But on its merit alone? I don't think so."

"What should I do?" Teresa sat up straight, a determined look on her face.

"You let me write a response. And we'll go from there. I guess I need to know if you want to fight for some kind of share. You're clearly eligible, or your father wouldn't be trying to cut you off."

"I don't need anything else from them. I'd like to stop short of being disowned, if that's an option. But I still want to stand on my own two feet. Which sounds rich given what I did to get access to my trust. But I'm not looking for more." Teresa tugged her hand out of mine and clasped her hands together in her lap. "From anyone."

I fought to keep her words from feeling like a jab. Did she think I suspected her of being a gold digger? Because I didn't. She hadn't realized just how many zeroes I had access to personally, let alone in our family fortune, before I laid it all out for her. And she'd fought me tooth and nail about putting her as a joint owner of my accounts.

She'd finally given in, but she insisted on having her salary from Bennett get deposited into the same account so she'd feel like she contributed something. I had a sneaking suspicion that she was keeping a spreadsheet to make sure she didn't accidentally spend any of "my" money.

Not that she spent much money on anything.

"Got it. That gives me a place to start. I'll keep you posted."

Bennett tipped his head to the side. "Why don't you take the rest of today off?"

"But—"

Bennett shook his head. "It's Friday. I have some calls to make and a letter to write. We don't have any appointments on the book. Go enjoy the sunshine."

She hesitated. "You're sure?"

"Absolutely."

Teresa turned to me. "Do you think we could go over and maybe look at a car? I found one last night that seems doable."

"Yeah. Of course." I stood. "Thanks, Bennett."

"Hey, I get to write scary lawyer letters. I'm excited."

I laughed. "Oh yeah. You're terrifying."

"I can be. When needed." He made a shooing motion. "Get out of here. Both of you. Go buy a car."

We left Bennett's office and paused in the foyer for Teresa to shut everything down and collect her purse. Once we were out on the sidewalk, I held out my hand, and my heart leapt when she took it.

"How about I take you to lunch, first. Then we can see about a car."

She studied me a moment before nodding with a shy smile that turned my insides to goo. "I'd like that."

24

TERESA

I pulled my car into the driveway at Christian's parents' house and parked. I snagged my purse and hopped out, pausing to grin at the sporty little convertible before hurrying up the stairs to the front door.

I rang the bell.

It took long enough that I was starting to get worried. I was about to text Linda when Gramps finally opened the door.

His face split with a grin. "Teresa, honey. What a nice surprise. Come on in."

"Actually, Gramps, I was wondering if I could take you out to lunch." I pointed down to where my car sat. "I'm told you've always loved convertibles."

"Oh, would you look at that." Gramps's eyes shone. "I can't say no to a beautiful young woman, but if I could, I sure couldn't say no to that car. Let me just get my hat."

I grinned and waited while he took his time collecting a denim bucket hat off the hall tree. After a moment, he sighed, and pulled a cane out of an umbrella stand.

"Ready when you are, m'dear."

When Gramps had maneuvered through the door, I pulled it

shut, then stayed by his side as he navigated the stairs. I wanted to slap my forehead—I should have insisted we take the elevator in the kitchen that went down to the garage. But between me, the banister, and his cane, he made it down in one piece.

I hurried over to open the passenger door and helped him get in and settled. "All set?"

Gramps nodded.

I shut his door, then went around and slid behind the wheel. I looked over at him. "Anywhere in particular you'd like to eat?"

"I love The Diner."

I chuckled. "Linda said you'd probably say that. But I wanted to ask."

"She knows you're getting me out of my cage, does she?"

I concentrated on backing down the driveway and getting onto the road pointing in the right direction before I answered. "She does. Only because I wanted to be sure it was all right. I didn't know if you had plans."

Gramps laughed. "I'm old enough that I don't make plans, as a rule. I just take the days as the Lord gives them to me."

"It's a good way to live. Probably a lot less stressful."

"Once you get used to it." Gramps tipped his face up so the sun hit his skin. "Takes a little bit though, if you're used to doing. And my oh my, I used to be a doer."

"That seems to run in the family."

"Sure enough. Lorings don't sit on their laurels. That's what my dad used to say. And his dad before him. Probably on back for a few generations. Family money is well and good, but you need to make something of yourself if you're going to enjoy it."

It was a good policy. Too bad my parents hadn't embraced it. Had my grandparents? More so than Mom and Dad anyway.

Gramps had his eyes shut and seemed to be enjoying the sun and wind, so I left him alone the rest of the way into town.

When I pulled into a spot at the diner and parked, he sighed and opened his eyes.

"Grammie would have loved a car like this. I'm going to talk you into more rides, young lady. Maybe you'll even let me behind the wheel if I promise to stay on the road in front of the house?" He shot me a wink. "Linda doesn't need to know."

"Um."

He laughed and pointed a spindly finger at me. "You should see your face. Ah, well. It was worth a try. Maybe we can get my daughter to give us permission. Would that be all right?"

I nodded. "I wouldn't know how to live with myself if you got hurt, Gramps."

I got out of the car and hurried around to help Gramps. He was already trying to push himself to his feet with the help of the door and his cane when I got there. A tiny bit of extra oomph was all it took to get him upright and moving.

"Not as young as I used to be. That's for sure." Gramps started toward the entrance.

I fell into step beside him. "But it's a blessing to have you around."

"I like to think the family feels that way. I think most of the time, they do."

I got the door for him and he moseyed up to the hostess stand.

"Hi, Mr. Loring. It's great to see you. You want your usual booth?"

Gramps turned to look at me. "I like a booth with a view. Do you mind?"

"Not at all. That sounds great."

"Follow me." The hostess made a mark on the seating chart on the stand, then led us over to a two-person booth by the window from which I could just make out the marina.

Gramps levered himself down and put his hat and cane on the seat beside him.

I slid onto the seat opposite and reached for a menu.

"Can I get your drinks started?"

I glanced up at the hostess. "Sweet tea, please."

"I have to go unsweet. Linda says I'm on the edge of being too sweet and Christian backs her up on it. But bring those yellow fake packets, would you? They're the only ones that aren't disgusting."

"Sure thing, Mr. Loring. Jenny will be over soon to get your food orders."

"Do you want a menu?" I reached for where they were stashed behind the little mini jukebox on the table.

He waved a hand. "I'm in the mood for a patty melt today. And fries. And I hope you'll not mind telling Linda about it. If she asks, don't lie. But maybe don't volunteer the information? She'd want me to get a salad, and I just don't see the point."

"My lips are sealed." Hopefully Linda wouldn't ask. She hadn't tried to dig into why I wanted to take Gramps to lunch in the first place, so maybe she hadn't figured out how much she could pry with me yet.

Jenny came by with our drinks and took our orders then disappeared again.

"So. What can I do for you?" Gramps folded his hands on the table and watched me with a steady gaze.

My face heated. I thought about trying to deflect, but what was the point? I'd wanted to talk to him, and he'd caught on. I might as well just dive in. I took a sip of my tea. "At lunch the other day, when Caroline was in town?"

He nodded. "Two, three weeks back?"

"Yeah. You mentioned that you and Grammie had married after just six weeks. And I wondered if you'd tell me about that."

His eyebrows lifted. He pulled four of the fake sugar packets out and flicked them back and forth before tearing them open and dumping them into his tea. He stirred with the straw, sipped, wrinkled his nose, and stirred some more. "We met at the beach. No surprise there, probably, seeing as how I've lived on Loring Island my whole life. But it was her first time at the ocean, and the pure joy and rapture on her face took my breath away."

I smiled, trying to picture Gramps as a young man on the beach.

"Of course, I had to go say hello."

"Just like that?"

Gramps nodded. "Of course. I've never been shy. No, that's not a struggle I've ever had. Keeping my mouth shut? That's another story. Anyway, my Edna, she didn't seem to mind my direct approach. And when I asked if she wanted to go get a milkshake in town, she agreed. She was there with her roommates and I don't think she even let them know where she was going."

"Was it love at first sight then?" I'd been hoping for something else. Something different. What that was, I wasn't sure. But I was a little let down.

"I guess you could call it that, but it wasn't like in the movies." He paused while Jenny brought out our food and checked that we didn't need anything. "It was more a connection. A feeling that she understood me. She saw me for who I was."

I looked down at my food and pondered that.

Gramps reached over and put his fingers on top of mine. "Let me bless the food real quick."

He said a short prayer, then picked up a fry and dunked it in the little tub of ketchup.

"But when you married her, you were in love." I didn't ask it as a question. It had to be that way, didn't it?

"We were. But sometimes I think people get the idea of love wrong. It's not something that's on or off. Love, when its fed and nurtured properly, grows every day. I loved her when we got married. But that love was nothing to what I felt for her the day she died."

"So...how did you know you loved her enough at the start?" I pulled the toothpick out of one half of my club sandwich and took a bite.

Gramps cut off a bite from his patty melt and chewed it thoughtfully before answering. "There was that connection, certainly. Like we were old friends right from the start. And then, of course, she was the most beautiful creature I'd ever laid eyes on. That certainly didn't hurt. But I think the thing that pushed me over the edge, was knowing that she treated me with all of the virtues in 1 Corinthians 13. And she made me want to embody those virtues when it came to her."

I wiped my fingers on a napkin and dug out my phone. "Do you mind if I look that up?"

"Course not." He smiled and picked up some more fries.

I opened up the Bible app and found the passage. Patient. Kind. Humble. Forgiving. Christian was all of those things. More than I deserved.

"Does he pass?" Gramps caught my eye as I stowed away my phone again. "My grandson?"

I nodded. "But I'm not sure I do."

"It can be hard, sometimes, if you come from a family that struggles to show love in healthy ways. Edna's family was like that. Her mother never did learn to like me. Nothing I did was ever right. But then, nothing Edna did was ever right either. Her mother was a God-fearing woman, but I half wonder if she didn't stand at the throne of Jesus her first day in heaven and give Him what for about the way things were going on earth." Gramps chuckled quietly. "The key, I think, is wanting to love."

I blinked. "Wanting?"

"Sure. Just like you can choose to love your neighbor or your enemy, you choose, every day to love your spouse. And you have to want to make that choice. Some days you have to want it more than others. If you ever stop wanting to love someone? You will." Gramps frowned. "I suspect that's what happened to Caroline. Grady, I love that boy so much, but he's a trial most days. And I think the choosing and the wanting got to be too much for her. And Travis—and the rest of the family—didn't see how thin she was wearing in time to help her."

I ate some more of my sandwich as I considered that. It was the first time anyone in the family had given Caroline a real benefit of the doubt. Bennett sounded like he was trying. Maybe everyone was trying. Gramps just did it.

Was that a choice, too?

Gramps put his fork and knife down and patted his belly. "I'll take the rest home for a snack. I can't eat as much all at once these days. Did I help?"

"You did."

He smiled across the table at me. "And do you love my grandson?"

Did I? Did I want to? That was easy, yes. So, if that's what I wanted, then I just had to choose it? It seemed wrong. Too easy. And not anything like the swooping birds and hearts like in the movies. But then, how many of those movie couples would still be together in five years? Or ten?

Christian saw me. I was pretty sure I saw him, too. The connection was there. And attraction? Oh, yeah.

"You know, I think I do."

Gramps gave me another of his huge grins. "I'm glad to hear it. Make sure you tell him, too."

My stomach twisted. That...was a daunting thought. He'd told me he cared about me. Was that a sort of soft launch for him sharing his feelings? Knowing him, it absolutely was. He was so careful with me, not wanting to push or do anything that would make me uncomfortable. And I appreciated it. So much.

But maybe it was time for me to change the pace.

The next time Jenny came by, she brought boxes and the check. I overruled Gramps's offer to pay and gave her my card. When she brought it back, I carried both of the boxed up meals and slid my arm through his while we walked out to the car.

"You have a radio in this car?" Gramps was eyeing the dash.

"Sure. Would you like music on the way home?"

He nodded. "See if you can find the oldies station, would you? I'll think of my Edna with the sun on my face and the breeze flying by."

It took a little fiddling, but I finally found a station playing music from the 1950s. Gramps tapped his fingers on his leg in time to the music, so I left him alone to his thoughts as I took us back through town and out to the road that led to the family homes.

I was going to tell Christian that I loved him.

The thought still sat a little uneasily in my belly, but I wasn't going to let nerves get in the way of things. I'd gotten pretty good at ignoring nerves in Nashville—not that it had mattered all that much in the long run. But I did leave with a handful of contacts who'd said to reach out if I ever had a song to sell.

Hm.

A thought started to form in the back of my mind as we arrived back at the house. I helped Gramps back up the stairs to the front door, then handed him his leftovers.

"Thank you, Gramps."

He smiled and held his arms open in invitation. I stepped in for the hug. "It was my very real pleasure."

He kissed my cheek, then went inside the house.

I returned to my car and sat for a moment. Was I ready?

Could I do it? All the usual questions circled, but I squashed them. If I could be brave and tell my husband I loved him, I could send a song to Danny Granger.

I swallowed and started the engine.

The one thing I wasn't going to do was think about how badly rejection would hurt.

From either of them.

25

CHRISTIAN

Teresa's car was already in the garage when I pulled in. It made me smile. I hadn't minded living alone, but gosh it was amazing to come home and know someone else was there. Someone who would be happy to see me. And I wouldn't have to spend the whole evening wishing for an emergency call just to break up the boredom.

Laughing at myself, I parked, grabbed my things from the car, and started up the stairs into the house. I turned the doorknob and pushed it open as I called out, "Honey, I'm home."

"Hey! I'll be right there." I heard her call down from her rooms upstairs.

I sighed and took my bag over to the shelf where I kept it, then kicked my shoes off in the general direction of the shoe storage. Her rooms were still upstairs.

It was fine. It was. We'd only been married three weeks. And we'd known each other what, five weeks? More if you counted from Easter, but it wasn't like we'd had an in-depth getting to know you conversation then. I would have loved to, no question, but it hadn't seemed appropriate under the circumstances.

Would she ever come around? I closed my eyes and sent up

the same short prayer I'd been making for the last three weeks. *Lord, let her love me.* Maybe, if I stopped to consider it more carefully, I'd find it pathetic. But I wasn't going to spend my time analyzing things just now. I loved her.

She just wasn't ready to hear it.

"Hey." Teresa paused as she came into the kitchen and looked at me. "Rough day?"

I shook my head. "Not really. Last minute stitches kept me a few minutes late. Toddler stepped on a seashell."

"Ouch." She winced.

"Yeah. The kid was handling it better than mom though. You would've thought I was doing brain surgery with all the hand wringing on mom's part."

"Aw." She patted my arm. "Will it help if I tell you I already made dinner?"

"You did?" My eyebrows lifted. We'd gotten in the habit of spending the first ten or fifteen minutes after we were both home discussing what to eat and then making it together. Neither of us were amazing cooks, but we weren't going to starve. Or poison ourselves.

"I did. Why don't you go sit down at the table, and I'll bring it out."

I frowned. "I don't mind helping."

She made a little shooing motion. "Go sit. I'll just be a minute."

I hesitated, then did as I was told. If she didn't need my help, I wasn't going to complain about getting off my feet. It had been a busier than average day at the clinic, and the hysterical mom had just capped it off in the not-so-perfect way.

I pulled out a chair and sat. She'd already set the table. I smiled slightly. I wasn't one of those "let's go back to the 1950s" guys, but coming home to a nicely set table and dinner already cooked every now and then was definitely appreciated.

I'd have to return the favor. She'd probably like it just as much.

A couple of minutes later, Teresa came in with two bowls and a plate precariously balanced in her arms. She set them on the table without mishap, then held up a finger. "The tea. I'll be right back. Help yourself."

The first bowl was heaped with mashed potatoes and I took a big scoop and dropped it on my plate before reaching for the second bowl. Green beans. Yum. I was in the process of spooning what looked suspiciously like my mother's green beans onto my plate when she returned with a pitcher of iced tea. She filled my cup, then her own, and then sat.

"I got the green bean recipe from your mom, so I hope I did it right. The only thing I've ever done with them is either casserole with the crunchy onions on top or cold with some ranch."

I made a yucky face. "Cold?"

"With ranch." She shrugged. "It's like a salad."

"No. It's not like a salad. It's a cold, slimy green bean smothered in ranch." I stuck out my tongue. "Pass."

"You have to try it before you knock it."

I shook my head. "Nope. Not after I turned thirty. After that, I reserved the right in perpetuity to knock things and not try them if they sound awful."

She laughed. The sound lifted my spirits. "We'll see."

I pulled the plate closer, then looked up at her. "Meatloaf?"

I nodded. "Linda said it was a favorite. Not the only favorite, but it seemed like something I could manage."

"It is a favorite. Mom and Dad both hate it, so I had to beg for it when I was little."

"What kid begs for meatloaf?" She wrinkled her nose.

"What's not to love? It's meat. Shaped like bread. And ketchup." I took a generous helping of meatloaf, then nudged the serving dishes closer to her.

When she'd put food on her plate, I reached for her hand. Tonight, she didn't hesitate like usual. I squeezed her fingers, then said a quick blessing over the food.

"What brought this on?" I cut off a corner of meatloaf, dragged it through the potatoes, then stabbed a green bean to make the perfect bite.

"I had a really good day." She paused and cleared her throat. "I think I sold a song."

I set my fork down, grinning. "Really? That's excellent. Congratulations!"

"We have to figure out the best way to do things, since I don't have an agent, but maybe now that Danny Granger wants to buy this song, and he's interested in three others that I told him about, maybe I can find an agent." She shrugged, but excitement pumped off her.

"I'm so proud of you." I reached for her hand again and pulled it to my lips. "So proud. I would have taken you out to celebrate."

"I wanted to do this." She didn't tug her hand away, and I wasn't in a hurry to let go. "Plus, I took Gramps to lunch."

"You did?" I tilted my head to one side. "How come? I mean, Gramps is great, I get that. It just seems a little out of left field."

"I can see that. I had some questions. Um. You remember when Caroline came to that Sunday lunch?"

I snorted. "Not likely to forget that anytime soon. Grady is still having nightmares about being taken away."

Her forehead wrinkled. "He is? That's awful. But—" she blew out a breath. "Obviously I don't understand their family dynamics. I can't imagine a child being that scared of his mom."

"Can't you?" I looked at her. She wouldn't meet my gaze.

"It's not exactly the same."

"Maybe not." I should drop it. It wasn't a conversation we

needed to have again. Not after everything her parents had put her through. "How's Gramps?"

Her face lightened and she smiled. "He's a treasure. And he had the answers I needed. Which is even better."

"Oh?"

She nodded and took a deep breath, as if steeling herself. "I wanted to know how he knew he loved your Grammie. They got married so fast—he said, remember?"

"Yeah. He tells that story a lot."

"Well, we got to talking and it made me realize. Um. I love you, Christian."

"You love me." For some reason, my mind couldn't process the words.

The joy that had been on her face started to fade. I could almost see her pulling back into herself. "I shouldn't have—"

"No. No you should." I kept hold of her hand when she tried to pull away. "I just didn't think...I love you."

She blinked. "You're not just saying that?"

"No. I'm not just saying that. I thought it was too soon. I didn't want to push." I scooted my chair back and wriggled my hand free. "Hang on. Wait there."

I hurried from the room to the shelf where I stored my bag. I unzipped it and dug around until my hand closed around the black velvet box I'd tucked in there after a visit to a jewelry store on my way home from a hospital shift. I dragged it out and zipped back to the dining room.

"Where—"

I put the box down on the table beside her. "I didn't know when, or even if, I'd ever get to give this to you. But I've been carrying it around so you didn't stumble across it."

She stared at the box, then looked up at me.

I nudged it closer. "Open it."

"Christian."

"You love me, right?"

She nodded.

"And I love you." I reached for the box and flipped open the lid. "I think we should get married."

She laughed. If the sound bordered on hysteria, I could overlook it this time. "We're already married."

"Oh. Right." I winked. "Then I think you need some rings."

I plucked the wedding set out of the box and held it up. After a brief hesitation, Teresa held out her left hand. I slid the rings on.

"They fit." She looked up at me, confused. "How did you know what size?"

"Remember when Mom dropped by the office with some of Grammie's rings for you to try?"

"Seriously?"

I shrugged. "Only part of it was sneaky. Grammie was very vocal about wanting all of us to give one of her rings to our future wives. Mom was really just doing what Grammie wanted. It helped me out too."

"I wondered why she had me try them on my left hand first and then my right, when they were obviously designed as right-hand rings." She held out her hand and admired the rings. "I love them."

"I'm glad." Everything felt warm and as if nothing in the world could ever go wrong again. I knew that wouldn't last— there would be problems. We were living in reality, not a romance novel. But right now? I didn't care. If there'd been a lamp post handy outside my house, I would have given my best shot to swinging on it while singing.

After a moment, her face fell. "What about you? I need to get you a ring, too."

I pointed to the ring box.

She picked it up and removed the simple gold band that remained inside. "But I didn't pay for it."

"Sure you did. You have your salary deposited in our checking account, right?"

"Yeah."

"I spent money out of the checking account. So, we're good." I held out my hand. "Will you put it on me?"

"It doesn't feel fair."

"I need a ring. You have one to give me. What's not fair?" I held her gaze steadily. This was important to me, this idea that we were a unit. I wanted her to know what was mine was hers. I wanted her to trust me with what was hers.

"All right." She slid the ring on my finger. "But make sure you remember that I paid for that one."

"Yes, ma'am."

Teresa rolled her eyes before taking another forkful of dinner. She frowned. "Do you want me to heat yours up? I think I'm going to zap mine."

I made another perfect bite and shook my head. "Nope. That's the beauty of meatloaf. It's good hot. It's good cold. It's good lukewarm."

"If you say so." She stood and took her plate into the kitchen.

When she returned, she told me more about her conversation with Gramps, and her decision to reach out to Danny Granger.

"He responded like ten minutes after I sent the email. And it was him, not an assistant or something. It was surreal. We'd bumped into each other in that café I think I've told you about, Melody's? But I didn't expect him to remember."

"That's so cool. I didn't even realize he was still recording. Not since his wife died."

Sorrow flickered over Teresa's face. "That was tragic. But I guess he's getting back into it. The rest of the band is pushing for it, he said. And he's out of excuses. I should spend some time tonight looking up agents again, maybe sending some emails."

"Or," I held up a finger, "I know it's important. And if that's what you think you need to do, I will support it one hundred percent. But I was thinking it might be a good night to put on a movie and not even pretend to watch it." I held my breath as I waited for her reaction. Maybe it was one thing to say she loved me and another to want to make out on the couch. And it didn't have to be anything big, but I ached to hold her. To do more than just hug her when she was down.

Her cheeks burned bright pink, but her eyes held an impish light. "You know what? That's a much better idea. Let's do that."

I did a mental fist pump and stood up, to clear my plate.

She stood and wrapped her arms around me. "Let's leave the dishes for later."

When her lips found mine, I decided I didn't mind that idea at all.

26

TERESA

I pulled up to the curb in front of my parents' beach house and pursed my lips when I saw the "For Sale" sign in the yard.

"You all right?" Christian rubbed my leg.

"Yeah. I should have expected this. I guess I hoped they might keep it as a way to see me—us—every now and then." I shouldn't be this hurt, but it stung worse than I'd imagined it could.

"Sorry."

"Not your fault." I pushed open my door and climbed out of the car. "Let's go get it over with."

Christian got out of the passenger side of my car and took my hand when he fell into step beside me. We walked up the driveway and the stairs to the front door. Dad pulled it open before I could hit the bell.

"Let's do this fast. Your mother and I want to get on the road as soon as possible." He waved us toward the sitting room on the left side of the hall.

"Hi, Mom." I leaned in to kiss her cheek.

"Teresa." She managed a slight smile, but her eyes were glassy. Definitely not sober. But when was she ever?

"Mrs. Duvall." Christian leaned in to kiss her cheek as well. He straightened. "We'll miss having y'all as residents on Loring Island."

Dad scoffed. "You'll find someone else to bilk out of taxes. Property like this? It won't sit vacant long."

I could have debated that. I thought I remembered Rob, or maybe it was Travis, saying something about how long it had sat on the market before Dad bought it. Long enough that Rob was thinking of adding it to his rental portfolio. With Dad, though, there was no point. Facts only mattered to him if they were the facts he wanted to believe.

"Have a seat." Dad nodded to the chairs facing the settee where Mom sat, then he perched on the edge of the cushion beside her.

Christian waited for me to sit, then he took the chair next to mine. The whole time, he kept a firm hold on my hand and it anchored me in ways that suggested a little snippet of a song. I filed the thought away for later. Jesus was the sure and steady anchor, but sometimes the other people in our lives could be a more physical manifestation of that care. It was important to sing about both.

"According to your lawyer, and now ours, my initial plan has gone out the window. Your mother and I will be modifying our wills, however, to leave you a small sum. I'm not cutting you out completely, because I'm told that would make it easier for you to contest. I've tried to convince your grandparents to do the same, but thus far they remain intractable." He scowled. "So, you may get something you're not owed after all. Just not from us. Clear?"

I nodded. How was it possible for him to break my heart another time? Wasn't there some point when his ability to hurt me would stop?

Christian gently squeezed my hand, a little bolstering touch that loosened my tight chest.

"We're asking you not to contact us. If, at some point in the future, we decide to reach out, we shouldn't have any trouble finding you. Questions?" Dad's expression suggested that I'd better not have any.

But I did. Why? What had I ever done to them? But I also knew there was no point in asking them that. They wouldn't be able to explain it, they'd just go on about how I didn't trust them to know what was best and give examples of me doing ridiculous things like getting my arm fixed when it was broken.

At the thought, I absently rubbed the newly-uncasted arm. It was good to have that off. Even better to have full use of both my arms. I'd been getting by on the guitar, but it hadn't been easy.

"No. I guess not." I sighed, dejected. "Is that all?"

"It is. You're dismissed." Dad stood.

I stood as well, and sent one more look toward Mom. She avoided my eyes. "Come on, Christian."

Christian stood and gave my father a long look. "Your daughter is an incredible woman. I'm blessed to have her in my life. Blessed to have earned her trust and love. I hope that some-day, you'll see that she gave both of those to you, as well, and you threw them away."

With that, he turned and put his hand on the small of my back as he ushered me out of the sitting room and to the front door. He paused on the stoop. "Was there anything of yours here that you wanted to get before we go?"

"No." I turned and looked back over my shoulder. My gaze landed on Dad, with mom on the settee behind him. "No, there's nothing left for me here."

Christian wrapped his arm around my shoulders as we made our way to the car. He opened my door, waiting for me to slide behind the wheel and get settled before closing it and circling back around to get in on the passenger side.

As he pulled the seatbelt across his chest, he looked at me. "You know what? I could go for some ice cream. Do you want ice cream?"

I glanced up at the closed doors of my parents' house, then started the car. "I could go for some ice cream."

"Let's head over to MacLachlan's. I think Evan said they had tiramisu flavored ice cream this week."

"That sounds...amazing. I'm in." I checked for traffic and made a tight U-turn as I pulled away from the curb. Before long, we were on the bridge on our way into Bennett. Christian kept the conversation light, steering us away from anything that would circle back to my parents. I appreciated it.

I'd want to talk about it later. He'd be there for that, too. But right now, ice cream seemed like a lot better of an idea than a breakdown.

At MacLachlan's, I pulled into a space toward the rear of the lot. It was crowded today. Christian was at my door just as I was getting ready to push it open. I grinned at him and took his hand as I got out of the car so we could walk over to join the line that snaked through the parking lot.

"Busy today." I leaned back against Christian's chest as we stopped at the end of the line. He slipped his arms around me.

"End of summer. Labor Day is next weekend. School's starting up most places, if it hasn't already. But ice cream is always a good idea."

I laughed. "Maybe it's good we have to cross the bridge to come here."

"Probably. Although we have some good ice cream on Loring, too. But you don't have the thrill of finding out what flavors are available. They always have the same thing."

"Some people—maybe even most of them—would consider it better to be predictable."

He shrugged. "Maybe so. But just think, if I'd been predictable, we wouldn't be married."

I turned in his arms and leaned up to press a kiss to his lips. "Predictable is overrated."

"I wish your parents hadn't been so predictable." He searched my face. "You have a family who loves you. Even if it doesn't seem to include the ones who raised you."

One corner of my mouth quirked up. "I wasn't surprised. Not really. And I'm finding I can tune out Dad's voice a lot better now. Jericho and I have been reading that book about finding our identity in Christ and it's helping replace his voice with the loving voice of the Father. You help with that, too."

"I'm glad. I want to do that for you." He kissed my forehead, then spun me back around so we could inch a few steps forward.

When we finally reached the ordering window, the owner of the ice cream shop, Jon peered out at us, his characteristic grin on his face.

"Christian, what's this I hear about you getting married? This is your wife?"

Christian beamed and lifted my left hand, complete with sparkling diamonds, to his lips. "This is Teresa. I think you've met before. But we weren't married yet."

"Maybe so." Jon squinted. "Get a lot of new faces coming through. What can I get y'all?"

I eyed the menu board and considered the flavors. "I heard there was tiramisu."

Jon laughed. "Word gets around. We're gonna run out before long, but we're still stocked today. Cup or cone?"

"Cup, please."

"I'll have that, too, but in a cone." Christian let go of me so he could reach in his pocket for his wallet as Jon rang up the order.

We scooted down to the pickup area and within a few minutes, we were carrying our treats back to the car.

"Do you want to eat here, or go find a place to sit by the water?"

I poked at my ice cream with the spoon. "Let's go down to the water."

He nodded and opened the door so I could get in, then went around and got in the passenger seat. I drove us carefully through town toward the bridge, but I pulled around to the mainland side marina instead of crossing.

We got out of the car and walked until we found an empty spot where we could sit. Christian sat first and I settled between his legs, and leaned against his chest.

"This summer hasn't been at all what I thought it would be."

Christian licked his ice cream. "Disappointed?"

I twisted so our eyes met. "Not in the slightest. Well, that's not true. It was a pretty terrible summer right up until we got married at the marina. Since then? It's been better than a dream."

Ice cream forgotten, he lowered his mouth to mine. If someone had told me I'd end the summer married I would have laughed them out of the room. Thank the Lord sometimes things don't go as planned.

EPILOGUE

Evan

"Excuse me!"

I looked over at the woman shouting from her car window and frowned. The science station wasn't open to the public except for various pre-arranged educational programs. None of which took place at five p.m. on a Friday night. I finished locking the door, then hitched my messenger bag up and crossed to her vehicle.

"Can I help you?"

"Yes, I'm wondering if you can tell me how to get in touch with the director here. Doctor Jantz? Debra Jantz?"

Aunt Deb was listed on the website as the director, but anyone who dealt with the science center knew I ran things now. "Who are you?"

The woman bristled and her lips thinned. "Dr. Rebecca Farnsworth. I've been writing about loggerheads—"

"For Nature Magazine. I've read your work." I tilted my head to one side. From her articles, I wasn't sure she'd actually seen a loggerhead outside of a magazine.

She sighed. "And you hate it, right? Look, they edit my stuff. But I need the publishing credits, so I suck it up. I'd really like to speak with Dr. Jantz about the possibility of working here through hatching. Maybe I could write a paper that someone other than Nature would publish and then I could get out of adjunct professor misery and get a full-time job."

My lips quirked at the exasperation in her voice. Aunt Deb would tell me it was my call. Because, well, it was. But she wanted to meet Dr. Jantz, so... "She's already gone home for the day, but we can stop by her house. Follow me."

"Oh. I don't want—"

At least she stopped talking when I walked away. I went to my bicycle and unlocked it from the bike rack. I took a minute to put on my helmet, turn on the headlight, and adjust my messenger bag so it wouldn't be in the way, then I got on and took a few powerful pedals in her direction. I waved as I rode past and started down the driveway to the road.

"Oh, for crying out loud."

I laughed as her exclamation reached my ears. She was irritated now? Wait until she actually talked to Aunt Deb.

I couldn't wait.

ACKNOWLEDGMENTS

This book, y'all.

When I finished book 1, I thought it would be no problem to get the next one written and out in a reasonable timeframe. If you're reading this right away, you know that didn't happen. Lots of reasons. Or maybe excuses. But it is what it is. Either way, I hope you enjoyed Christian and Teresa's story. Writing could happen without readers like you, but there would be considerably less joy. I appreciate, more than I can say, that you picked up my book and spent time in its pages.

As ever, none of this would be possible without the amazing people I have in my life. First and foremost, my husband and my boys. They give me space to write. Sometimes they even push me to go write when I'm frittering time away doing unnecessary things. And they are my biggest cheerleaders.

Additionally, I remain incredibly grateful for the encouragement and support of my amazing friends Katie and Mel. I honestly am not sure how I got this old without y'all, but now that you're here, there's no escape. In addition to being the absolute best human on the planet, Katie is also my editor extraordinaire. If there are mistakes in here still, it's because I ignored what she said to do. I do that sometimes.

Last, but absolutely not least, I am grateful to Jesus for continuing to give me stories. It's my prayer that something in this books helped you get a little glimpse of His love. Because He loves you.

WANT A FREE BOOK?

If you enjoyed this book and would like to read another of my books for free, you can get a free e-book simply by signing up for my newsletter on my website.

OTHER BOOKS BY ELIZABETH MADDREY

Beachfront Billionaires

Second Chance at the Seaside

Married at the Marina

Billionaire Next Door

The Billionaire's Nanny

The Billionaire's Best Friend

The Billionaire's Secret Crush

The Billionaire's Backup

The Billionaire's Teacher

The Billionaire's Wife

Postcards, A Novel

So You Want to Be a Billionaire

So You Want a Second Chance

So You Love to Hate Your Boss

So You Love Your Best Friend's Sister

So You Have My Secret Baby

So You Need a Fake Relationship

So You Forgot You Love Me

Hope Ranch Series

Hope for Christmas

Hope for Tomorrow

Hope for Love

Hope for Freedom

Hope for Family

Hope at Last

Peacock Hill Romance Series

A Heart Restored

A Heart Reclaimed

A Heart Realigned

A Heart Redirected

A Heart Rearranged

A Heart Reconsidered

Arcadia Valley Romance – Baxter Family Bakery Series

Loaves & Wishes

Muffins & Moonbeams

Cookies & Candlelight

Donuts & Daydreams

The 'Operation Romance' Series

Operation Mistletoe

Operation Valentine

Operation Fireworks

Operation Back-to-School

The 'Taste of Romance' Series

A Splash of Substance

A Pinch of Promise

A Dash of Daring

For the most recent listing of all my books, please visit my website.

ABOUT THE AUTHOR

USA Today bestselling author Elizabeth Maddrey is a semi-reformed computer geek and homeschooling mother of two who lives in the suburbs of Washington D.C. When she isn't writing, Elizabeth is a voracious consumer of books. She loves to write about Christians who struggle through their lives, dealing with sin and receiving God's grace on their way to their own romantic happily ever after.